# NIGHT OF NINE TAILS

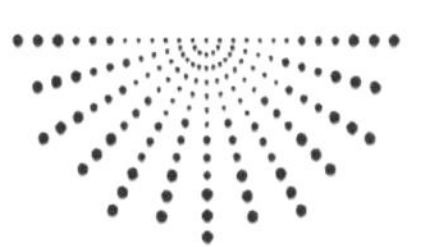

# NIGHT OF NINE TAILS

## REG RAWLINS, PSYCHIC INVESTIGATOR #4

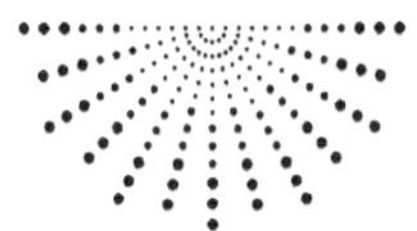

## P.D. WORKMAN

ISBN: 9781989415337 (IS Hardcover)

ISBN: 9781989415320 (IS Paperback)

ISBN: 9781989415290 (KDP Paperback)

ISBN: 9781989415306 (Kindle)

ISBN: 9781989415313 (ePub)


pdworkman

ALSO BY P.D. WORKMAN

*Reg Rawlins, Psychic Detective*
What the Cat Knew
A Psychic with Catitude
A Catastrophic Theft
Night of Nine Tails
Telepathy of Gardens
Delusions of the Past
Fairy Blade Unmade
Web of Nightmares
A Whisker's Breadth
Skunk Man Swamp (Coming Soon)
Magic Ain't A Game (Coming Soon)
Without Foresight (Coming Soon)

*Auntie Clem's Bakery*
Gluten-Free Murder
Dairy-Free Death
Allergen-Free Assignation
Witch-Free Halloween (Halloween Short)
Dog-Free Dinner (Christmas Short)
Stirring Up Murder
Brewing Death
Coup de Glace
Sour Cherry Turnover
Apple-achian Treasure

Vegan Baked Alaska

Muffins Masks Murder

Tai Chi and Chai Tea

Santa Shortbread

Cold as Ice Cream

Changing Fortune Cookies

Hot on the Trail Mix

Recipes from Auntie Clem's Bakery

*Zachary Goldman Mysteries*

She Wore Mourning

His Hands Were Quiet

She Was Dying Anyway

He Was Walking Alone

They Thought He was Safe

He Was Not There

Her Work Was Everything

She Told a Lie

He Never Forgot

She Was At Risk

*Kenzie Kirsch Medical Thrillers*

Unlawful Harvest

Doctored Death (Coming soon)

Dosed to Death (Coming soon)

Gentle Angel (Coming soon)

**AND MORE AT PDWORKMAN.COM**

*For those who fight the darkness every day*

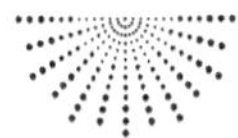

# CHAPTER ONE

Reg climbed out of bed, the dread from her nightmare still squeezing her heart so tightly it hurt. It had been a long time since she had felt that anxious without knowing what it was she had to fear. She was keenly attuned to the possible dangers in her life, always staying one step ahead of the authorities or anyone who might have figured out her latest scam, but the heart-squeezing dread was different. It wasn't connected to any specific risk she could identify.

She could write it off as the vestiges of her nightmare, but she didn't want to ignore the warning. It could be something that her subconscious was trying to warn her about. If something was bothering her, she needed to know what it was to address it. If it was time to leave Black Sands… she didn't want to, but if it were the only way to stay safe, then she would.

Starlight was sitting in the window looking out at the back garden. He looked over at Reg and let out a low, mournful howl. Reg went over to him and petted him and let her tuxedo cat rub the top of his head against her chin and neck.

"What's the matter, Star? Did you have a nightmare too?"

He sat back and started to wash, giving her the cold shoulder. She felt his rebuff keenly. She knew very well that he wasn't unhappy because he'd been having a nightmare. She was being silly, but in doing so, she had made light of his problem, which, as far as he was concerned, was far more important than her petty human problems.

"Okay, I'm sorry." She stroked him again. "What is it?"

She peered out the window. She could see Sarah working in the garden, something that lifted her heart just a little. Not so long ago, she had been worried that she was going to lose Sarah for good. Suffering the effects of losing her powerful emerald amulet, Sarah had been on the brink of death. It had been a hard-won battle to bring her back. Seeing her puttering around in the garden was something that Reg had never expected to see again and it warmed her heart.

She kneaded the back of Starlight's neck. "Are you looking for your friend?"

This time he didn't rebuff her. She could feel the warmth of his confirmation, but also the emptiness and longing that the other cat had left behind.

Reg had only seen the black cat he watched for twice. Then, Reg's mind had been on more important things; finding the emerald and proving that she wasn't the one who had stolen it. It wasn't easy for someone with a past like Reg's to prove her innocence. While no one in Black Sands knew her full history, both Corvin and Detective Jessup had a pretty good idea that she had stolen and fenced jewelry and other valuable goods before.

"I'll ask Sarah if she's seen any sign of him," Reg told Starlight, kissing his velvety black ears.

He stared at her reproachfully with his mismatched green and blue eyes. Reg coughed and corrected herself.

"I'll ask Sarah if she's seen *her.*"

She chuckled as she grabbed a housecoat to pull on over her shorts and t-shirt and walked out to the kitchen. Starlight remained in the window watching for any sign of the black cat rather than following Reg into the kitchen and demanding breakfast. He really was worried about the black cat.

Reg turned on the coffee machine. She looked at her phone for any new mail or messages while she waited for it to brew a pot of coffee, trying to immerse herself in something other than the tightness around her heart. If she just ignored the feeling, it would go away. If it was just general anxiety, then distracting herself with something else should help.

But even before she filled her first cup of coffee, she knew that it wasn't going away. It wasn't just the vestiges of a bad dream, brought on by imagination or watching TV too late into the night.

Something was really wrong.

She just didn't know what it was.

* * *

Reg slipped on a pair of pink flip-flops and went around the cottage to the garden, where Sarah was standing, hands on well-padded hips, looking at the bent and broken plants, shaking her head. She glanced at Reg and shook her gray head.

"It looks like a hurricane was through here."

Reg sipped her coffee, which was really still too hot to drink.

"I'm sorry," she acknowledged. She wasn't apologizing for something she had done wrong, just saying that she felt sorry for the state of things. She was sorry that Sarah was feeling bad.

It was, in fact, not Reg or a hurricane that was responsible for all of the beaten-down plants in the garden. The damage had been done by Sarah herself, in a demented frenzy as she had tried to chase off the black cat that Starlight was looking for as he sat in the window. Reg hadn't seen it—hadn't seen her —since.

"I half-remember doing it," Sarah said, her forehead wrinkling into frown lines, "but it's like it happened a long time ago to someone else. I know I was angry, uncontrollably angry, but I can't remember feeling that way. Not... really."

"You were not well. But now you're feeling better... and I bet it won't be long before you have everything whipped back into shape again."

"I think it's taken a bad enough beating already. I need to remove all of the detritus and tie up some of the plants until they are strong enough... a lot of them won't bloom again this year. It's such a meaningless loss. It didn't have to happen at all..."

Reg tried another sip of coffee. "Do you want a cup?" she offered Sarah. "I just brewed a pot."

"No, dear. I have found that since my... reanimation... caffeine just puts me over the top. I have more energy than I know what to do with."

"I could make you some tea."

"I'm fine. I've had my breakfast and I don't need anything else. I just need to figure out how to get started here." Sarah sighed. "You're up early. Do you have an appointment?"

"No. I'm just having nightmares. I thought I might as well get up."

Sarah nodded. "I could make you a potion to help with nightmares."

Reg shook her head. She assumed that Sarah just meant some herbal remedy with valerian and whatever other brain-calming herbs she could think of, but Reg wasn't about to swallow anything called a potion. She wasn't that far gone yet.

"It's okay. I'm sure they'll pass in a few days."

"You need to make sure you get a good sleep. It can affect your productivity. Especially your psychic abilities."

Uncomfortable, Reg changed the subject. "So, I was wondering if you saw that cat around here again."

"Which cat?" Sarah frowned and motioned to her wrecked garden. "The one that caused all of this?"

It certainly hadn't been the cat's fault that Sarah had freaked out, trying to beat it with a broom and flattening most of the garden.

"Uh, yes. The black cat."

"It's a stray," Sarah said dismissively. "It will be in someone else's yard."

"Well, probably," Reg agreed. "I'm just looking for it… Starlight is looking for it. Her." She looked at the cottage window. "He's sitting there watching for her. But I haven't seen her since that day."

"I don't want another cat wandering around here. Starlight is inside, and that's fine; I don't want a cat out in the garden chasing away my birds."

"I know. But Starlight is very… convincing. He really wants me to look for her."

"You're not going to become the neighborhood cat lady, taking in all of the strays in the neighborhood. Not while you're living in my guest cottage."

"I don't want more than one cat."

"Then what are you going to do when you find it?"

"I don't know." Reg just knew that Starlight wanted her to look for his new amour. "I guess… maybe I would find a good home for her, and I could take Starlight there sometime to visit with her?" She rolled her eyes. "I don't really know anything about cat relationships. Do you?"

"No. Nor do I want to."

"So, you haven't seen her around anywhere?"

"No, I haven't. And if I do, I'll chase her away again."

Reg nodded. When Sarah said that she didn't like cats, she had meant it. Even though she was polite to Starlight and would even feed him when she came to see Reg, she was still not a cat person and didn't want them anywhere near her birds.

There was a loud crash, and Reg whirled around, putting her hands up, ready to defend herself. But there was no imminent attack. Just the rattle of a truck as it continued to drive down the street in front of Sarah's house. It had hit a bump or a pothole along the way, that was all. Sarah raised her brows at Reg, amused.

"A little jumpy today?"

"I just thought…" Reg trailed off. "Yeah, I guess I'm a little jumpy today. I don't know what is going on with me… I'm feeling anxious all the time… like something is going to happen. Something is wrong."

Sarah picked up a ball of twine, finally deciding where to start on her garden refurbishment.

"Well, you could help me with the garden. It's a very relaxing hobby."

"I'm not really looking for a hobby. I need to stay focused on my business if I'm going to support myself."

"Are you worried about failing? I thought that your psychic services business had been going quite well."

"It is. I can't complain about that. You've been a real help to me with all of your contacts and I'm always getting new clients. It's just that… I don't think this anxiety is related to my business; it's something else."

"But you don't know what it is?"

"No."

Reg watched Sarah as she approached a droopy, bent-over plant and lifted its branches tentatively as if trying to gauge whether it were still alive or beyond repair. She started to tie it to a nearby stake.

"Maybe you're picking up someone else's anxiety, then. Maybe it's not even your own."

Reg still had a hard time believing she actually had a psychic gift. She was good at reading people, that much was certain, but all of the other odd things that had happened since she had moved to Black Sands seemed like magic tricks. Someone using sleight of hand to gaslight her into thinking that she really did have unexplained powers. But she couldn't think of a way to explain everything that had happened using science or illusion.

She couldn't deny that she was often influenced by others' moods, though. Maybe that's all that Sarah was saying. She had recently met with someone or been around someone who had been very anxious, and she had just taken on those emotions herself without realizing it.

"Yeah. Maybe that's it."

"Have you had a client recently who was worried about the future?" Sarah suggested. "I imagine that a lot of the people who hire you are concerned about the future. That's what tends to worry humans the most. Not knowing where they are going."

"I can't think of anyone offhand, but there must have been. That must be what I'm doing. I'm just… empathetic."

"Exactly," Sarah agreed. "Maybe have a nice, calming cup of tea instead of caffeine in the morning, take some time to meditate and center yourself. I'm sure it will help to smooth away your anxiety. And if not… I do know some recipes. Or I could help you to find a healer who could help you if you don't trust my skills."

"Oh, it isn't that. I'm just not used to… magical solutions." Reg tried to explain it in a way that wouldn't offend Sarah. "I'm sure that your potions are just as good as the other charms and protection spells around the property. You're very good at what you do."

Sarah sighed, tying up another branch. "I think I'm going to have to find someone who can fix gardens. It's going to take forever to repair one plant at a time, and then to wait to see how they respond. I need a spellcaster who is good with flora."

Reg couldn't offer much help in that direction. "Maybe… Letticia would know someone."

"I'm sure I have a name in my Rolodex. I'll just have to take a look. It's been a long time since I needed to hire someone to do this." She put her hands on her hips again, surveying the minuscule amount of work she had done. "I really don't want to be tied to my garden all day. I want to be out, having a good time."

For a woman who, according to Jessup, was several centuries old, Sarah had a remarkable level of vigor, which had grown with her recent healing.

If Reg hadn't known that taking the emerald away would kill Sarah in short order, she might have been tempted to have it for her own.

# CHAPTER TWO

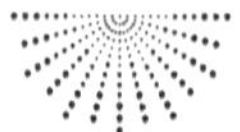

*O*nce Sarah decided to get someone else to come and help her to put her garden in order, she headed back to the big house, and Reg returned to the rental cottage to report to Starlight on her non-progress.

The cat made a snorting noise that suggested to Reg that she wasn't trying hard enough and finally left his perch on the windowsill to yowl around his bowl, insisting that Reg find something better than the stale kitty kibble that remained in his bowl. He rubbed against Reg's legs and then the fridge to encourage her to make the connection between the cat and his need to eat something tasty and nourishing from the fridge.

"I'm not that stupid," Reg said, "I actually do know what you want."

He sat back and looked at her, his gaze steady. If she knew what he wanted, then why did it take her so long to comply with his requests? How hard was it to go to the fridge and use her huge paws with their opposable thumbs to get him something good to eat?

Reg sighed, shook her head, and did as she was told, poking through the leftover fast food boxes and Tupperware containing offerings from Sarah. She found some beef stew that she needed to get rid of one way or another. She spooned some into Starlight's dish, and he pushed his head in to start eating before she had even finished dishing it up.

Reg watched him chow down noisily for a few seconds, then picked up her coffee and watched the house, feeling for Sarah. She knew without having to see that Sarah was going out again. Since her miraculous healing, she had been going out nearly every day. She was meeting with this friend or that new beau or somebody else who Reg had never heard of. Having decided that she wasn't going to do the garden work herself, she was now free to go gallivanting off yet again.

It was pretty sad that a centuries-old woman had a better social life than Reg. Reg didn't have a boyfriend, though she wasn't sure that she wanted one. And she didn't have very many people she could actually call friends. There was Sarah, of course, but she and Reg didn't see each other socially unless Reg happened to be eating at The Crystal Bowl, which was where Sarah usually ate, or they were both at a community event together. There was Detective Jessup, but Reg was not happy with her, primarily due to the fact that Marta Jessup had considered Reg the prime suspect in the investigation of Sarah's missing emerald. It was true that multiple witnesses and Reg's past had all made her look guilty, but she *wasn't* guilty, and if Jessup had been a friend, she would have known that.

But that was fine, because it wasn't a good idea for Reg to have a friend who was a cop. She knew that there were a lot of cons and cops who were close friends, but she had never understood how it worked, and she couldn't see herself fully trusting anyone who had anything to do with law enforcement. Back in Bald Eagle Falls, her foster sister Erin's boyfriend was a cop. But Erin had a legitimate business baking gluten-free products now. The fact that she kept finding bodies or getting involved in police investigations didn't help matters, but in spite of all of that, she seemed to have a pretty good relationship with Officer Handsome.

Reg needed to find some new friends. She was usually good at making friends quickly. She had been moved around a lot as a kid, so she'd had to develop some good social skills if she wanted to play with anyone other than her imaginary friends.

Corvin had suggested that Reg's imaginary friends hadn't been invented, but ghostly, but Reg thought he was either pulling her leg or he was mistaken. She hadn't learned until later in life that she could pretend to talk to dead people and get money for it. As a child, she had just been entertaining herself by peopling her surroundings with interesting characters, like a writer writing a book. The psychologists had always said that she had a vivid imagination, if they could just get her to put it to good use.

Which was precisely what Reg was doing.

* * *

After Corvin's hearing, a security guard had walked Reg out to her car. He hadn't been an unattractive guy and had shown an interest in her. He had given her his card, but she couldn't remember what she had done with it. She tried to remember what she had been wearing that day. It was probably still in her pocket or her purse. She wouldn't have thrown it out.

She tried her purse first, but it was the sort of cavernous bag where miscellany went to die. Who knew what kind of crud had collected in the bottom of it. She was always putting little things in there for an emergency or to put to good use later, and could never find them again when she wanted them.

She looked through the top few layers, including pulling out her wallet and checking to see if she had put the card into one of the slots, but there was no sign of it. She didn't want to dig all the way to the bottom or to dump it out, so she decided to try her pockets instead. She always put her clothes back in her dresser or closet if they didn't need washing. She couldn't see the point of washing an item every time you wore it if you didn't sweat or spill and it still looked fresh and unwrinkled. Her wardrobe was pretty small, and she didn't want to have to do the laundry every two or three days.

She was pretty sure she had been wearing pants, not one of her gypsy skirts when she went to the trial. She had driven to Letticia's house that day, and it was a long way through the woods. She hadn't known whether she was going to end up having to hike up a trail or something else requiring a full range of movement, so she had worn pants rather than a skirt.

Reg went through the pockets of a couple of pairs of pants. She hated how women's clothing so seldom had pockets and refused to buy any without pockets. It was easy to sew pockets into a skirt, but tailored pants were another story. It was much easier to hide things quickly if one had proper pockets. What else was she going to do, stuff something down her bra? While that might work for smaller items, something larger would end up looking odd.

In the second pair of pants, her fingers touched a card. Reg pulled it out, feeling a warm rush of satisfaction over having found it. She turned the card over to look at the name on it. Damon Knight. She didn't know much about him, but it sounded like a magical name. He had appeared to have some magic the day of the trial, able to put out a small fire with his powers without even turning a hair. And he hadn't escorted Reg to her car because she was causing trouble or because he wanted to protect her from an ugly mob. He'd walked her to her car because he wanted a chance to spend a few minutes alone with her and to give her his number.

Reg left her bedroom and walked over to the wicker couch. She had left her phone on the coffee table in front of it. She didn't have any appointments in the next couple of hours, so the time was hers to use as she liked. She sat down on the couch and curled her feet up beneath her, trying to get comfy. The wicker couch always seemed to be lumpy or poky somewhere. But it was a piece of furniture that she hadn't had to buy herself, so what did she have to complain about?

"Come on over, Starlight."

The cat was washing in a bright sunbeam. He stopped and looked at Reg as if he couldn't believe that she had interrupted his ablutions.

"Come on." Reg patted the cushion next to her. "I'll scratch your ears."

He looked at her for another minute, then consented to join her. He jumped up beside her and accepted the pets and cuddles and ear scratches. She touched the white spot on his forehead, the star that gave him his name. His third eye, Sarah called it.

"What do you think?" she asked him thoughtfully. "Think Damon will answer the phone, or will it go to voicemail? He might be working. I don't know if he works regular hours or only special events. He could be an accountant or something boring the rest of the time."

Starlight rubbed against her hand, purring, lapping up the attention. Reg focused on him for a few more minutes before picking up her phone to call Damon.

"Here, lay down now and cuddle," she encouraged, patting the couch to encourage him to lie down. Starlight continued to rub and bump against her. She rolled her eyes and tapped Damon's number into her phone.

It only rang once or twice before a click told Reg it had connected. It was so fast that she was sure it had gone to voicemail and she was trying to think of what she wanted to say in her message. Did she even want to leave a message, or should she try him again another time so that they could actually talk to each other and judge each other's temperature?

"Damon," he said.

Reg waited for the rest of the recording, then realized that was it. She wasn't talking to a machine; she was talking to the warlock himself.

"Oh, hi, Damon. I don't know if you remember me, but I met you at Corvin Hunter's hearing…"

"Reg Rawlins," Damon said, a smile in his voice.

Reg smiled back. "Yes. That's right. You do remember."

"I was hoping you would call."

"Well… I did." Reg rolled her eyes at her response. How quickly the conversation was dwindling to something she was likely to have had in sixth grade.

"How are you?" Damon asked politely. "Did you hear the verdict about Hunter?"

"Yes, I did. I got a delivery."

"Good. They're supposed to notify all of the concerned parties, but sometimes someone gets missed. Whether by accident or on purpose…"

"So they decided to shun him."

"Yes."

"Are you… part of Corvin's coven?" Reg asked tentatively. She didn't know how big the magical community was and whether there were multiple covens or just the one. Were all warlocks automatically admitted to the coven, or did they have to qualify to get in? Or did they have a choice as to what coven they wanted to go to?

"No." Damon gave a low chuckle. "I'm more of a lone wolf. Which is one of the reasons that I can work security at something like that. You couldn't do security if the warlock on trial was someone from your own coven. Too close of a relationship."

"So the two of you are not friends?"

"No. I don't have anything to do with Hunter. Not because I have anything against him… he was just never my type. You know. The kind of guy that I would associate with."

"What kind of guy do you associate with?"

"Well, as I say, I'm sort of a lone wolf. So… not a lot of people. I have a couple of close friends, but other than that… my circle is pretty small."

"Mine too," Reg admitted. "I need to make some new friends."

"Old ones just not holding up?" he teased.

"No." Reg let out a sigh that was all too real. "I need someone I can hang out with. I haven't had a lot of luck in making friends here. I mean… I haven't made enemies, but I'd like to get to know some people who are… more like me."

"Psychics?" Damon suggested.

"No way," Reg said immediately. She had only associated with one other psychic so far, and Marian was not the kind of person she wanted to be around. She didn't want to be around anyone who was going to try to read her or to influence her feelings. Marian was good at manipulating people, and Reg wanted to stay in full control of her own thoughts and feelings.

"No way?" Damon repeated, laughing. "You sound pretty adamant about that!"

"Have you ever been in a room where everyone is trying to read everyone else?" Reg asked. "I'd go crazy. I'll keep my thoughts to myself."

"That makes sense." Damon didn't say anything for a moment, and Reg tried to figure out how to take control of the conversation and steer it in the direction she wanted to go. "So did you decide to take me up on my offer?"

Reg frowned, trying to remember the conversation. What offer had he made?

"Umm… I…"

"I offered to take you out to dinner, show you around town. I didn't hear from you right away, so I thought maybe you weren't interested."

"Things have just been a little crazy with me lately. Well, forget lately, they've been a little crazy ever since I hit town. But yeah, I would be interested in getting out… getting to know Black Sands a little better."

"Excellent. Are you free tonight?"

"Let me take a look at my appointment book. Hang on. I should have done that before I called you, but I forgot."

"Sure."

Reg went to the kitchen, where her appointment book was lying on the island. She kept it out where Sarah could access it so that if Sarah happened to make an appointment for her, she would not be surprised. She opened the calendar and quickly found the day.

"Yeah, it looks like I'm free tonight. About seven onward?"

"Seven it is," Damon agreed. "Can I pick you up at your house?"

"No, you don't need to do that. Why don't we meet somewhere?"

eg had been expecting Damon to suggest a restaurant. Dinner and a date, it seemed the natural choice. But instead, he had suggested a bowling alley. Did people even do that anymore? It brought to mind pictures of Fred Flintstone dancing up to the alley and throwing his stone bowling ball to knock down the pins. She wasn't sure what to do when she got there. Damon found her standing on the worn red carpet looking around at the various counters, baffled.

"Hello, stranger! You're looking a little lost."

"Yeah. What exactly am I supposed to do here?"

"Come with me; we need to get you a ticket, shoes, and a ball."

"Can't I just wear my own shoes?"

"Not unless you have bowling shoes, and I gather by your expression that you are not a regular bowler."

"I don't like wearing other people's shoes."

With all of the foster homes she had been in, Reg had put up with all kinds of hand-me-downs, and shoes were the worst. She hated putting her feet in someone else's stinky shoes.

"No one does," Damon agreed. "But they sanitize them. You won't get someone else's foot fungus."

"Ugh." Reg was seriously reconsidering a date with Damon. She hadn't even thought about foot fungus.

"Come on. Try it once. If you don't like it, then you know for next time, and we'll do something else instead. You choose next time."

"I don't know."

"Just try," Damon urged. "It's a lot of fun."

Reg shook her head, but she followed Damon to the ticket counter, then the shoe counter where she got the ugliest flat red-laced shoes she had ever seen. They didn't feel right on her feet. Of course they wouldn't, since other people had been wearing them. Who knew how many people.

The bowling balls were cool. There were a lot of different colors, and she liked the sparkles and swirls that some of them had. Damon helped her to pick out the size he thought she should use, and got a slightly bigger one for himself. At least he hadn't brought his own ball, so she knew he wasn't too crazy about bowling. If he'd brought his own… she would have known that he was too far gone and she couldn't ever go out with him again.

"So you've never bowled before?" Damon asked as he led her to the alley they had been assigned and pointed out their seats and the computer that would keep track of their scores.

"I think I might have once or twice when I was a kid, but I don't remember very well." Reg had an impression of crowds of kids yelling and throwing their balls down the alley. Bright lights and loud music and way too much sensory input. Since most of her foster families had not had the money to do much, it had probably been through one of the organizations that took disadvantaged youth places. She had gone to all kinds of camps and movies and other events with community outreach organizations.

"Okay, let me just walk you through the rules and the scoring then. I'm assuming you don't watch it on TV or already know all of that?"

"Assume I don't know anything," Reg agreed.

He gave her a warm smile and put an arm around her shoulder. Reg tensed. She wasn't ready for physical contact yet. Especially with a warlock whose powers she knew nothing about. She gave her shoulders a little shrug to dislodge his arm.

"Sorry," Damon said, raising an eyebrow questioningly.

Reg moved an inch away from him to regain her space and took a deep breath.

"Corvin Hunter," she said.

He looked around, but since she didn't actually mean that Corvin was there, he looked back at her, even more confused.

"The only experience I've had with romance with warlocks was with Corvin Hunter," Reg explained, her face getting warm with what she knew would be a bright red flush to match her red box braids.

"Ah." Damon nodded. "But not all warlocks are like him. He's… special."

"Oh yeah, he's special," Reg agreed. "And I'm not going to walk into anything like that again. So you can expect me to be Miss Prim and Proper until I know you better and know what your powers and your motives are."

He smiled reassuringly. "You don't need to worry. As I'm sure you've been told, Hunter's powers are very rare. And dying out, with any luck. You don't need to worry about running into another warlock who can steal your powers like that."

"Just because they are rare, that doesn't mean there aren't any more. And who knows what other powers I need to worry about. It seems like the magical community doesn't like to talk about the bad stuff, so they're not going to tell me if someone else like you has powers that I should be concerned about."

"No one warned you about Hunter?"

Reg sat down to retie her shoe. She grimaced. "Well, a few people told me to be careful of him or to stay away from him, but they didn't tell me why or what I needed to be careful of. So I was warned… but I wasn't warned."

"And you are the kind of person who doesn't take well to being told what to do?"

Reg hoped that her face wasn't going to keep burning the whole night. She shook her head. "No, I'm not. My parents were always frustrated with not being able to tell me anything. But I guess all of that came out at the trial. Now everyone knows that I'm not the kind of person who listens to warnings, however well-intentioned."

"Not everyone in the community was at the trial," he reassured her. "It wasn't that big of a crowd. And I don't think that's what they got out of the trial."

"Oh, what do you think they got out of it?"

"That you are a strong, independent woman who isn't going to be pushed around by the patriarchy."

Reg coughed. She checked the lace on her other shoe and stood up. They still didn't feel right. "Well, I guess you got that part right. You wouldn't happen to be psychic, would you?"

"No, just very sensitive."

She looked at him and shook her head. She wasn't sure that a sensitive man was what she was looking for. Damon's grin back at her was too mischievous to take his words seriously. He didn't consider himself a sensitive man; he was just teasing her.

"Oh, you're a handful," she told him.

Damon's grin got wider. "You are a psychic!"

Reg snorted. "Okay, why don't we play? I want to get this over with."

"Really? I'm hurt. If you knew how much fun this is, you wouldn't be in such a hurry to get out of here."

"Prove it."

"Why don't you go first?" he offered, motioning to their alley.

Reg looked at the other bowlers playing nearby. "Since I'm the newbie here, why don't you show me how it's done? I want to see your technique."

"Ladies first."

"Age before beauty," Reg countered.

"Oh," Damon put his hand over his heart. "What makes you think I'm older than you are?"

"From what I've seen so far, all of the witches and warlocks are older than they look. So I'm assuming you're at least seventy."

He laughed. But he picked up his bowling ball and didn't argue.

Reg watched him closely as he strode forward, swung back, and then delivered the ball in a smooth forward motion, his leg jutting out behind him at an angle as he squatted low to the floor. He knocked down a few of the pins but did not get a strike. Reg tried to put herself into his body as he took another turn, trying to feel what it must be like, how each action would naturally flow into the next. The rest of the pins went down, so according to the rules he had given Reg, that meant it was her turn.

She picked up her ball and held it in one hand. Could she connect psychically to a bowling ball? Lately, when she'd been angry, things had been breaking or falling around her. She still wasn't sure that she believed it was anything to do with her mood, but if the others were right and she could affect physical objects telekinetically, than why not to direct a bowling ball down the lane?

She took a deep breath and tried to imitate Damon's approach and release. When she reached the line and released the ball, it went directly into the gutter and rolled down to the end. Reg watched it in dismay.

Damon laughed. "Don't look so heartbroken. It was only your first try."

"Yeah, but… I thought… I just thought I would be better than that."

"Just get a feel for it first. Don't try to use perfect form; just get a feel for what it feels like to roll it."

Reg went to the ball return machine and waited for her ball to pop back up. The midnight blue ball returned and she picked it up.

"I get another try, right?"

"Yes, one more this frame."

"And then it's your turn."

"Right."

Reg tried again, this time not trying to imitate Damon's form, but just to get the ball closer to the center instead of throwing it directly into the gutter. She tripped over the toe of one shoe and just about did a faceplant before reaching the line.

She dropped the ball with a crash that made everyone turn and look at her, and it didn't even go down the lane, but rolled back to her feet and looked up at her like a lost puppy. Reg covered her face.

"Can I leave now?"

"No, you can't leave. You're just getting warmed up. Don't worry about what anyone else thinks. This is your first time. You're going to be just fine once you get settled in."

Reg groaned and picked up the ball, eyeing the people on either side of her that were glaring like she had intentionally broken the rules by dropping her ball. She didn't try to approach the alley again, she just threw it down the lane, making it crash again as it hit the polished wood floor, and it rolled most of the way down the alley before falling into the gutter.

"Can I just give up now?"

"Be patient. Don't be so hard on yourself."

"I don't like this game."

"You don't know yet. You've only bowled one frame."

"I know already."

Damon took his turn, getting a strike. He sat back down before she even had a chance to sit down.

"How long have you been doing this?" Reg questioned. "It isn't fair to bring me to something that you're already a pro at."

"I'm not a pro. I just do it for fun now and then. I'm not in a league or anything."

"Is this where you bring all of your girlfriends on a first date?"

He cocked his head, looking at her. "Believe it or not, I don't date very much. And you're the first girl that I've brought here... at least in a couple of years."

"Then why me? Why not take me somewhere else instead of humiliating me?"

"Are you really feeling that badly about it?"

Reg rolled her eyes. "No. I'm dramatizing—a little. I don't like being shown up like this. If I'd said that I liked to bowl or was good at bowling… then I'd forgive you for bringing me here. But it seems a little… show-offy to bring me here just to show me how good you are when I'm so awful at it."

"You're really not that bad. You've only bowled one frame."

Reg picked up her ball and walked toward the lane.

"If you still hate it by the end, I promise I won't try to bring you back here," Damon promised.

"Yeah. I heard you."

Reg retrieved her ball. She looked at the lane, closed her eyes, and rolled the ball. Nothing bad happened. She waited a few seconds before opening her eyes, just in time to see the ball hit the last pin on the right-hand side of the triangle.

"There you go!" Damon encouraged. "That wasn't so bad, was it? You knocked one down."

"Just one," Reg groused. But secretly, she was encouraged. She had managed to hit one pin without even looking. It hadn't gone into the gutter every time. Maybe there was some hope for her after all.

She again closed her eyes and released the ball. It wobbled back and forth down the lane, weaving this way and that until it reached the end, and it knocked down the front pin and a couple of others.

"See that?" Damon crowed. "You're a natural. Center pin."

Reg shook her head, but was pleased. At least she hadn't put every ball in the gutter. Damon took his turn, not getting a strike, but ending up knocking down all of the pins except for the outside two. He pouted dramatically, but she didn't feel at all bad for him.

Reg picked up her ball again.

"Do you want me to show you the proper form?" Damon

offered, approaching her without waiting for her answer, and putting his arms around her to readjust her position. Reg flailed, knocking him in the gut with her ball and then dropping it on the ends of his shoes as she pulled out of his grasp. Damon went white and gasped for breath while trying to lift both feet at the same time to clutch at his toes. He ended up on his butt on the worn, dirty carpet, holding the ends of his shoes and drawing in a big, wheezing breath. Reg was horrified, but at the same time angry that he had touched her after she had already warned him once.

She bent down to talk to him, aware that everyone around them was laughing or watching her closely, eager to see what was going to happen next.

"Are you okay?" She offered him a hand to help him up, but then pulled it away before he could take it. "I'm sorry, I didn't mean to…"

He rubbed his toes through the shoes, hunched over to protect his stomach. "No, my fault," he said in a strained voice. "You did tell me once already…"

"I know, but still, I didn't mean to hit you or to drop my ball."

"It's your turn. Why don't you go ahead and take your turn?"

Reg turned to look for her ball and picked it up. "Really, I didn't mean to wreck everything…"

"I think maybe next time we'll do something else. Something that doesn't include a built-in weapon." Damon groaned and pushed himself back up to his feet.

"Are you okay? I mean, really?"

"I'll be fine. Just a small bowling mishap. Happens all the time."

"If this is what it's always like, then maybe we shouldn't do it again," Reg agreed.

Damon gave a weak laugh. Reg looked at the pins and walked forward, not even aiming, just wanting to get her turn over with and be done with the night. The faster she could finish, the sooner they could be out of there, away from all of the prying eyes. The ball made its way straight down the alley and hit the front pin.

Reg was turning away, then stopped and watched as they all fell down. She glanced aside at Damon, then back at the pins as they all toppled over and the machine lowered to reset the pins.

She blinked, and the pins were all upright again.

"Your turn," she said to Damon, trying to sound casual. He looked at her; one eyebrow raised inquiringly.

"You have to take your frame first," he reminded her.

Reg looked at the pins and at the screen showing the scoring. She was going to tell him that it was her turn, she'd just gotten her first strike, and then she realized that her ball was still in her hand. She looked down at it and frowned, trying to reconcile what she was experiencing with what had just happened.

"What the...? But I bowled. I got a strike..."

"You got a strike?" Damon repeated. "I think I would have noticed that."

"But... I did."

He motioned at the scoring screen. Reg signed in exasperation. He hadn't been paying attention, and for some reason, the scoring machine had missed it. Her first strike, and it had gone unnoticed. Except that didn't explain why she was still holding the ball in her hand. If she had already bowled her frame, then it should have been in the return slot, and Damon should have been stepping forward to take his turn.

She shook her head and stepped forward to roll the ball again. She didn't want Damon thinking she was a complete lunatic, so she didn't argue it any further. It must have been some brain glitch or deja vu.

Not deja vu, but prescience. She had seen what was going to happen next.

Reg swung her arm and released the ball and watched it blast down the center of the lane and hit the front pin. But it knocked down only a couple of pins, and the rest remained standing. Reg sighed and shook her head. If that was the level of her prescience, she'd better not be laying any bets based on her visions of the future.

"Good job," Damon praised. "That was a nice throw. It was just a quirk that it wasn't a strike. Sometimes that happens. Nothing you can do about it. Try again, maybe you'll get a spare."

Reg looked at the pins standing on either side and shook her head. Not likely. How was she supposed to hit pins on both sides at once? She'd have to bowl down one side the first time and then down the other side. If she was lucky, she could wipe them all out in two more shots. But she wasn't expecting to get lucky.

She retrieved her ball and tried once more. She tried to aim it just left of center where most of the pins were, but the ball just went straight through the hole that she had created the first time. Reg shook her head. Damon didn't try any encouraging statements this time. She had missed her shot at a spare. There seemed to be an awful lot of technical language for something as simple as rolling a ball into some pins.

She flashed back to bowling as a child on one of those youth group field trips. She could see one of the supervisors who had escorted them there helping her with her stance, reaching out as Damon had to readjust her positioning. His hands on her shoulders, brushing her legs, encouraging her to pull in her belly. His warm body pressing up against hers as he gave her one last squeeze and encouraged her to go for it.

Reg felt suddenly sick. She turned and ran for the restrooms. She had seen the ladies room next to the shoe rental counter when they had been getting everything they needed.

"Reg?" Damon called after her, his voice concerned.

But she didn't care what he thought of her taking off like that and didn't have the time to stop and explain what was going on. She just ran for the bathroom without looking back.

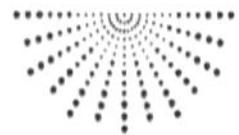

# CHAPTER FOUR

She had thought that she was going to throw up, the pain that had seized her in the gut had been so intense. But once she made it to the bathroom stall and hovered there, the feeling passed, and she was just anxious and uncertain. She didn't want to throw up, but she felt like she wouldn't be able to get rid of the memory if she didn't. It would keep pressing in on her, wrecking her night. She didn't want to be there bowling. Why had she agreed to in the first place? Who did Damon think he was, dictating that they had to play a game that Reg knew nothing about and he was so expert at? He was just showing off. He was doing some kind of macho positioning thing, showing his superiority, and she didn't need to play along with him like that. He knew her feelings about being pushed around by a man. He had first met her as she defended herself and explained what had happened between her and that predator, Corvin Hunter.

Hunter was a good name for him. Reg didn't know why she'd never thought about that before. He was a hunter, just like his name suggested. He looked for those with powers, and he hunted them down so that he could take it from them. She should have been warned just by his name.

Damon. Did his name mean something too? Should she know

by what his parents had named him what kind of a person he would grow up to be? Did Damon mean demon? Was he black and evil inside, and she was supposed to be warned by his name? She drew a blank on his last name and she hadn't brought the business card with her to check it.

It had been a bad idea to come out on a date. She obviously wasn't up to it. Maybe the nightmares she had been having signified that she wasn't safe in Black Sands. She should leave. Or at least, not have anything else to do with warlocks. There had to be plenty of non-magical people in Black Sands. Why did she have to pick someone who had powers?

Reg stayed in the bathroom stall for an extended time, waiting for the pain and the profuse sweating to go away. She didn't want to go back out and have to face Damon until she was sure she was settled down and calm again. She didn't want to play the part of a hysterical woman. She wasn't *hysterical*. She took the flashback as a sign that she should not be dating Damon. And she should not be bowling. She should have listened to her instincts in the beginning and refused. She shouldn't let someone talk her into something she didn't want to do just because she wanted to please him and not cause a social scene.

Next time, she would cause the scene. After all, that was what she had ended up doing anyway. She had ended up attracting more attention to her and Damon than she would have if she'd just insisted that she wanted to do something else.

Finally, Reg flushed the unused toilet and walked back out to the sinks, where she washed her hands and splashed water on her face, then sponged it off with a scratchy paper towel. She was just fine. She was perfectly calm. There was nothing to be concerned about. She would tell Damon it was a mistake and she was going to go home. The date was a failure. How was she to have known that without trying? Sometimes a person just had to try and fail.

She took one more deep breath and then walked out of the restroom.

She had thought that he would still be in their bowling lane, but Damon was hovering near the bathrooms. His attention was distracted the moment that she exited the bathroom, looking over at something at the shoe rental table, but then he turned his eyes back toward the ladies' room and saw that she was out. He hurried toward her.

"Reg? Are you okay? Are you not feeling well?"

"No, I'm not." She latched on to the excuse. "I should go home. Sorry to wreck our evening together, but…"

"I was having a good time. I'm sorry you're not feeling very well."

He was having a good time? Getting hit in the gut with the ball and having her drop it on his toes? Or watching her toddler-like struggles to figure out how to roll a ball down an alley? Did he get off on watching her fail, on exulting over how superior he was to her at the game? It was a stupid game, anyway.

"I think I should go home."

His mouth was turned down in a frown. "Do you want to go out somewhere? Maybe we should get you something to eat. You may just not be feeling well because you're playing on an empty stomach. We could go out and get something to eat. Or we could eat here," he motioned to the commissary. "I was going to take you out somewhere to eat afterward, so I didn't order any snacks, but we could have something here. We could have a snack here so that you were feeling up to bowling the rest of the set, and then we could go out somewhere fancier to eat…"

"I really don't want to play anymore. I don't think I can."

He looked disappointed, but he nodded and didn't argue with her about it. Reg was momentarily angry with herself. Now she was playing the part of the weak female and putting him into the role of protector? Why would she do that, when he was the one who had made her feel the way she did? He wasn't an innocent party, who just happened to be there when she got sick. He was the reason that she wasn't feeling well.

In fact, she felt just fine. The initial nausea had passed. She just didn't want to bowl anymore.

It wouldn't teach him anything if he thought that she was just sick and that everything had been going fine between them. The next time, he would just choose mini golf, and he would put his arms around her to readjust her stance, and she would have to jab the golf club into his gut to make him back off.

"Look, I'm not enjoying myself," she told him, making her voice strong. She had the right to her feelings and didn't have to cave to his just because he was a man and she didn't want him to think she was a witch. "I'd just like to go home."

His eyes widened, and she could read how startled he was. He'd really thought that she was having fun, or that she would have at least changed her mind about bowling by the end of the night.

"Oh. I didn't realize… I thought that…" He tried to find a way to put it back on her, to indicate that it was her fault for not communicating with him. But she had said from the start that she didn't want to bowl and that she wasn't comfortable there.

Reg bent down to untie her shoes, and slid them off. She was glad to get out of them. They felt oppressive to her. She knew how it felt to have to strip off her clothes and put on a uniform. How it was supposed to make her feel vulnerable and uncertain and to make her more likely to do what she was told by whatever authority was over her. Stripping off her shoes felt like taking back her control. She wasn't that little girl who'd had to stand there and let the supervisor put his hands all over her under the guise of helping her bowl. She had a voice, and she could use it.

"I don't like it," she told Damon in a quiet, firm voice, "and I'm not going to stay here."

The music and other noise of the bowling alley were too loud. Reg looked around in irritation. She just wanted quiet. The piped-in music stopped abruptly. All of the bowlers stopped talking and looked around to see what was going on. Reg could hear someone behind the commissary counter calling out to whoever was in charge of the music equipment to fix the problem.

"I'm leaving," she told Damon.

"Reg—" He reached out to catch her shoulder and stop her, then froze and didn't touch her. "Let me take you out to eat. If that's okay. Bowling was a stupid idea. I'm sorry. You told me you didn't want to do it and I should have just listened. Okay? I screwed up."

"Well… I don't know…"

"Let me make it up to you. You can choose the place. Where do you want to eat? We can even go out to the city if there's somewhere nice you'd like to go."

Not that Black Sands didn't have some nice restaurants. But the city did offer more options.

"Okay. If you're sure you still want to hang out with me. Your night hasn't exactly been all fun and games either."

He looked surprised that she should suggest such a thing. As if punching him in the gut and dropping a bowling ball on his toes hadn't made any impression on him.

"No, I'm having a good time. I mean… I don't mean it that way. I'm not having a good time if you're not happy. But I could be having a good time. If you were happy." He trailed off, knowing it must sound pretty lame.

Reg rolled her eyes and laughed. "Let's just get our shoes on and go."

They retrieved their shoes and returned their rented balls and shoes, advising the ticket person that their lane was available for use. She frowned at them, then shrugged and cleared the scoring screen.

* * *

They went back and forth on what restaurant to go to. Reg wasn't familiar with a lot of the eating establishments. She went to The Crystal Bowl, which was where Sarah frequently went for dinner and where she occasionally saw Corvin or others she knew from the magical community. And Corvin had once taken her to the Eagle Arms, but that was a fancy, expensive place, and Reg didn't want to suggest that Damon should take her somewhere so high-brow. They probably required reservations to be made two weeks ahead of time or some significant name-dropping in order to get a table.

"What do you like?" Damon asked. "Seafood? Burgers? Italian?"

"I'm pretty good with anything." Reg shrugged. Having been on the skids from time to time, she would eat pretty much anything that was put in front of her. After rejecting Damon's choice of activity, she didn't want to be pushy on the restaurant choice.

"There's a cool little diner on the west side," Damon said. "They have an all-day breakfast menu and make great waffles."

"Sure, that sounds good," Reg agreed. She could handle a waffle and syrup piled with strawberries and whipped cream. It was like having dessert for dinner.

"Yeah? You're sure?" Damon checked.

Reg nodded. "I'm sure. Waffles would be good."

So he took her to Wickedly Waffle, a charming 50's-style diner that was popular, but not too busy. Reg opened the menu and was pleased to see that nothing was in cursive writing and there were plenty of pictures as well as the written descriptions. She preferred not to have to read an entire book to figure out what she wanted to eat. The breakfast section of the menu was a few pages long, and Reg found what she was looking for, a picture of a waffle smothered in berries and cream. Damon took longer to choose what he wanted, flipping back and forth between pages. And it sounded like he'd already been there enough times to know what he liked.

Once they had both made their choices, they relaxed and made an effort to start the evening over fresh.

"So, have you always lived in Black Sands?" Reg asked Damon.

"Most of my life. I wasn't born here, but my family moved here when I was just a kid."

"And I don't know how this works… is everyone in your family magical, or…?"

"We all have certain gifts… things that come more naturally. But not everyone has decided to pursue them. My mother was always very involved with her coven. My dad wasn't big on developing his gifts. I have five older brothers and sisters, and I'm the only one who decided to go all-out in pursuing my powers."

Reg nodded, fascinated by this little window into the world of magic and how people chose to live with their gifts when they knew about them from birth, or whenever they knew that they had gifts. Out of everyone in Damon's family, only two chose to be part of the magical community. She would have thought that anyone with paranormal powers would be interested in developing them. At least, if they lived in a place like Black Sands where there was a big magical community. For Reg, growing up without knowing anyone else who had that kind of gift, she hadn't understood her abilities and it had been safer to be like everybody else. Was the same true in a place like Black Sands? Was it still best for children to lie low to keep from being bullied or abused? Despite the extensive network of magical persons, was it still something that was frowned upon?

"So is it impolite of me to ask you about your gifts?" she asked tentatively. "I haven't worked out the etiquette yet."

"I don't mind you asking. But I don't share very much. I work private security and, as you saw at Hunter's hearing, I do have the ability to deal with minor magical curses and psychic phenomena. I'm good at calming people down, deescalating violence. Abilities that have led me to the position that I'm in."

Reg nodded slowly. She ran her finger around the rim of her glass, thinking about that.

He had been able to hold off her angry reactions to Corvin and to calm her down enough to let the hearing continue, though it had been pretty much over by the time Reg blew a gasket. He had kept her feeling calm as it came to an end and had walked her out to her car. She had felt good being around him.

But what about bowling? He had not been able to keep her calm throughout their game and had not been able to convince her to stay and finish. Was that because he hadn't used his powers on her, or because she had been able to overcome them? She looked at him speculatively.

"It isn't polite to use your powers on someone without their permission," Damon said as if he were reading her thoughts. "It's different when I'm at work. Kind of like it's okay for a cop to arrest you and put you in handcuffs when you've broken the law, but if he breaks out the handcuffs when you're having an intimate moment, then he'd better have your permission before he slaps them on."

Reg laughed. She liked the picture that came into her head as he described it.

"So if I wanted you to help me to calm down, you could do that? But you wouldn't do it without my permission unless I was causing a stink at an event you were working?"

"Yes."

She took a sip of her water, thinking about that. "And what Corvin does, taking someone's powers away for his own use, that's why he's supposed to get his victim's consent before doing it."

"Yes. Exactly," Damon agreed, studying her with his dark, serious eyes.

"But who would ever consent to him taking their powers? No one would if they really knew what he was doing."

"I'm just the security guard at these things. I don't have to make the decision about whether someone is guilty or not."

"You don't like Corvin, though, do you?"

"Why would I like someone who takes advantage of women, even if it is his inborn nature?"

Reg couldn't help liking the guy, even if he had made her bowl. She smiled at him and took another sip of her water, hoping that the waffles would arrive soon. "So you think that Corvin could control himself, if he wanted to, and not take advantage of women?"

"I wouldn't like to speculate. I don't have anyone in my family like him. But I do know that in my family, we have each chosen whether we wanted to pursue our magical nature or whether to live normal lives."

"You think he had that choice too?"

"I don't know." He shrugged. "It's not my problem. Whether he did or whether he didn't, the results are still the same, he preys on women and I don't have to accept that."

Reg's stomach rumbled. She put her hand over it, hoping that Damon hadn't been able to hear it.

"Well, I guess we should have planned dinner before anything else," Damon observed. "You should have told me you were hungry."

Reg looked away, embarrassed. But the conversation made her think more about Corvin.

"I felt Corvin's hunger," she told Damon. "Two times. And it's…" She shook her head, trying to find the words. "It's overwhelming. It's like a hole eating right through him. I don't see how anyone could ignore something like that. That's why I don't know what to think of him. He's not just a predator… he's human too, and he has human emotions, and he has this driving need to fill his hunger. I don't think I'd be able to deny it."

"But you don't have to. And neither do I. That's his curse. Not ours. We all have our own troubles. No reason we should have to be responsible for his too."

"No, I don't mean that. I just mean…"

"You feel sorry for him."

"A little, okay. Yes. It's true. It's a dreadful feeling."

"But he might have just projected that onto you. You don't know that's what he was feeling."

"He couldn't give it to me if he didn't feel it, could he?"

Damon raised an eyebrow. "Couldn't he?"

"Well… I don't know. I don't know enough about magic or the way it all works…"

"I don't know much about psychic abilities. That's your wheelhouse. But I think he could make you think he's worse off than he is."

Reg hadn't thought of that. She had just assumed that what she had felt had been the true state of how Corvin felt. And not only on that day, but from one day to the next, always on the brink of starvation because he wasn't allowed to feast on anybody without their permission.

"Have you found Hunter to be… an honest and open person?" Damon prodded.

Reg shook her head, laughing, even though it wasn't really funny. "An honest and open person? No. Definitely not. He's always hiding something, holding something back. He's always trying to convince me to do something I don't want to, and he uses every bit of guile to do that. The time that I actually gave him permission…"

Damon waited for her to finish the thought. Blood rushed to Reg's face until it felt like it was on fire. She didn't want to finish. She had no intention of telling him about that experience. Her tongue had gotten ahead of her brain. Something she could not allow to happen.

"I… I don't want to talk about that."

Damon shrugged. His eyes were curious, but he had to understand why she wouldn't want to talk about such an intimate subject and to tell him exactly what he had done to get her cooperation. Another wave of heat went over Reg's face, and she took a drink of water to cool it. It might work better if she splashed it on her face. She was going to turn a permanent beet red if she kept it up.

* * *

The waitress arrived with their dinners. Or their breakfasts. Whichever they were, they provided a welcome distraction from Reg's embarrassment. She exclaimed over her waffles with rather more enthusiasm than would typically be expected, and while the waitress smiled and nodded, there was a little crease between her eyebrows as she looked at Reg, obviously wondering what planet she came from.

Reg remembered how Marian had tried to influence her feelings on more than one occasion, and tried to send reassuring feelings toward the waitress. The crease smoothed out. The woman nodded once more and left them to their food.

"Sorry. I'm feeling a little… off balance tonight," Reg tried to explain, as she sank her fork into the waffles and consumed her first few bites.

Damon appeared to be enjoying his stack of pancakes topped with a fried egg. He shrugged his shoulders. "I don't think you have anything to apologize for. You haven't done anything wrong or inappropriate."

"No?" She looked at him for reassurance.

Damon shook his head. "Would I lie to you?"

"I barely even know you. I would guess that if you had a good enough motive, you would."

"Well, I'm not lying to you, okay? Try to relax and enjoy yourself. You're… trying too hard."

"Am I?" Reg thought about it and decided he was probably right. Why was she trying so hard to impress him and make him think that they were a good match? What if he wasn't a good match for her? She didn't want to end up caught in a relationship that didn't work. She'd rather know early in the relationship if they were not right for each other. If she wanted to know whether or not they were compatible, the best policy was to be herself.

"Okay. I'll try to calm down."

She did her best to relax and enjoy herself, but that nagging feeling of foreboding was still sitting in the back of her mind, dark and cold.

# CHAPTER FIVE

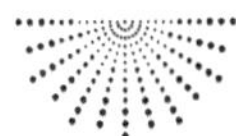

The rest of the evening had been as enjoyable as it could be with the feeling of dread still probing at the edges of her consciousness and with the poor start it had gotten off to. Reg tried to forget about the childhood memories and her anxiety over the possibility that Damon would try to magic her as Corvin had. She tried to pretend that it was just a regular date like she might have been on before she moved to Black Sands. But she found herself trying to read Damon's face and body language, to see his aura, and to feel the feelings that he was projecting. It was hard to be relaxed when anything could happen. She had no idea what to expect from him.

Eventually, they had finished eating dinner, had drunk their after-dinner coffee, and it was time for them to go their separate directions. Reg had insisted on arriving in her own car because she didn't want to be put in the position of having to invite Damon into her cottage or to send him away. She didn't want an awkward doorstep kiss or expectations.

Damon insisted on walking her to her car, as he had the day of the hearing. Reg tried to remember how she had felt with him beside her, how she had been happy to have the company and someone who seemed to be on her side instead of siding with Corvin's accusations. At least someone had stood by her.

It was dark. Reg felt all the more worried as they moved from one circle of light pooled beneath a streetlight to the next. She was in an unfamiliar neighborhood with an unfamiliar man, and it was darker than she would have liked.

The oppressive feeling was getting closer and thicker, pressing in on her like a wolf pack circling in the darkness, just outside the pool of light. Without even thinking, she grasped Damon's arm and moved closer to him, seeking safety in someone bigger and stronger than she was. He put his hand comfortably over hers for a moment, nice and warm and secure. He reached to put one arm around her shoulders, but paused before setting it down.

"Is it okay? Do you mind if I...?"

Reg grasped his hand and wrapped his arm around her like it was a warm scarf. She nestled against his side and looked around. He would think she was a coward for being so nervous. There was no one around them who was a danger to her. A few people walking on their own, a few walking with a friend or partner. No one who looked the least bit threatening.

So why did she feel so threatened?

* * *

Reg forced herself to separate from Damon when they reached her car.

"It's been a nice night." She hoped that her smile looked sincere. It didn't feel natural. It had been a nice dinner, but not spectacular. She didn't get swept away by him like she did by Corvin, but that was a good thing. She didn't want to lose herself or to lose control of the situation.

"Sorry about the bowling," Damon apologized, moving a little closer to her again and trying to put his arms around her waist or his hands on her hips or some other intimate gesture that would seem natural. But he wasn't sure how she was going to take it, so it was awkward. Reg took both of his hands in hers. Friendly, but not too friendly.

"Yeah… sorry about that. Just… some bad memories. I don't think… I don't think I ever want to go bowling again."

He gazed into her eyes. He did have nice eyes. He was taller than she, with a five o'clock shadow that gave him a rugged, manly look, but it was his eyes that were the most striking.

She could see herself getting involved with him. Ending the date with a kiss of promise instead of just holding hands and saying empty words. She could almost feel his lips on hers.

It was only with an effort that Reg was able to pull herself away from the imagined scene and see what was really before her. He had a slight cleft in his chin. And beautiful dark eyes.

"We'll do something else next time," he promised. "You can tell me what you like to do. No more bowling."

She sensed, though, his sadness at this promise. What emotional attachment did he have with bowling? Maybe he had gone with his parents as a boy, or maybe that was where his parents had met and fallen in love, and he saw it as something fun and romantic rather than a pointless game. She didn't let his regret change her mind.

"I'll call you."

She let go of his hands and turned to unlock her door and get in. As soon as her back was turned, she sensed a shift in the atmosphere. Danger loomed up so strongly that she whirled around, hands up to defend herself. Damon was just standing there and stepped back in alarm at her sudden movement.

Reg darted a glance back and forth, looking behind him and in the periphery. Something that set off her internal alarm. There was some danger close by. But it didn't seem to be Damon himself.

"What is it?" Damon asked.

"Something… I don't know what it is." She searched for some sign of it. "Something in the shadows."

* * *

Reg couldn't help pressing her foot to the gas a little bit too hard. She knew she was speeding and hoped that she wouldn't get pulled over by the cops, but she was more worried about what was behind her than about the police. If the police came, then maybe their weapons and lights would scare off whatever was behind her.

As a child, she'd been pursued by a nameless darkness more than once. It followed her from one home to another. She thought that if she moved around enough, she would leave it behind, and eventually, she had. She had always expected it to return, but it never did.

But it was back.

She looked in the rear-view mirror, watching for any glimpse of something dark. There had to be others in the magical community who could see or feel it. She couldn't be the only one.

Unless she were going crazy. Maybe the stress of the last few months was getting to her. Her brain couldn't handle all of the crazy stuff anymore and she had cracked. Now she was seeing bogeymen where there wasn't anything. They would end up locking her up. She would no longer be in control of her own life and they could keep her there for years, until they decided she had been cured.

There was nothing unusual in the rear-view mirror. No shapes in the darkness. Just that feeling of dread.

It only took fifteen minutes to get home. Reg didn't see anything or get pulled over. The feeling didn't go away, but she didn't feel like it was quite as imminent. Maybe it had stayed behind with Damon. Or maybe it had tried to follow her but hadn't been able to keep up with the car. Spirits could travel long distances, but if it were something tangible, it might not be able to move quickly without a vehicle.

Damon.

Demon.

Could demons drive?

Damon wasn't evil. He was just a warlock; one who had been nice to her, but who had terrible taste in his choice of recreational activities. He wasn't a dark wizard, trying to catch her in his net of evil magic.

Was he?

# CHAPTER SIX

She sat in her car for a few minutes before getting out, looking around and watching for any unusual activity. Feeling her way ahead of her, as she had learned during the past few investigations. There was no need to run straight into trouble. Not when she could psychically scan Sarah's house and the guest cottage in the back yard to make sure that there were no monsters or demons there waiting for her.

Sarah was in her house. No one was in Reg's. She could sense no traps.

Reg got out, locked the doors of the car as soon as she was out, and walked at a brisk pace around the house and down the path in the backyard to her door. She flicked her eyes around before going in her door, looking for the black cat. But it did not appear to have returned.

She put her hand on the cottage door and reached out once more before putting her key in the lock and letting herself in. Nothing. Starlight was there, snoozing peacefully. No one else. No disturbances.

She swung the door open silently and reached over to turn on the inside lights before stepping in. Nothing appeared to have been touched. She pulled the door shut behind her, locking it securely. She often left it unlocked for Sarah until she went to bed, but not on a night there was a nameless shadow skulking around Black Sands. Sarah had a key. Or she could ring the doorbell. Reg didn't know whether Sarah could unlock doors with magic; she'd never had a reason to ask. Were there practitioners who were able to unlock doors without a key? Maybe her cottage wasn't as secure as she had thought.

But Sarah had set wards for Reg's protection. Hopefully, they were strong enough to keep out the dark force.

Starlight jumped off of Reg's bed with a soft thump and wandered out to the kitchen, where he meowed inquiringly at Reg, wondering what had taken her so long to get home and why she seemed so disturbed.

"It's nothing," Reg said. "I'm sure it's nothing. Just letting my imagination get away from me."

Starlight looked at her sharply, as if she had said something worrisome instead of something reassuring. Reg went to the fridge, even though she was not hungry after the meal at the diner. She was just looking for something to soothe the stress away. She'd had plenty of sugar and fat, but maybe if there was chocolate… Failing that, she might try one of Sarah's soothing teas. Maybe that would settle her down enough that she would be able to sleep without dreams.

Starlight jumped up on the island counter behind her. Reg turned and looked at him.

"You know you're not supposed to be up there."

She reached toward the tap to turn on the water and flick it at him. Starlight gave a cross yowl. She looked at him, sensing something more than his usual impatience with her. She looked at the island, where her appointment book waited for her. Starlight pawed at something underneath it. Reg slid the appointment book to the side to reveal a few flyers. Sarah was still trying to get her to go to community events so she could meet more of the Black Sands residents and be more involved. Reg wasn't sure she wanted to be more involved. She seemed to have enough on her plate already.

She looked through the flyers to make sure there was nothing important. One of them was not advertising an event or special sale, but had a picture of a black cat photocopied onto it. Reg scanned the 'lost cat' headline, the brief description of a cat named Nicole, and a few details about the area she might be in and three different phone numbers at which to reach Nicole's owner.

Black cat, female, no markings, no tattoos or identification. Why had Nicole's owner let the cat out without any tags or identification? That wasn't very responsible pet ownership.

Of course, Starlight had escaped not that long ago, let out by Sarah when Reg was away. He hadn't had any tags either. Though he had been tattooed by the animal shelter in case he was ever brought in again.

"Nicole," she said to Starlight. "Is that your friend's name? Are you looking for Nicole?"

He sat looking at her. Reg sighed. "I suppose I should call in the morning and let them know that she's been around here. But I haven't seen her lately, so I don't know whether that will be of any help."

Starlight flicked his ears and didn't have anything to say about it one way or the other.

* * *

Reg tossed and turned, trying to find a comfortable position in the bed, to turn off her brain's constant replay of the date with Damon, and to push away the feeling of darkness and dread that threatened to overwhelm her. She'd had two cups of one of Sarah's soothing teas, but that just made her have to run to the toilet after an hour of waiting for it to have some effect. She wanted desperately to get to sleep and to escape the oppressive feelings, but it just wasn't helping.

Eventually, she gave up. She couldn't bear lying in bed and

trying to shut everything out. It made her body ache and her head throb. She could be sitting up watching a late movie, or posting to community websites to drum up more clients. She could bake a cake. Anything was better than trying to sleep when it was far beyond her ability to shut off her brain and find rest.

She was a psychic. She did midnight seances and readings. She was used to being up late. So why bother going to bed so early? She could wait until two or three and try again when she was suitably tired.

Starlight made a noise as she got up out of bed, a soft, startled purr-meow. He was in the window again, looking out into the garden for Nicole, the missing cat. When she walked out to the living room, he jumped down and followed her. He went over to the fridge and rubbed against it, suggesting that things would be better if she made them both a midnight snack. Reg resisted at first. She turned on the TV and surfed through a few channels. The TV was small and she rarely ever used it. She kept busy with other things, and when she wanted to watch something, she often watched on her phone screen, which was even smaller.

Starlight kept calling to her and, eventually, Reg got up and joined him in the kitchen.

"Don't you know that anything you eat this late at night goes straight to your hips?" she demanded. "Your body doesn't have a chance to burn it off before you go to sleep, so it goes straight to storage. We'll both get as fat as pigs."

Starlight was a nocturnal animal. He wasn't going to sleep. He was at the active part of his day. So why shouldn't he eat at night? Feeding him in the morning before his sleep was more likely to make him fat, if she were to follow her own logic.

"Fine, fine, let's see what's in here," Reg conceded.

She was trying not to eat too much high-calorie food. She ate out a lot and too much fast food did not do her body good. But the picture of a nice chocolate cake was stuck in her mind, and she wanted something sweet and calorific.

She hadn't had dessert at the restaurant.

But who wanted dessert after a pile of syrup, strawberries, and whipped cream? And a waffle was more like cake than a sandwich. When she thought about it, she'd had dessert for dinner. So her snack should be something savory and healthy. Exactly what she didn't want. She went through the containers in the fridge and pulled out the remains of a fried chicken breast sandwich. She removed the meat from the soggy bun and put it on the cutting board to cut into strips for Starlight. He purred and rubbed around her legs, opening his mouth so that his purr filled the room.

"Okay, okay, I know, you like my choice," Reg laughed, looking down at him. She swiftly cut the chicken breast up for him and put it into his bowl. She licked off her fingers and watched him. That was one problem solved. She still didn't know what she was going to eat. She didn't have any cake, but that was what she was craving. She looked in the fridge once more, but no chocolate cake had magically appeared there and none of the other offerings appealed to her.

"Why don't I ever buy cake?" she groused aloud.

Starlight looked up from his chicken, then went back to chawing it down.

Reg grabbed an apple and closed the fridge.

An apple wasn't what she wanted. But it was what she had, so it would have to do. She sat down again and looked at the TV.

News. Yuck.

She started flipping channels again. A late-night black and white zombie movie. No. A sports station showing—believe it or not—a bowling tournament.

No.

She kept going, looking for something to occupy her mind until she could get tired enough to fall asleep in spite of her anxiety.

Maybe she should see a doctor. She'd had anxiety pills prescribed in the past and she knew it wouldn't be hard to get them again. But she didn't want pills. She wanted the feeling to go away without any pills. She wanted to be normal. She always felt so defective when a doctor suggested that she needed medication to control her anxiety or her wild, runaway-train imagination. She was normal. She just happened to have a highly active brain.

The sound of her phone ringing just about sent her rocketing out of her seat. Who would be calling her so late at night? Yes, she was often up into the wee hours of the morning, but etiquette usually dictated that people call closer to regular business hours. She wasn't running a psychic hotline that people could call late at night to get a reading. Though that wasn't such a bad idea if she were going to be staying up late every night. She could refuse to schedule anything in the morning, and shift her schedule so that she was always sleeping in the morning instead of at night. Maybe she wouldn't feel so anxious about sleep if the sun were up and she didn't have to worry about shadowy shapes in the darkness.

It was as bad as when she had been a kid and thought that there were monsters under the bed. Or ghosts. Or vampires. Or some other supernatural but equally frightening force.

The phone rang again, and Reg jumped again. She knew it was going to keep ringing, so why would she be startled that it did?

Reg picked it up from the side table and looked at the screen.

Corvin Hunter.

What was he calling her about? Especially in the middle of the night? She never encouraged him to call her. And she had certainly never called him at that hour.

Well, maybe she had encouraged him to call. In the early days, before she knew what he really was. That the attraction she felt to him was part of his powers, not just the usual chemical attraction to a handsome man.

She swiped to answer the call. There was no reason she should want to talk to Corvin Hunter, knowing how dangerous he was, but she wanted someone to talk to, and he was available. He would distract her from the unsettled feelings.

"Hello?"

"Regina." The way that he said her name, correctly

pronouncing it Reh-JEE-nah rather than like the Canadian city, never failed to send a shiver of pleasure through her. Even though he wasn't in the same room as she and therefore couldn't send his rose-scented pheromones and charms in her direction, she still felt the little tug at her heartstrings, like watching a Hallmark commercial.

"What are you doing calling me so late?" Reg demanded, keeping her voice stern, not letting him know how close she was to turning to mush just at hearing his voice.

"What are you doing up so late?"

"I could be doing a seance, you know. You could be interrupting something very important."

"I assume that if you were doing a seance, you would have your ringer turned off."

That wasn't a bad idea, but Regina had never bothered to turn her ringer off for one. "I don't plan on people calling me this late, so no, I don't usually bother."

"Well, since you answered, I assume that either you aren't holding a seance, or the spirits don't mind. Maybe they'd like someone else to talk to."

Reg snorted. "They wouldn't want to talk to you."

"Trust me, there are plenty of spirits who would be interested in talking to me," he assured her, ego as big as anything.

"So why did you call? What do you want so late at night?"

"What I always want." He let that statement sit and fester for a few seconds. Reg's face heated as she considered the statement. "Just a chance to talk to a friend."

"We're not friends."

"Reg." The voice he put on was hurt, but Reg knew enough not to take it seriously. "You wound me. We're not friends? After all that we've been through together? After all that we have shared?"

"We haven't shared anything. You've taken."

"I don't think you're remembering correctly." His voice took on a velvety tone that reminded her of the night that they had spent together. It had been an incredible night and she couldn't deny that they had been connected more intimately than any other relationship she'd ever had. Maybe that was why it was so hard to leave him alone, even knowing what he was.

She cleared her throat. "Why did you call? You just wanted to chat? It's a bit late for that, don't you think?"

"I knew you were up. I saw your light on."

Reg glanced uneasily toward the door. "Stay away from here."

"I'm not there. I just drove past and happened to see your light. I wondered…" His voice was serious, dropping the teasing, intimate tone. Reg waited for him to finish his question, goosebumps rising on her arms for no reason.

"Wondered what?" she prompted.

"I wondered if maybe it was keeping you awake too."

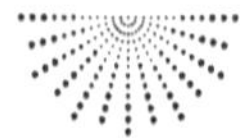

# CHAPTER SEVEN

*R*eg frowned at the phone. She didn't say anything right away. Corvin wondered if *what* was keeping her awake? She remembered when she had first moved to Black Sands and had been struggling to deal with a new environment and Warren's restless spirit. Corvin had said he was having problems sleeping due to a disturbance in the spiritual balance of Black Sands.

"What are you talking about?"

Corvin answered carefully. "There is something… dark at work."

Reg breathed into the phone. Starlight jumped up beside her on the couch. He nosed at her, trying to get her attention.

"Tell me what you mean." Reg struggled to keep her voice steady.

But Corvin probably read all he needed to from her response. "I thought that if anyone else in Black Sands could feel it, it would be you."

"What is it?" Reg didn't bother denying that she had felt something too.

"I don't know yet. But it's very powerful."

"Is it like when Warren was unconscious? When Hawthorne-Rose was operating?"

"Yes... but more powerful than that. Like someone or something has moved into the neighborhood."

Reg nodded her agreement. She scratched Starlight's ears. He rubbed his head on the bottom of her chin and scraped his jowls against her phone.

"It's really..." Reg tried to put it into words. "It's really creepy. I feel sick and worried all the time. And when I was with Damon..."

"Damon?" Corvin repeated sharply.

"Yes."

"What were you doing with Damon?"

"None of your business."

"Okay... then... when you were with Damon, what? What happened?"

"I thought it was coming after me. I felt it... closing in."

"Hmm." He didn't sound like he doubted her. More like he was concerned. "Damon didn't feel it?"

"No. Nothing."

"He's not sensitive, but I thought if it was that close, maybe he would have felt something."

Reg made a murmur of acknowledgment. It was hard for her to believe that with how strongly she'd felt the presence, Damon had felt nothing at all.

"When did it start?" Corvin asked. "When did you start to feel it?"

"A day or two after we got Sarah's emerald back. I thought... it would just go away. I was hoping that it was just from a nightmare, or just because so much had been going on lately, and once I got into something else, it would just disappear."

"But it didn't."

"No. When did you notice it?"

"About the same time. I had given Sarah a lot of energy and had just gotten notice of the tribunal's decision, so it seemed natural that I'd be having bad feelings. But as you said, it didn't go away. I replenished my energy, I ramped up my business with people outside of the coven and kept myself busy. But it didn't work. The feelings just kept getting…"

"Worse?"

"Yes. Growing. Like something is gathering power. Or multiplying. It's not a good feeling."

"No," Reg agreed. She stroked Starlight's fur, thinking. "So it's not just after me? I thought… that it might be looking for me."

"Looking for you? I don't know. Why would it?"

"I don't know. It's just that… I've felt this before, and last time it followed me. For a long time."

"Can we get together to discuss this?"

"No." Reg immediately pushed him away in her thoughts. He said he had seen her light on, so he had been past the cottage. He might have returned. Or he might have been there the whole time, lying about just having driven past. She tried to put blocks up around her. She hadn't learned how to protect herself against psychic or magical forces, but she really should. She didn't want to be so vulnerable around Corvin. Or around anyone else. She needed layers of protection.

"Regina. I really do want to discuss this. But I don't think it is something that we can flesh out over the phone. You know that I'm not just making it up. You've felt it too. The two of us need to get together. If we're the only two who are aware of this force, it's our responsibility to at least try to find out what it is. Find out if we need protection, and how to stand up against it."

"You and I can't get together. You know that. You know that as soon as we do, you'll be tempted to steal my powers, and I'll be subject to your charms. Things can never end well for us."

Corvin was silent. Reg reconsidered her statement. It could never go well for her. But for Corvin… if she succumbed to his charms, then he would get exactly what he wanted.

"We can go somewhere public. Invite someone else who can help to… make you feel protected. We could figure this out and get ahead of it. We don't know what kind of havoc it might create in Black Sands if we don't confront it early. You can't let these things get a foothold."

Reg had tried going to public places with him before. She had been places where she thought she would be safe because there were other people around. But somehow, she kept falling for him.

"Reg…" Corvin pleaded. "We need to do this. Do you want *that* to take over? Do you want it to gain power here?"

"How do I know this isn't something that you've engineered just to make me let down my guard with you? It could be something… a curse you put on me to make me think that there was some danger in Black Sands. That… *being* in the parking lot could have been you. You might have been manipulating me this whole time."

"Why would I do that?"

"Because you want my powers. And maybe because you want a friend since you've been shunned from your coven. Those are two really big incentives."

"Okay, so maybe I would do that," he admitted. "It would be a good ploy. But I promise you, I haven't. I haven't put any spell or curse on you. We haven't even seen each other, so how could I have? And I couldn't have been near you the whole time you have been feeling this. It's been too long."

Reg sighed. Unfortunately, he was right.

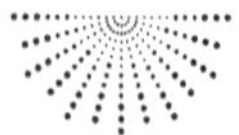

# CHAPTER EIGHT

"*R*eg? Are you still there?"

Reg tried to pull herself out from her dark thoughts to focus on the conversation.

"You expect me to help you out with this after the garbage you pulled at the tribunal?"

There was an intake of breath. "Uh…"

"You tried to blackmail me into speaking on your behalf instead of talking about what you had done to me. You attacked my character. You even tried to bring up stuff from the past."

"Well—" he tried to protest.

"Stuff from before I even came here," Reg pointed out. "And that means you went digging into my past."

He cleared his throat. "I can see how that might bother you, but in all honesty, the reason I looked into your past wasn't to attack you, it was to find out more about who you are and where you came from. Where your psychic powers came from. I've told you before, and I know others have as well, that you are very strong. Your powers are significant. Powers like that don't just show up randomly. It came from somewhere. *You* came from somewhere."

Reg didn't want to know where she had come from or where her psychic gift had come from. She was her own person, strong and independent.

"You still snooped around in my life without my permission, and you tried to use it against me at the tribunal. If I hadn't—"

"If you hadn't set me on fire, I would have succeeded?" Corvin said dryly.

Reg swallowed. She didn't know whether to laugh or to yell at him. She had been so furious at the time, but she could see the humor in it now. She had fought back against him unconsciously, exercising powers she didn't even know that she had—if it had been her doing and not that of someone else in the room—and she had put a stop to his inflammatory words.

She giggled.

She couldn't help it. It was just a stress relief valve. All of the anxiety and darkness had been building up inside her, and the giggle was just a way to bleed off a little of the pressure. It *had* been funny. Seeing imperturbable Corvin tearing off his cloak and his jacket as they each burst into flames. The glare of exasperation he had leveled across the room at her when she had disrupted his testimony and nearly derailed the hearing. He had gotten his comeuppance.

"How about this," Corvin continued in his stiff, dry tone. "If I try anything, then you can simply light me on fire."

"I don't actually know how to control it. And if you charmed me, I don't know if I could."

"We need to get together."

"Not tonight. Everybody else has already gone to bed. We'll try to sort something out tomorrow."

"Witches don't go to bed by midnight. I suspect there are more magical folk awake than asleep at this point. In the morning, they will all be heading to bed. Call someone. Call all of the witches you know. Put us all in a room together so that they can keep track of me and make sure I don't try anything with you."

He was being overdramatic, and he knew it. He was trying to force her into action, and Reg didn't understand why it was vital that it be right away. She looked at the black window behind her and felt a wave of cold that raised goosebumps all the way up her arms and down her back.

Whatever was out there, it was getting stronger. Corvin was right; they couldn't keep arguing when the force was growing stronger and gathering in power. Who knew what its goal might be and what kind of destruction it might have planned? If it were, as Reg suspected, something that she had known in her childhood, if it were focused directly on causing her harm, then shouldn't she have as many on her side as she could get? So far, Corvin was the only other person who seemed to be aware of the dark force at work, so he was the only one who could help to protect her. He was the only one who could help her to convince anyone else that there really was something at work in the darkness and it wasn't just her imagination.

Starlight prowled around as Reg got ready to leave, not liking her going out so late at night. Reg wasn't so sure of it herself. There she was, afraid of the dark, so she was going to go back out into the night where she was unprotected?

Corvin didn't seem to think that she would have any problems on her way over to his club, but Reg wasn't so sure. There weren't any protective wards on her car like there were on the cottage. And something *had* been following her earlier.

"There will be a lot of people over at the club," Corvin had assured her. "You don't need to worry about being alone. You bring along whoever you want for personal protection. I'm not trying to take advantage of you. I want to meet and see whether we can figure out what is going on."

"How about Starlight?" Reg teased. Starlight seemed to have

some power over Corvin. Even though Corvin claimed not to be able to hear Starlight telepathically, he still spoke to the cat as if he knew exactly what Starlight was telling him.

"Familiars are not generally welcomed at the Club," Corvin said stiffly, "I realize that we took Starlight there once, but that was out of necessity."

Reg hadn't been serious about taking Starlight anyway, but she enjoyed goading Corvin however she could.

Starlight being out of the question, Reg decided to call Damon to see whether he would oversee things at the club. She'd tried to rely on women to supervise before but, of course, Corvin had some influence over them as well, even though it didn't seem to be as strong as his ability to charm Reg. She had a feeling that a male escort would be a different story. Damon wouldn't let Corvin get away with anything. And he wouldn't trust Corvin if he didn't have eyes on him at all times. He was a security guard by trade, so who better to provide Reg with some magical protection?

She walked quickly back to her car, looking up and down the street for anything out of the ordinary. The presence was still there, in the background. Not the feeling that she'd had in the parking lot with Damon when she'd been afraid it was going to attack. She got into the car and locked the door and turned on the headlights before putting her phone in its holder and calling Damon on speakerphone so that she could drive safely.

"Hi," Damon said, surprise in his voice. Reg couldn't tell whether she had woken him up. He didn't sound too fuzzy, but if he hadn't been asleep for very long, it probably wouldn't take much for him to wake up enough to answer the phone. "I wasn't expecting to hear back from you so soon. To tell the truth... I wasn't sure whether you would call me at all, after the bowling thing..."

"Yeah. Something has come up, and... I have to go out. I don't want to be alone. Are you already in bed, or could you come and... act as my escort to make sure that nothing happens?"

"Of course," Damon said immediately. She could hear him start to move around as he spoke. He hadn't said whether he'd gone to bed yet, but she imagined that soft background noises she could hear were the rustling of his sheets and clothing as he got up and dressed. "So… what exactly came up? What's going on? Does it have something to do with what you… felt in the parking lot?"

"Yeah. Sort of. Someone who might know a little bit more about what is going on. But I don't want to meet with him alone."

"No, that wouldn't be a good idea. Who are you meeting with?"

Reg cleared her throat. She knew he wasn't going to like her answer. "Corvin Hunter."

"Hunter?" His voice held disbelief. "Why are you meeting with Hunter?"

"Like I said, he might be able to shed a little light on whatever it is that's going on. It's not just a nightmare or the stress of living in a new place. It's more than that. He can feel it too."

"So he says. What makes you think that he isn't just trying to con you? He could very well be the one making you feel so anxious. He could be following you around, casting some spell to make you uneasy, even when he isn't around."

"I thought of that. He said he isn't, but… I don't exactly trust him. It doesn't feel like him. But I want to have someone with me, whether he's got anything to do with it or not. Even if he says he just wants to help me, I know what's going to happen the minute we're in the same room together."

Damon growled something under his breath and Reg didn't bother asking him to repeat it. She could guess. He'd heard the testimony at the hearing; he knew her history with Corvin.

"Where are you meeting him? Somewhere public, I hope? Not his own lair?"

"This club he belongs to. He said there would be plenty of people around, but that I could bring whoever I wanted to along for protection. So I thought…"

"I'm happy to help. You do not want to be getting mixed up

with this guy. Not again. I'm not sure why you would even agree to meet with him again."

"I know."

"Tell me where it is."

Reg was a little surprised that Damon didn't already know where Corvin's club was, but Corvin had said before that it was exclusive. Even Jessup, a police detective, hadn't known anything about it. She gave Damon the address and directions and described the entrance door, which was a small, nondescript side door that no one would think led into such a lavish, exclusive place.

"Okay. Got it. Are you on your way over there now?"

"Yes."

"It will take me a few minutes to get there. Stay in your car until I call you back. I'll walk you in."

"I can go in ahead and wait for you. There are staff."

"No. You stay in your car until I'm with you. If I'm going to provide you with protection, you have to follow the rules."

Reg felt like a scolded child. But she had asked him for his help; she knew she needed to do what he said.

"Okay. I'll wait for you."

"Good. I'll see you in a few minutes."

Reg hung up the phone. She was reaching for the gear shift when she saw a shadow down the street. She squinted, trying to get a better look at it. Was someone out there, watching her and waiting for her to leave? Or was it just an animal? A stray pet or wildlife? She didn't like to think of what things could be lurking in the treed areas around the houses. There were more than just raccoons and foxes like back in Maine where she'd grown up. There were things like alligators and snakes.

But it wasn't slithering across the road. It scurried like a cat or a fox.

She pulled out, keeping an eye on the spot where the shape had merged into the shadows.

As she was watching, a cat darted out from under one of the

cars, making her jump and swerve before hitting the brakes. The cat stopped in the road and looked back at her.

A black cat. She couldn't see whether it had any markings or tattoos, but it certainly could be Nicole. Reg rolled down her window.

"Nicole?" she called softly, trying not to spook it. She made kissy calling sounds to see if it would come to her.

The cat continued to look in her direction but did not approach the car or react to the name. There were probably a lot of black cats in Black Sands. Cats were a common familiar for witches and warlocks and, of course, a black cat was the stereotypical witch's companion.

Reg released the brake and the cat dashed away. Reg tried to relax her shoulders and then the rest of her muscles. It was just a black cat. Maybe it was Nicole and maybe it wasn't. She would call or text the owner later and describe what she had seen, and the owner could come over and look around and call for her.

If the cat in Sarah's garden had been Nicole, she'd been out on her own for a while. The cat had been skinny and had obviously been outside for more than just a day or two.

Trying to put any other distractions out of her mind, Reg focused on her driving. She had only been to the club once and was relying on the GPS to get her there, but the GPS wasn't always reliable. If she lost satellite reception, she'd be in trouble, and she didn't want to be driving around aimlessly late at night with whatever had been following her.

* * *

She made it to the club and sat in the car parked on the street, since she didn't know how to get access to the underground parking that the members were allowed to use. She scanned the road for any activity and then looked down at her phone. Damon wasn't there yet, so she'd have to sit there and wait for him. She knew it would be safer inside the club. She hadn't told him how close it was to the pixies' realm. Maybe that would have made a difference. She knew that the pixies didn't like the sun, so they were probably out in force at night, scurrying around her in the dark. She looked up again, searching for any sign of movement. Still nothing.

She closed her eyes and reached out with her mind. She could sense the presence of magical powers in the club, a sort of a warmth that throbbed around the building like a beating heart. Corvin was probably in there already, though she had a hard time picking his signature out of the rest of the warlocks in there.

She opened her eyes again, sighing to herself.

She nearly screamed when she saw the dark shape outside her window.

But she hadn't felt the evil presence there and, when she was able to look more closely, she saw that it was Damon.

Unlike earlier, at the bowling alley and the restaurant, he was dressed in a long black cloak, a peaked hood pulled up over his head that hid his face, making it hard to see him until he shifted his head and a streetlight fell across his features. Reg put her hand over her pounding heart. She opened the door.

"You scared the hell out of me! What are you doing sneaking up on me like that?"

"I wasn't sneaking."

"Well… you should let me know you were there. I just opened my eyes, and you were standing there, I thought that you were…"

He raised his brows. "Thought that I was Corvin?"

"No. A… I don't know. Something else. Something… dark." Reg climbed out of the car, glad that he couldn't see how flushed she was.

He cocked his head to the side slightly, then shook his head, bemused. He couldn't feel the dark presence, so of course he was confused. He didn't know what was out there.

"Did you see anything?" she asked, looking around. She shut

her car door. She didn't want to be taken unaware by pixies or by the dark force. She shouldn't have agreed to meet Corvin at night. What had she been thinking? She knew it was a bad idea, but she had let herself be talked into it. She always let him talk her into things.

"No, I didn't see anything." Damon took a glance around, but his manner was loose and unconcerned. "Our crime rate in Black Sands is pretty low. It's good to be careful, but I'm more concerned about what you're going to face when you go inside than I am about what could happen out here. You are not likely to get mugged. But Hunter… no one likes him or his ilk. I don't trust any club that would allow him membership."

"I thought… it was a place that all warlocks went. I mean, I know he said it was exclusive, but all guys like to make themselves look important. Exclusive usually just means no women allowed or they have really expensive fees."

"I don't know what kind of place it is, but I'm not a member, and I don't think anyone else in his coven is. It's best to stay away from places where beings like him gather."

Reg suppressed a shiver. She and Damon walked up to the door that Reg had previously used. Maybe she should take Damon's advice and not go inside. She could call Corvin and tell him that she'd come to her senses and they would have to meet somewhere else, somewhere of her choosing, in the daylight. With lots of other people around who were not 'his kind.'

Reg couldn't imagine what it would be like to be surrounded by them. How could she raise any defenses against a coordinated attack, when she couldn't even protect herself against one warlock? Did she think that having Damon there would be enough protection? Corvin might not be able to charm another warlock the same way as he could influence Reg, but she was sure that he had other magic too. He had to make a living in the magical community, and he didn't do that just by stealing powers from unsuspecting psychics.

Reg took one more nervous look around, then raised her hand

and knocked on the door. There should at least be some weird Victorian door knocker on the door. Something magical and mysterious looking. It didn't seem right that she should have to use her fist to knock. Maybe a doorbell that made deep chimes within the building to set the mood.

The door opened almost immediately. A tall, slim, pale woman stood before them. She had a smile of bright red lipstick that looked like an artist had applied it. Her dress could have been painted on by the same brush, it was so form fitting. Reg averted her eyes, embarrassed by the fact that she would have been able to see any lines from the woman's undergarments, but there were none.

"Miss Rawlins, so nice of you to visit again," the woman greeted pleasantly.

It was good that she recognized Reg since Reg was so tongue-tied, she had no idea what to say to the hostess. It wasn't the same woman as she had seen there before, so she shouldn't have been able to recognize Reg, but she supposed that Corvin had told her he was expecting a guest, and there weren't too many people around town with red hair in braids like Reg's.

The woman's eyes turned to Damon. "And we are happy to welcome you here…?"

"Damon," he told her crisply. "Damon Knight."

She nodded but showed no recognition of his name. If he was hoping to make an impression on her, he appeared to have failed.

"Mr. Knight. We are always happy to welcome new guests. I'm sure Mr. Hunter will be happy to host you."

Reg snorted. Mr. Hunter would definitely not be happy to host Damon. He had repeatedly suggested that Reg could bring whatever witches she wanted to. He had not suggested that she bring a warlock or an actual security guard.

"Mr. Hunter is waiting for you in a private room. I will take you there…"

Reg stood inside the doorway and shook her head. "No. He

said it would be in public. Where there were a lot of people around. Not alone in a private room."

"Well, you won't be alone, you have Mr. Knight."

"No. You must have a dining room here, or a game room or library where people get together to talk. Take us there. You can tell Corvin to come to us."

She looked at Reg, clearly dismayed. They were sworn to do whatever it took to keep the club members happy, and this was not going to make Corvin happy. She tried again.

"You will be perfectly safe in the private room. There is nothing to fear. We take our guests' security very seriously here."

"You take your *members'* security very seriously. I am not convinced about your guests'. My friend was nearly assaulted here. And I'm sure you know that Corvin isn't the safest guy to be around. I am not meeting him in private. He agreed to meet in public."

"You'll be more comfortable in the private room. I can bring you drinks. We can provide whatever you need. In one of the public rooms, you won't be able to have the privacy that you desire for your discussion…"

"No. Is this going to be a problem? Because I can just leave now."

The woman reached out and touched Reg's arm. "No!"

Damon shifted forward, his big frame crowding Reg and the hostess in the entryway. His eyes were like lightning. "Don't touch her."

The hostess withdrew her hand immediately, eyes wide.

"Don't try that again. Are you going to accommodate Miss Rawlins, or are we going to leave?"

"Please don't leave." She seemed almost afraid. Would she face severe consequences if Reg decided it wasn't safe and walked back out? Would she be fired or physically punished? Something even worse? The woman swallowed and tried to keep a calm demeanor, but even though she managed to control her face and her voice, Reg could still feel the emotions pouring off of her.

"I'll stay if you take me to one of the common rooms, where there are other people," Reg asserted. "Then you can go talk to Corvin and tell him that you convinced me to stay, but that he's going to have to come down off of his high horse and meet me in front of other people like he promised."

The hostess nodded woodenly. "Please come with me. I will update him on the situation after you are settled."

# CHAPTER NINE

The dining room that Reg and Damon were escorted to was not full by any measure, but it wasn't empty. There would be other witnesses if Corvin decided to do something threatening. Reg wasn't sure anymore whether that would be enough of a protection. Obviously, the other people who frequented the club were going to be just as privileged and self-centered as Corvin himself. They would be loyal to their own kind, not to someone like Reg who came from outside of the community and barely knew which way was up in the magical world. She didn't know what kind of reputation Damon might have, but the hostess had not recognized him or his name. He had said that he was a lone wolf. She hadn't thought about it before, but that meant that he didn't have the weight of a coven behind him. He didn't have anyone watching his back. They were just two people against Corvin and the staff of the club and the other members and their guests.

Conversations ceased when they were escorted in. People didn't recognize them, and they weren't there with another member, so Reg supposed that was worthy of note. She explored the emotions of the room, looking around at the diners and trying to discern who they needed to be careful of and who might be friendly. Some people were naturally the protectors of strangers and the weak, but she didn't get that vibe from any of them. They were curious. Some of them were irritated by the introduction of strangers into their ranks. But no one was there who cared whether something happened to her. She might be fractionally safer in a room with other people than she was in Corvin's private room, but Reg sensed that it wasn't by much.

Damon looked around, assessing whatever angles he had been trained to. When the hostess indicated one table, he shook his head and selected another empty table instead.

"We'll sit here."

Reg couldn't see any difference in safety between the two. She suspected that he was just showing his control of the situation. He wanted them to know that he had the upper hand and they weren't going to be calling the shots. Reg sat down where Damon indicated. They could both see the door that Corvin would enter through. Reg was aware that there was also a kitchen door and an emergency exit. She couldn't watch them all at the same time. Damon glanced around and sat down.

"Nice little place he's got here," he commented.

"Yes. It must be really expensive. And from what I understand, they'll go to any lengths to satisfy their members' needs."

"I'm not sure I find that reassuring."

"No. Me neither."

"Are you sure you want to go ahead with this? You can change your mind. If you don't feel safe here, you can dictate the terms. You can tell him that you'll meet him at another time and place."

"I know. But I want to get this over with. I want to find out what he knows about this force. What's going on in Black Sands."

"I doubt you'll get any answers out of Hunter. He'll pump you for what you know, or try to get whatever it is that he invited you here for, and you'll leave here none the wiser. Hunter looks out for one person, and that's himself."

"I get that."

He gazed at her for a minute, then nodded. "I guess you do."

Low lights and flickering candles lit the dining room. Damon's hood was still up over his head, his face mostly in shadows. He looked rugged and dangerous. Maybe a match for someone like Corvin, who seemed to be more refined and careful.

It was a few minutes before Corvin appeared. He was not escorted by the hostess. Of course, he knew where the dining room was and didn't need her to point his guests out.

His jaw was clenched. He sat down in the seat next to Reg at the round table rather than the one across from her. He didn't get angry at her for insisting that they meet in a public place, didn't object to Damon's presence; he just sat down and got down to business.

"Thank you for coming to see me," he told Reg in a low voice. She didn't feel the warmth that she usually did from him. He hadn't turned on the charm, so he seemed just like a normal man. An unusually handsome one, yes, but she didn't feel magically drawn toward him: no special tingles, no rose scent, no shivers.

"So, what exactly do you want to know that you couldn't have asked over the phone?" Reg asked. Was there really something that he needed to be face-to-face for? Other than trying again to seduce her and steal her powers?

"You and I are the only ones that I know of who are aware of the force at work here," Corvin said, leaning forward.

Reg reflexively held her breath, expecting the heady scent of roses to envelop her. She couldn't hold it forever, and when she released it and breathed in, the air was clear, filled only with the smells of the food cooking in the kitchen.

"Right," she said. "Why is that important? What does it mean?"

"There are other psychics in town who I would expect to have noticed it. Other witches and wizards have some level of sensitivity to the changing spiritual or magnetic forces in Black Sands. But so far, it's just you and me."

"So?"

He rubbed his jaw, fingers rasping over the short whiskers of his beard. "I think that if only you and I have felt it, that it must be something that connects the two of us. There is something that affects the two of us personally, that is unique to just you and me."

Reg shook her head, frowning. "Like what? I don't know what you mean."

"I'm not sure that I do either. I wanted to see what I could feel if we were together, to explore any connections that we have and to try to get a better picture of what it might be. I was hoping that you would meet with me in a private room where we would be more free to talk without distractions."

"No."

He sat back, shaking his head. "I'm not trying to ensorcel you, Reg. I'm trying to figure out what danger you are in."

"Me and you."

"What?"

"You said that you and I could both feel it, so if I am in danger, then you must be too. If it affects the two of us, won't it affect us the same way? If it wants to attack me, then doesn't it want to attack you too?"

Corvin contemplated her suggestion. Reg was impatient waiting for his answer, but leaned back to let him work through it and to decide whether she was right or wrong.

"I'm not sure I am in any direct danger," Corvin said slowly. "I think that Black Sands itself is under a pall and that you specifi-cally are in danger. But I'm not sure that I am in any more danger than the rest of Black Sands."

"But something is going to happen. It isn't just me. When I… lose direct contact with… whatever it is… it's still here. It's still doing something that threatens…" Reg struggled to find the right words. She wasn't a scholar, hadn't ever done very well in school with her disrupted life, learning disabilities, and differences from the other children. But she wished for once that she could find the exact right words to express herself. She had an impulse to connect with Corvin, to establish a telepathic link into his head so she could tell him without words just what it was that she meant. She glanced aside at Damon, wondering whether it would be safe if he was sitting right there. She would never do it alone, but with magical security there, Damon could pull her back if Corvin tried to control her, couldn't he?

"Something that threatens the balance and the peace of the community," Corvin suggested.

It was as close as Reg figured they were going to be able to get using just words. She nodded. "It didn't come here because of me and it isn't staying here because of me. It has… purpose."

Corvin nodded. "Okay. But why is it that you and I are the only ones who can sense it?"

Reg reviewed the possibilities. As Corvin said, there were plenty of other psychics and witches she would have thought would be able to sense such a profound influence in their community. It was so strong to her that she felt that even non-practitioners should be able to feel the oppressive pall.

But what if it wasn't that much stronger than other influences in the community, it was just that Reg was extra sensitive to it? Why would Corvin also be able to feel it so strongly? He didn't ordinarily have strong psychic powers. He could feel shifts in the magical balance, but it wasn't his gift. She could remember the expression on his face when he had been in possession of her powers. How he had marveled at how strong the voices in his head were and he had experimented with exercising the powers that he'd taken from her. Powers that she had never really understood that she had.

"When you returned my powers, you said that you still retained something," Reg said slowly, "you compared it to the droplets of milk that stay in the carton when you pour it out."

Corvin's eyes were quick. He immediately caught on to her train of thought. "So maybe the reason that you and I can both sense it is that I retained something of your gifts."

Reg nodded. "Yes. Exactly."

He closed his eyes, and Reg could feel him exploring inside his head, trying to verify what she had suggested. She wondered whether his awareness of his own psyche was so strong because that was a natural gift or because he had grown up in the magical community, where his abilities were accepted and spoken of openly. Reg had been forced to deny her gifts and to stuff them down, so that she didn't know or understand them at all.

The minutes drew on. Reg glanced over at Damon. His eyes were on Corvin, alert for any changes.

"You have memories connected with this force," Corvin suggested, opening his eyes again.

Reg shifted uncomfortably. "I'm not sure if it's exactly this force, but… something like it."

"What happened?"

"Nothing happened. I… tried to run away from it. I hid from it. Moved from one family to another. Eventually… it was gone."

"It was just gone?"

"Yes."

Corvin took a sip of the ice water in front of him. He grimaced and raised his hand to motion to a waiter. He ordered a drink and raised a questioning eyebrow at Reg and Damon. "On me, of course. You need something stronger than water."

Reg ordered a glass of wine and Corvin argued for a moment with the waiter about the vintage. Damon waved off the offer of a drink. He was on duty and taking his role seriously.

"You do not remember correctly," Corvin challenged Reg.

Anger immediately lit up Reg's brain. "You think I'm lying?"

"No. As I said, I don't think you're remembering it properly. I think that like with much of your childhood, you've suppressed it."

"You don't know anything about my childhood," she snapped. And hoped that it was true.

"I knew about the imaginary friends, didn't I?"

"You guessed."

"And you suppressed. You weren't allowed to see spirits, so you had imaginary friends. And when you were too old for imaginary friends, you did your best to ignore them and block them out because you didn't want to go to the loony bin. And you made yourself forget about your imaginary friends, or at least the part about them being real people."

Reg gritted her teeth. "Yes. Fine. That much is true." Except that she hadn't blocked them to stay out of the loony bin, she'd blocked them to get back out. She knew that if she kept hearing them, she would never be released.

Corvin nodded. He took a sip of his scotch and set it back down. "You also had nightmares."

"Everybody has nightmares."

"Tell me about yours."

Reg hesitated. She didn't start with the nightmares she was currently having. She thought back to when she was little, when they had been so frighteningly real that she would wake the household up with her screams.

"All little kids have nightmares."

"Did you have the same or similar ones over and over again? Is there one that stands out more than the others?"

"I don't know. I would dream about... a shadow man. Someone who was there in the dark, when the lights went out. Waiting for me. Trying to find me."

"Did you see his face? Did you talk to him?"

"No. No, I just ran away. He was so scary. I'd wake up soaking wet."

"Did you get counseling?"

"I was always in counseling or therapy of one kind or another. They wanted to fix me. Make me normal like all of the other kids."

"What did they talk to you about?"

Reg shook her head. "I don't know. Shrink stuff."

"Like what?"

Reg eyed her glass. If she were going to hold herself to one glass of wine, she was going to have to ration it, not just to gulp the whole thing down like she wanted to do.

"Um… relaxation exercises. Thinking about good things. Not watching TV before bed. Asking me about what happened when I was really little. Just whatever they thought would help me not be afraid at night."

"What happened when you were really little?"

"I don't know." Reg anticipated his next question. "They said… it would help me overcome past trauma. Stuff that I couldn't even remember. Like… my mom dying."

"How did your mom die?"

"In an accident."

It was Damon who cocked his head at Reg's answer, his forehead creasing. Reg ground her teeth in irritation. Corvin might not have pursued it any further, but with Damon's easy-to-read face, Corvin knew in an instant that something did not pass muster.

"What? It wasn't an accident?" Corvin asked, looking from Reg to Damon and back again.

"Damon doesn't know anything about it," Reg snapped. "We just met."

"Damon is a diviner. He has a gift for recognizing the truth. Or lies."

Reg looked at Damon, scowling. "Why didn't you tell me that?"

"Would it have made any difference to anything?"

She tried to review the entire evening at once. How many times had she lied to him? And what about? Reg might not be a pathological liar, but she wasn't exactly dedicated to the truth, either. She was a good liar. She had to be. And most people couldn't tell.

"How did your mother die?" Corvin demanded.

"I don't remember."

Corvin looked at Damon.

"I'm not a lie detector," Damon said. "I'm here to keep Reg safe, not to be your human polygraph."

He drew the hood down farther, hiding his face in shadow. Too little too late.

"What do you remember?" Corvin pried, focusing his gaze on Reg once more.

"Why does this matter? What does any of this have to do with what's going on here?"

"That's what I want to find out. What does it have to do with what's going on in Black Sands now? How is it connected? You have the answer inside you somewhere."

"I don't," Reg protested. "I don't know what's going on or what it is that's out there. You're the one with the magical expertise."

"Then listen to me when I tell you something. The answer is in your head. This feeling and these nightmares are connected to your past. Maybe something to do with your mother, maybe not. But it's a good starting point."

"She was killed. I don't know how. I was too young to know anything. I didn't have any family, so they put me into foster care. But I was always trouble and no one would adopt me." She shook her head in irritation. "What does any of that matter?"

"What do you remember from the day she died?"

"Nothing. I don't remember anything. I was too young."

"What do you remember about the place you lived at the time? With your mother?"

"Nothing." Reg stopped and thought. She shook her head again. "No. nothing."

Corvin looked over at Damon, but he didn't need Damon's gift to tell that something was stirring in Reg's brain, keeping her from being sure of her answer. Every time she said she didn't remember anything about it, her brain did a little twist. A little tic that made her unsure of herself.

She had been too young to remember anything about her mother or about the place they had lived.

The voices in her head were growing more and more insistent, harder and harder to ignore. One of them, in particular, was louder than all the rest. Reg pressed her thumbs into her temples.

"What is it?" Corvin asked.

"Leave me alone. Just be quiet."

He frowned, looking at her. Reg pressed her temples harder.

"Shut up. Shut up. Shut up."

But Norma Jean's voice came through, her accent and cadence unmistakable. Reg had lost her own accent in all of the years moving from one family to another. But her mother's was still as clear as a bell.

"Regina, honey, listen to me. Don't push me out."

"No," Reg insisted. "Just go away. Shut up. Stop talking."

"You need to know what happened. You can remember. If you decide to remember, you can."

"I can't. I can't remember. I was just a baby at the time. That's all. Just a baby."

"Sweet child, you were more than just a baby. You were almost school age. Kindergarten, anyway. You would have been going to kindergarten at the big elementary school come fall."

"I don't have to listen to you."

"I know they didn't treat you right at the homes you went to after I died. I tried to help. Truly I did. But they didn't know how to take care of a traumatized little girl who had just seen her momma die. They didn't know how to care for you when you were taken away from everything you had ever known."

To say nothing of a child who could still hear her dead mother talking to her.

Reg felt a hand on her face and for a moment, thought that it was her mother's touch. It had been so many years since she had felt her mother's touch. Almost a lifetime.

"Hunter, back off," a man's voice snapped.

"Shh. I'm not hurting her." Reg recognized Corvin's purr.

She tried to sort out what was going on. But she was so

consumed by Norma Jean's voice, she didn't know how to get back out of her own head.

"Corvin. Unhand her."

Reg felt the hand withdraw from her cheek and with it, the warmth and tenderness that she had been craving. Her mother's voice grew more strident. "You can't forget what happened to your mother. You know what they did to me."

Reg broke through violently, forcing her way past her mother's barriers and opening her eyes. The world swam in front of her. She reached out to Corvin to steady herself. She couldn't remember that he was dangerous, she only knew that he would feed her strength and he could help her to figure out what was going on in her head, why that locked box had been breached.

"Corvin." She could barely whisper his name.

"I'm here, Regina."

She held on to his arm, clutching tightly like everything else in the world might disappear and she would be left alone and stranded.

"You shouldn't trust him," Damon growled. "Why am I here if you're going to ignore what I tell you and he can just waltz in and do whatever he likes?"

Reg blinked, trying to focus on Damon. He seemed far away, on the other side of a dark room.

"Damon? What's going on?"

"Don't touch him. Don't let him touch you. He'll consume you."

Reg looked down at her hand, holding on to Corvin's strong arm for support. She dug her fingers into his arm, feeling the buzz of energy through his thick suit jacket. She took a few deep breaths and forced herself to let his arm go.

"What was that?"

"*Who* was that?" Corvin countered.

Reg breathed heavily like she had been running. She tried to stay in control of herself and not to open the door even a crack to let Norma Jean back in.

"Norma Jean."

"Your mother?"

Reg swallowed and nodded.

"You were communing with your mother?" Damon asked. "What did she say?"

"You couldn't hear her?"

"You're the only one who can hear her," Corvin advised.

"You could hear her," Reg insisted.

"No. I was trying. But your bulldog here wouldn't let me. Why don't you tell him to go home; then you and I can continue. Or we could go somewhere more private."

"He was trying to freaking mind meld with you." Damon's voice was hard. "I know what he can do, and so do you. I'm here to stop him."

"Yes," Reg agreed. But she wished that he had let Corvin complete the connection. She wanted him to see and feel it instead of her having to struggle to put it into words.

"Have a drink." Corvin nudged her wine glass toward her. "Quit trying to make it last all night. You need it."

What she needed was the energy he was feeding her, his hand held a few inches away from hers, hovering and radiating energy like a heat lamp.

"Have a drink and tell me what your mother wanted you to remember. Just get it all out, like ripping off a bandage."

Reg raised it to her lips with shaky fingers. The wine warmed her, but she would have preferred Corvin's touch. She remembered how it felt to be held by him, and she wanted to crawl into his arms where it was safe.

She had to settle instead for Damon, reaching out to grasp his hand and hold it tightly. No electricity. No warmth except for his normal body temperature.

"So?" Corvin prompted. "What happened?"

"They tortured and killed her." Reg's heart hurt like it had just happened. All of the years she had spent burying the memories and the pain, and it was as raw and fresh as if it had just happened.

"Who did? Did you see?"

"The man with the hair." Reg's voice was that of a little girl. She cleared her throat and tried to take over from the scared child inside her. "Long, black hair. In braids." Reg fingered her own braids. She looked at Corvin, the horror blooming up through her body, like ink spreading through clear water. "No, not braids. Dreadlocks. It was the witch doctor."

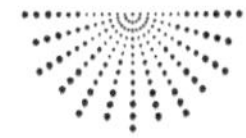

# CHAPTER TEN

*D*amon wouldn't let Reg drive home, but insisted that she leave her car at the club and he would drive her. She could get her car at another time, or Corvin could have the club return it to her house.

"You can't drive in this state. You're too emotionally distraught."

She felt defensive. He hadn't said that she shouldn't feel what she did, but it still felt like a criticism. Like the foster parents and therapists she had dealt with over the years, he was telling her that she should be over it by now. Her mother had died decades before. It wasn't like she was still in mourning. She knew Damon didn't mean it that way, but she had been told too many times not to feel the grief. She had worked hard to wall that part of her life off and go on in a new direction. A fresh start. How many times had she been given a fresh start, and thought that maybe this time it would work? Maybe she would be able to go somewhere she could be at peace and start a productive life and live the same way as anyone else.

"I've been driving myself for years," Reg said crossly. "I know my way home. I'd be just fine driving myself."

"Let me do this favor for you. To make up for taking you out to bowling earlier, okay? This is my do-over."

"Some do-over," Reg grumbled. "I didn't want to go bowling and I don't want you to drive me home."

"You wanted me to provide personal protection. This is just part of the service."

Walking to his car, Reg hung on to his arm, still feeling shaky. She looked back toward the club. She couldn't see Corvin. He hadn't insisted on following them out. But she could still feel him and sense his restlessness and unease.

He hadn't known anything about the 'witch doctor' who had been working with Hawthorne-Rose when Reg had first moved to Black Sands and been caught up in the mysterious disappearance of Warren Blake. Reg had seen the black man with the dreadlocks and the round, white-rimmed eyes in Warren Blake's memories. He was one of the few players whose face she'd been able to see. She had thought that when Hawthorne-Rose had been caught and turned over to the authorities that they had busted up his smuggling ring and that Black Sands was safe once more. They had all thought so.

But something was going on. The Witch Doctor was once more operating in Black Sands. Reg didn't know if he was smuggling or doing something else. Why did she feel so unsettled? Was it just because he was close by and she associated him with the man who had killed her mother? Maybe seeing him in Warren Blake's memories had triggered new nightmares because he reminded Reg of her past. Perhaps the Witch Doctor wasn't operating in Black Sands at all, she was just having a delayed emotional reaction to a traumatic memory.

"Are you okay?" Damon rubbed Reg's hand, still clutching his arm, in an attempt to soothe her.

"I'm fine. Now I know what it was that was bugging me, so I'll probably sleep great tonight. I'm so exhausted, I'll just fall into bed, and I won't even dream."

She knew the nightmares were still there. She could feel them.

"Tell me the truth." Damon's voice was low and calm.

Of course. The diviner. He knew she was lying about being fine and about being able to escape the nightmares for once.

"I'm shaken up," Reg admitted. "I wasn't expecting… anything like this. I don't know what I was expecting, but it wasn't this."

"Do you really think that the man who killed your mother is in Black Sands?"

"No. The Witch Doctor just reminds me of him. Because of the dreadlocks. It was just an accidental association. The Witch Doctor probably isn't even here."

A strong, painful throb of her heart testified that it wasn't true. The Witch Doctor was there, and he was back at his evil business of smuggling magical objects and endangered animal organs used for spells.

But that was all. He didn't know or care about Reg. He wouldn't attack her. He didn't have evil plans to deal with her.

"You're hurting yourself," Damon said.

Reg loosened her grip on his arm, then realized that he'd said she was hurting herself, not him. She shook her head. "What do you mean, I'm hurting myself?"

"When you lie to yourself like that, you do damage to your soul. You cause a breach when your brain and your body know the truth and you choose to deny it or tell another story. Every time you lie to yourself, you are causing harm."

"I don't know what the truth is. I'm not lying to myself."

He looked at her for a minute, and Reg knew that he could still feel something from her. She didn't know how his gift worked and if he could tell what she was thinking and feeling if she didn't say anything, but he seemed to have a sense of it even when she was silent.

"I don't know how. I don't know the truth, so how can I lie to myself about it?"

"Maybe because you do know the truth."

Reg sighed in exasperation. Damon motioned to a big black

pickup truck. "This is me." He gave a little shrug. "Sorry, it's not that easy for someone who is… smaller than me… to get into."

"I'm short, but at least I'm not wearing a dress today."

Damon nodded. "That might be awkward." He pressed the button on his key fob to unlock it, opened the door for her, and then looked like he was going to pick her up and put her in the seat. Reg held up her hand.

"I can actually manage by myself."

He stepped back a few inches, but was still hovering and acting like he might have to catch her if she fell. Reg stepped onto the running board, grabbed the inside of the door frame, and hauled herself up into the cab of the truck. She sat down and pretended to readjust an imaginary skirt.

"See?"

"Very ladylike," he approved. He shut the door and went around to the driver's side. He didn't have any trouble stepping up into the cab. He started the truck with a roar, then turned on the heat and pointed one of the blowers toward her. "I think you might be a little bit in shock. We'll get you warmed up a little."

Reg wanted to tell him to back off, she could take care of herself, but the warm air felt really good, so she held her tongue. They sat there in silence for a few minutes. He made no move to pull out.

She looked at him sideways. "Uh… do you need my address, or what?"

"I just thought… you might want to talk about it. I don't want you to feel like you have to invite me into your house to talk, so I thought if we talked in the truck for a few minutes… that might be more comfortable."

"I don't want to talk about it."

"You really didn't remember that your mother was tortured and killed?"

"If you can discern the truth, then don't you already know that?"

"Well… yes… but it seems so strange that you would be able

to forget something like that. I would think that it would be burned into your memory, something that you could never forget."

"You don't know what it's like to have something like that happen to you. I couldn't deal with it." She shook her head. "I don't think I can deal with it now."

"How old were you?"

"She said I was going to go into kindergarten, so I guess I was four or five."

"And you were there when it happened?" he asked tentatively, obviously aware that he was treading on thin ice. "Did you... see...?"

"It's muddled." Reg held her head, pressing it between her hands. She didn't know whether to try to remember or to try to forget. If Damon was right, then forcing herself to forget about it might be damaging to her. Maybe that was what had triggered all of her psychic or psychological problems to start with. She had forced her brain to do things it wasn't supposed to do, and in doing so, had made a mess of things. "I don't know what I saw or didn't see."

"You remembered when Corvin asked you about the house. Can you remember the house?"

There were flashes. Reg had disjointed impressions of the walls, floor, and ceiling. The sparse furniture. She could see bits of herself, her own white legs and bare feet, her arms wrapped around her knees. Was she hiding? It would make sense that she was hiding somewhere they couldn't see her. If her mother were being tortured and murdered, then of course she would hide.

Her mother had probably put her there or told her where to hide so that she was out of sight before the intruders could see her. It seemed like she was somewhere cramped, a cupboard maybe. Peeking out to see what was going on.

* * *

Reg's nostrils flared as she had a sudden instant of clarity when all of the pictures gelled into one, and she could smell the damp under the sink and the sweetish smell of mice and the foreign musky odor of the man with the dreads and his companions. She could feel the same terror, as if she were there again, four years old, crying and screaming at them to stop.

But she couldn't have remained hidden if she was crying and screaming. They would have heard her and dragged her out. They wouldn't have left her behind, a witness to their violence. That part couldn't be true. Maybe it was like in her dreams, when she would scream and nothing would come out. She had cried and screamed, but it had been without a voice, so that she could stay hidden and they would be ignorant of her presence.

"It's okay. You're safe. It's okay, Reg."

Damon was rubbing her shoulder, trying to comfort her while tears ran down Reg's face.

"I'm sorry. I don't know what's wrong with me. I'm such a mess." She tried to wipe away the tears with her hands.

"No, it's okay. You need to let these emotions out. You shouldn't suppress them."

She opened her eyes and looked at him. He didn't seem disgusted by her display. He didn't look panicked like many men did when a woman broke down and they didn't know how to stop the waterworks. He just looked compassionate and understanding.

"I don't want to feel them." Reg sniffled and wiped at the corners of her eyes, trying to shut the tears off. "Why would anyone want to feel so scared and alone? Don't you understand what happened? They tortured and killed her right in front of me. Maybe she wasn't a good mom, but she was still my mother. She was doing all she could."

"I'm sure she was." He stroked her hair, pushing a few of the thin braids back over her ear. "What was she like?"

That question was a little easier to answer since Reg had still been in communication with her mother for years after she died. It wasn't like she had to rely on the memories of a four-year-old for that. But the way that Norma Jean had been in life and the way that she had been after death were not identical. Even though she stayed with Reg, she was no longer in charge of feeding and clothing her and making sure she was looked after when Norma Jean went out to party. She was no longer able to discipline Reg physically, but could only communicate with her using the words in her head. The lovey words that came to Reg's mind when Norma Jean talked to Reg after death were not the same words as she had used in life. In life, she had only been so mushy and loving when she was really happy or really smashed.

"She was… southern… she was… I don't know how old she was. When I look back now, I think she must have been pretty young. But of course, you don't know that when you're a little kid. Everyone is a grown up to a little kid. She must have had me as a teenager or early twenties, I think. She bragged about how pretty she was when she was alive, but I remember… she had a couple of missing teeth, and her hair was brittle, and she wore a lot of makeup."

"Was she an addict? A prostitute?"

"I don't know. Probably both. She can be so honey-sweet now, but back then… she wasn't very nice to me."

Damon extended his rubbing to Reg's neck and the top part of her back. She didn't mind his touch so much. Not like earlier when she'd felt like he was just trying to push her into a physical relationship. Now he was emotionally supportive and trying to help her work through what had happened to her as a little girl. He wasn't on the make.

"She probably had a pretty rough life too."

"Yeah. Probably."

"And this Witch Doctor? Was he someone she knew, or… did he just show up one day? Did they have a relationship, or did he happen upon her one day…"

Flashes of memory, watching the strange man and her mother, having to look through the legs of the chairs and table in the kitchen into the living room, where he crouched over her.

"No. Don't hurt my mommy!"

Damon pulled Reg closer to himself and squeezed her firmly. "It's okay. It's just a memory. It isn't happening now."

Reg wasn't so sure. The flashes were disorienting and she didn't know where she was. She wanted to stop them.

"I don't understand why they would hurt her. She didn't do anything to them. The scary man… he wanted to know…" Reg trailed off.

"What did he want to know?" Damon asked softly.

Reg pushed him away from her. She took a few deep breaths. It was getting too warm. The chill had left her and the truck seemed suffocatingly warm and close. She fumbled for the window controls and inched her window down a crack.

It wasn't any of Damon's business. He was prying into something that he had no business knowing, and she didn't want to share.

"I want to go home. I told you I don't want to talk about this."

"Okay. You don't want to talk about it."

"I want to go home. I can drive myself; you don't have to drive me."

"I'll still drive you. Just sit back and relax."

Reg let out her breath in an angry puff and leaned back against the seat, closing her eyes and pretending to rest.

# CHAPTER ELEVEN

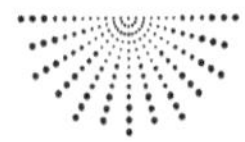

The truck came to an abrupt stop, throwing Reg unexpectedly against her seatbelt. She braced her hands against the dash, eyes suddenly wide open, and looked around in alarm.

"Sorry," Damon reached out and put his hand on her leg in a calming gesture. "Just a cat. Ran out in front of the truck."

Reg's heart was thumping a mile a minute. She took a deep breath, trying to fight the feeling of dread that knotted in her stomach, pulling tighter, stretching taut like something was going to snap.

"I didn't mean to startle you," Damon apologized again. "Are you okay?"

"It's not that. I'd rather you braked than ran over it. It's just…" her voice faded.

"The feeling again?"

"Yeah. Really strong here."

Damon glanced around as he released the brake and started to creep forward again. "Maybe it's just the location."

Reg blinked. "What do you mean?"

"The cemetery." Damon gestured to their right at a treed area

Reg had taken for a park. "Maybe you're just getting unsettling feelings because of restless spirits."

She looked out the window, trying to see something through the trees, but it was dark, and the vegetation around the cemetery was thick. "I don't know. Maybe."

She had the impression that he thought she was being overdramatic about her feeling.

Sometimes being psychic sucked.

They went on without a word. Reg didn't close her eyes again, wanting to be alert for any more cats or any spiritual manifestations. She didn't want to be taken off-guard. Damon turned right so that they rounded one corner of the cemetery and were still traveling with it on their right. Reg frowned at the emergency lights flashing ahead of them. Damon continued to drive, hoping to be able to see what was going on and to get past to drop Reg at home. But there was a police barricade across the road, not letting anyone pass. Damon rolled down his window to talk to the police officer.

"Sorry, you'll have to detour around," a familiar voice advised. "This road is temporarily closed."

Reg leaned over, almost into Damon's lap, to see the figure standing outside the truck, not looking terribly enthused with her job directing traffic. "Detective Jessup."

"Oh, Reg. I didn't see you. I didn't know that you knew…" Jessup looked at Damon.

"We just met," Damon advised. "First date. So what's going on?" A flick of Damon's hand indicated the cemetery. They couldn't see much from where they were, but there were floodlights and people coming and going, clearly a crime scene.

"Sorry, I can't tell you anything," Jessup advised. "You'll have to go around."

"What happened? Was it a murder?" Reg strained to see what was going on and to get a psychic read on the location.

"Nothing so exciting. It's really not for public disclosure."

"If it's not a murder," Damon said slowly, thinking it through, "then it must be theft. Grave robbers?"

Jessup looked irritated. "I can't confirm or deny," she snapped.

Reg didn't need to be a diviner to see that Damon had guessed correctly. Reg tried again to see through the vegetation around the cemetery. Who would be stealing from the graves? Was it someone looking for valuables? Or something more gruesome, someone looking for organs or some grisly souvenir? She wouldn't have been surprised by seances or even by vandalism, teenagers trying to scare each other or being stupid. But grave robbers? She didn't think that kind of thing happened in modern times.

"Don't they have... cement vaults that they put the caskets into?" she asked. "I thought that graves were sort of... burglarproof nowadays."

Jessup shook her head. "If I could encourage you to be on your way, folks. It's late, and you don't want to be roaming the streets right now. Get home and get some rest." She spoke in a flat tone as if they didn't know each other. And maybe they never had. Reg had thought that Jessup was at least partway to becoming a friend, but if recent events and Jessup's tone were any indication, she had been mistaken.

Damon rolled his eyes. He raised the window and performed a three-point turn.

"What a crock. They think that there's some danger in revealing that there was a grave robber in the cemetery? Like if they tell the public that, there's going to be a panic? Over grave robbing? Nothing like taking themselves too seriously."

Reg was silent, thinking.

"You know Marta?" Damon asked.

"Uh, yeah. We're acquainted."

Damon laughed. "Okay, then. Maybe that's a sensitive area. I won't ask."

Reg hoped that he wouldn't pursue it. She turned her head away from him to watch out the window as he worked his way back to the cross street and detoured around the cemetery.

*You don't want to be roaming the streets right now.* Did Jessup know something about the Witch Doctor and the feeling of doom he carried with him? Could she feel it too? Reg knew that Jessup didn't have much in the way of magical gifts, and whatever she did have, she kept quiet. So maybe she wouldn't have told anyone if she too felt the spiritual disruption in Black Sands. She and Corvin and Jessup had been involved together on other cases. Maybe there was a psychic connection among all three of them.

It made sense that Corvin could feel it after having held Reg's powers and retained some portion of them, however minuscule. But it didn't make sense that Detective Marta Jessup, being practically normal, would be able to sense it.

So it wasn't that. Either Reg had misread her, or there was something more going on.

* * *

"Can I walk you to your door?" Damon asked.

Reg looked at the dark yard. She felt for any danger, but couldn't sense anything above the level of anxiety she was already feeling from the Witch Doctor. She hesitated, not wanting an awkward scene at the door with Damon, or to have to invite him in. She had already learned about the dangers of inviting warlocks into her home.

Another car whizzed up to the house, a low, red sports car. Reg frowned and watched Sarah get out of the passenger side, laughing. She said something to the driver, and he screeched his tires, leaving rubber on the road as he pulled away. Sarah looked at the big black truck and waved at Reg.

"Getting in a little late, aren't you, Reg?"

Reg shook her head and laughed. "I could say the same about you," she said, getting out of the car. She waved at Damon and hoped that he would take the hint and just leave, as Sarah's consort had done. She walked with Sarah up to her door.

"Did you have a nice night?" Sarah asked.

"Uh… no, not really."

"Oh, dear." Sarah's face fell. "What happened?"

Reg shook her head. "What didn't happen?"

Sarah unlocked her door and motioned for Reg to go ahead of her. "Come in and tell me all about it."

Damon was still parked at the curb. Reg turned and waved at him again and went in.

"Lights on," Sarah ordered, and the room magically lit up.

Reg looked around, marveling.

"I'll never get tired of home automation," Sarah said. "Do you know, if I did that a few hundred years ago, I would have been burned at the stake. But nowadays, everyone has the technology."

Reg was a little let down to realize that it was just technology and not a magic spell.

"I'll make tea," Sarah announced. "Let's go to the kitchen."

They went to the back of the house, and Sarah put the kettle on. She puttered around for a few minutes, finding a half-eaten bag of cookies in the cupboard and putting a few out on a plate and displaying a range of homemade tea blends to Reg for her to pick what she wanted.

"You got anything in there for evil witch doctors?" Reg asked.

"Witch doctors?" Sarah frowned. "Well, it depends on what kind of sorcery he is doing."

"How about nightmares?"

"Ah, let's go with this one, then." Sarah picked one of the packets out and handed it to Reg, along with a cup. In a couple of minutes, the kettle was boiling, and they both filled their cups. Reg raised hers and blew on it, hoping to cool it down enough to drink.

"Tell me all about it," Sarah commanded.

Reg considered how much she wanted to tell Sarah. An experienced witch, Sarah might have some suggestions for Reg. But on the other hand, Sarah already knew more about Reg's life than she was comfortable with, and she didn't exactly want to share her innermost feelings.

Instead, she told Sarah about the bowling. Sarah laughed about Reg's dislike of the rental shoes and awkwardness in trying to bowl for the almost-first time. She raised her eyebrows and waited for more when Reg told her about going home and trying to sleep. She knew that something else had happened. Reg hadn't been home in bed when Sarah had gotten home.

"So then Corvin called."

Sarah's lip curled in distaste. "I thought you had decided not to have anything else to do with him. He is shunned; you have the support of the magical community behind you. You told him no, of course?"

"Of course," Reg agreed.

Sarah nodded, satisfied.

"Only then, he kind of talked me into it."

"Why do you let him do that? You know how dangerous he is. But…" Sarah's brow wrinkled, "it wasn't Corvin you came home with."

"No. Corvin wanted to talk about this feeling, about this… dark force that we've both been feeling. He said to bring whoever I wanted to to make sure that I was safe from him. So I called Damon again."

"You don't think it was just a ruse to see you again?" Sarah suggested. "You know how obsessed he is with getting your powers back."

"No… I mean, I know that, but that wasn't why he wanted to get together. He didn't try anything."

Sarah raised her eyes doubtfully.

"Well, I mean, he didn't try to charm me. He did try to… link telepathically, but that was to help me and see what was going on, not to try to steal my powers."

"You didn't let him."

Reg shifted uncomfortably. "I didn't try to stop him. I thought it might help… it felt good… but Damon stopped him. He did what he was supposed to."

"A good thing. You're playing with fire, Regina. I don't want to see you get burned again. He's not going to give you your powers back like the first time. That was exceptional circumstances. You know that they don't do that. I've never seen it happen before and never expect to see it again."

"I know. But Corvin wasn't trying to take my powers. We were trying to figure out what it was disrupting the… spiritual atmosphere." Reg felt a little silly saying it aloud, but Sarah didn't seem to find it was odd.

"So did you succeed in finding anything out?"

Reg skipped over the stuff about talking to her mother and what she had remembered. "We figured out that it might be the Witch Doctor. You know, the guy with the dreadlocks that I saw in Warren's memories. I don't know his real name."

"Why would he still be hanging around Black Sands? Once the smuggling ring was broken up, he would go somewhere else, start over where he wasn't known."

"Well, the police couldn't identify him, so isn't it possible that he figured he was safe to keep working here? He just had to gather together enough people to start working again…"

"I'm not a police officer like Detective Jessup, so I can't tell you exactly how these criminals think, but usually when you hear about a bust like this going down… things go quiet for a few years. They don't just start back up again. They move to other places where it is safer."

"I don't know." Reg shrugged irritably. "Maybe there is something here that makes it special. But he *is* still here."

"How do you know that for sure?"

"I saw him. I know that's who it was."

"How do you know, though? You saw him with your natural eyes, or in a nightmare?"

"In…" Reg didn't want to have to explain about her memories of her mother and how she had made the connection to the witch doctor. Was he even the same man? She couldn't say for sure, but Corvin had said that it had to be the witch doctor. That was why they were both feeling the dark presence. "In a vision," she said finally.

"What kind of a vision? It could have been symbolic, couldn't it? You can't always interpret these things literally."

"I'm... I'm not sure, but Corvin is going to look into it further. He'll be able to figure it out."

Sarah shook her head. "Well, leave it to him, then. But I still think it's just a ruse."

"It isn't just a ruse that I've been having these feelings. That's real, and I was having them before he called me to tell me that he was too. Explain that."

"I can't, dear. But I think he's using what you are feeling to take advantage of you. This was the first step. He'll call you back to tell you about the developments, then maybe go on some wild goose chase with you to get you alone..."

"I won't go anywhere with him alone. I promise."

"You let me give you some wards. They are not one hundred percent effective alone, but combined with your own will and your powers... I want you to have all of the protections against him that you can. Saying that you won't go with him isn't enough, you know the influence he has on you once you're in his presence. He is very strongly attracted to you, and that makes his power over you that much more intoxicating."

Reg felt her face flush. "Okay. Sure. Another necklace or garlic in my pocket or whatever you think might help. I'll do whatever you say."

Sarah nodded, looking a little bit happier. "So is that it, the end of your night?"

Reg sighed and tried to decide whether to tell Sarah about the cemetery. Did it have anything to do with the rest of her night? Talking about the cemetery would end up just sounding paranoid and overly dramatic.

"What?" Sarah prompted. She took a sip of her tea. "What else?"

"Nothing, I guess. Just, I ran into Detective Jessup."

"Oh, what was Marta doing?"

"She was redirecting traffic around the cemetery. Because something was going on over there."

Sarah nodded, "Yes, I heard about that. Isn't it awful?"

Reg closed her mouth. "Uh… what? She wouldn't tell us what it was all about."

"There were graves desecrated, vandalism, people breaking headstones and opening vaults and all kinds of nonsense. Kids these days have no sense of right and wrong. I would never have done something like that in my day."

"And… they think it was teenagers?" Reg asked, baffled. She might have done some wild things when she was a teenager; she certainly hadn't been above breaking the law. But she couldn't imagine destroying a cemetery while out on a ramble.

"That's what they're saying. You know how kids are. No respect for a place like that. They're always hanging out there, having their little rendezvous, trying to scare each other with ghost stories. Getting the girls wound up, you know, so that they can… comfort them later."

Reg blinked. "I didn't know. I never heard about anything like that."

"Kids will do anything. The doctors say it's because their brains aren't fully developed yet, they don't mature fully until they are in their twenties. In my day, girls were getting married as teenagers. We didn't have to wait until we were twenty to develop the maturity of adults."

Reg opened her mouth to protest that getting married as a teen didn't mean a girl was any more mature than the ones who were hanging out at the cemetery knocking down tombstones. Then she closed her mouth. She was tired, and the conversation wouldn't go anywhere. Kids probably had been more mature in Sarah's day. They'd had a lot more responsibility a lot earlier. Their brains still might not have been fully developed, but society's expectations were a lot different.

"Anyway… that's all. We had to detour around the cemetery,

and then we came home. Or, Damon dropped me off. He didn't come in. Obviously. You know that since you got home at the same time."

"Yes, I did, and I had a lovely time tonight."

"That's great." Reg forced a smile. She tried not to begrudge Sarah her nice evening. Not long ago, Sarah had been on her deathbed. Reg would not have been able to believe that she would soon be on her feet, bouncing around acting like she was thirty instead of… however old she really was. "You were out with a friend?"

"A group of us got together. I'm not really into dating one-on-one these days. I prefer a group just getting together to have fun. Not pairing off."

"That sounds nice."

"And you, my dear Reg, look like you have a headache and are badly in need of your bed. I shouldn't be keeping you up. Now, off you go. Do you need something for your head?"

Reg pressed her fingers into the center of her forehead where a deep, throbbing pain had settled. "Yes. No. I'll just go to bed. It's just because I'm tired. It will be better in the morning, I'm sure."

"Okay. Give me a call if you change your mind and need anything. I'll be up for a couple of hours yet."

Reg raised her eyebrows. She drained the rest of her tea and studied the leaves at the bottom of her cup. "You're not going to bed yet?"

"It's the witching hour. I have a lot to do."

"But you're up so early in the morning. How can you do that if you stay up for a couple more hours?"

"I don't need that much sleep anymore. I'll sleep when I'm dead. And in the afternoon, if I'm feeling fatigued. Nothing like a siesta to fill the tank for the rest of the day."

If Reg weren't already tired, Sarah's words would have done the job. She couldn't imagine keeping to the sort of schedule Sarah seemed to be on recently.

"Okay. Well, I'm going to bed. I'll see you tomorrow."

"Sweet dreams, Reg. I'm sure you'll sleep better now."

Reg wasn't so sure. She wasn't looking forward to more nightmares, or for the memories that would creep into her dreams. She rubbed her forehead for another minute. "Okay. Goodnight."

Sarah stood as Reg did. "You know..." she touched Reg on the arm, "if you're having that much trouble and don't want a potion, you could see a doctor. They might give you something to help you feel better."

Reg shook her head. "I've been there before and taken plenty of prescribed meds. This isn't... depression. It isn't normal anxiety. I know it's being caused by something going on in Black Sands. Like Corvin said."

Sarah shrugged. "Maybe so. We'll have to watch and see."

# CHAPTER TWELVE

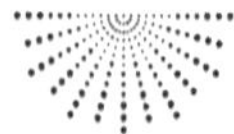

As Reg had expected, she had a restless sleep and when she awoke was still feeling groggy and headachy and didn't want to face the day. She tried her best to ignore Starlight, but the cat insisted on waking her up and being fed. Reg dragged herself out to the kitchen to find him something acceptable, then after a detour to the bathroom to relieve herself and take a bunch of Tylenol, climbed back into bed.

She didn't usually go back to sleep once she was up, and her body didn't like it. But her brain was still too exhausted to deal with life. Maybe she was fighting the flu or another bug. Or perhaps it was the results of whatever had happened the night before when she had been at the club with Corvin. The memories of her mother and communicating with her had taken far more energy than a simple conversation should have, and she was pretty sure she'd ended up drinking more than one glass of wine—maybe more than two or three, which was her usual upper limit. Damon had been there to protect her from Corvin, not from overindulging.

Maybe she was just hung over. In which case, some more sleep and water would help.

After Starlight finished eating, he jumped up on the bed and pushed his face into hers, purring and rubbing against her, encouraging her to get up. Reg shoved him away from her. "Why don't you go to sleep now? You were up half the night too. You need a catnap."

Starlight returned to sit on her stomach. He began to wash.

"This is not exactly comfortable."

He stopped and looked at her, and then started over with his washing routine. Reg pushed him off.

"Go look out the window."

He actually did what she said for once, jumping up onto the windowsill and staring out into the yard. After staring and sniffing sufficiently, he turned toward her and yowled. Clearly, he wanted her to do something about the missing cat. Nicole, Reg remembered. She had told herself a couple of times to call one of the numbers on the Missing Cat flyer and let Nicole's owner know that Reg might have seen her in the garden. And then again, the previous night, when she had gone out. She wondered what kind of a cat Damon had seen over near the cemetery when he had stopped the truck so suddenly. It had been dark out; he probably wouldn't be able to tell her anything more than that it was a cat. All cats were black in the dark.

Starlight yowled again.

"Yeah, okay," Reg agreed. It was evident that she wasn't going to be able to get back to sleep again. Despite how groggy she felt, she was awake, and her body wasn't going to let her return to slumber. She sat up, putting the pillows behind her back, and grabbed her phone off of the side table. She had taken a picture of the flyer so that she wouldn't lose it, so flipping back and forth between the screens, she was able to tap the first phone number into the phone pad. There were three separate numbers, but they didn't say what they were for or what order to call them in. Home, work, and cell, maybe. But no indication as to which to try at what time of day.

"Hello?" The voice was soft and feminine. Reg didn't think that she had wakened the woman, but her voice had a bit of a breathless quality to it.

"Yes, I saw your Missing Cat flyer."

"Oh, yes. Have you seen my little Nicole anywhere?"

She had an accent that Reg tentatively identified as French. When she said 'Nicole,' it wasn't with a short I sound, but like a long E. *NEE-cole.*

"I might have. It's hard to tell, since she doesn't have any markings, and I didn't get that close."

"Where did you see this cat?"

Reg gave her address. "We saw a black cat around here a couple of times, but my landlord chased it away, so I don't know if it will come back here again. I've been watching, but…"

"Okay. I will come over that way and have a look around. See if she will come when I call her. I do not know why she does not come home."

"Well, they can't really protect themselves out there," Reg said. "It's better if you keep her as an indoor cat so that she doesn't get hurt… hit by a car or eaten by an alligator…"

"Cats need to roam," the woman said firmly. "They are not like dogs. They need to be out in nature like wild animals."

Reg looked over at Starlight, shaking her head. She had been so worried when he had run away. She had been sure that something was going to happen to him. She would never let him run wild. Maybe that was why the cat she had seen had looked like it had been outside for a long time.

"Well, thank you for calling," the woman said. "I will definitely come over and see if she is somewhere close by."

"I did see a black cat last night too, when I was driving away. So maybe…"

"There are so many around. Every time someone calls, I go and look and call, and it's somebody else's cat." She gave a little laugh. "I am calling the other black cats the Nicoys."

"Nicoys. Like decoys. That's so cute."

"And there are so many Nicoys! I think everybody in this town must buy black cats. I do not know why they are so popular."

Reg hesitated, wanting to point out that witches liked black cats as familiars, but she didn't know whether the woman was a practitioner. If she weren't, she would think that Reg was off her rocker.

"I… didn't catch your name."

"Oh! I am so sorry. How rude of me. My name is Francesca St. Martin. We are new here. I've only been here for a few weeks."

"We?"

"Me and Nicole. Just the two of us. I don't have anyone else. I thought that Black Sands seemed like such a nice, quaint little place to settle down. It is like a storybook, no?"

A fairy tale, maybe, complete with wicked witches who might eat small children. Or cats. Black Sands had its good points, and Reg didn't want to have to leave any time soon, but it had its detractors as well.

"Yes, like a book," she agreed. "I'm Reg Rawlins. You can stop in and say 'hi' if you come by here. Have a cup of tea and meet my cat, Starlight."

"Oh, you have a cat too! I should have known. The people who call me about the posters are mostly people who have cats."

"Yes. Starlight is quite taken with your Nicole, if it was Nicole who was by here and not one of the Nicoys. He keeps watching for her out the window and wanting me to go out and find her."

She waited to see what Francesca's reaction would be to this suggestion.

Francesca laughed. "Sometimes it seems almost like they could talk to us, does it not?"

So she didn't believe in any kind of communication between cats and humans. It didn't sound like she knew anything about the magical community in Black Sands. She was just a normal person, moving into what she thought was a quaint little town in Florida.

"Well, stop in if you are by. I'm pretty new in Black Sands too. I wouldn't mind meeting someone else new."

"Yes," Francesca agreed. "I will see you… this afternoon if I can."

"Okay. See you then."

# CHAPTER THIRTEEN

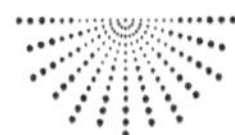

She took the rest of the morning easy, trying to recover her equilibrium and not to think about the things she had remembered about her mother and her death the night before. She had known that Norma Jean was dead, but it was a shock for Reg to remember that she had seen her mother murdered.

Had she been there to see it, or had Corvin just planted the idea in her head? She didn't like Sarah's suggestion that he was only pursuing the Witch Doctor angle because he wanted to get Reg somewhere that he could take advantage of her again. The last time, at the community dance, Reg had been rescued at the last moment by a fairy. She couldn't count on something like that happening again. She would get the wards from Sarah and learn everything she could about how to protect herself from him. But she needed his help to figure out what the Witch Doctor was up to in Black Sands.

She sat, staring at the crumbs of toast on her plate after she was finished eating. Could one read toast crumbs like they could read tea leaves?

*Was* it the Witch Doctor? Was he active again in Black Sands, so quickly after his smuggling ring had been shut down? And was he the man who had killed her mother, or was that only an association that Reg had made because of his black dreadlocks? It really couldn't be the same man. Not thousands of miles away and decades later. That defied belief.

She couldn't help closing her eyes to visualize the man who had stood over her mother. She didn't want to go back there, but she wanted to know that it wasn't the same man. It was just an unconscious association in Reg's memory.

His face resolved in Reg's brain. It became clear enough that she could hold it in her mind and look at it, turning it this way and that. He looked almost identical to the man she had seen in Warren's memories. And that meant it couldn't be the same person. If it had been the same person who had killed her mother, he would have been a much younger man at the time. He wouldn't look the same. She had contaminated the memory with the image of the present-day Witch Doctor. That happened with witnesses all the time. Show them a picture of someone a few times, and they would become convinced that was who they had seen. That was why they insisted on proper lineups and photo arrays.

The phone rang. Reg looked at the screen, not in the mood to talk to anyone. She wanted to sit and think and analyze the memories. She needed to explore them and decide what she wanted to do with them. Wall them off again? Deal with them, now that she was an adult with adult emotions and the ability to look at it dispassionately? How would it change her life if she processed the memories? Would it stay the same if she buried them again, or had remembering them once already changed her forever? She didn't know what to do about it.

The phone rang again, and Reg realized that even though she was staring at the phone, she hadn't really seen it and processed the name on the screen. Of course, it was the one person she really didn't want to talk to—and really did.

Corvin.

She took her time picking up the phone and deciding whether

to answer the call. It would be easier if he just gave up or it went to voicemail. After a couple more rings, she touched the screen lightly.

"Corvin."

"Regina." His purr gave Reg the usual shiver of anticipation. How could her name sound so good on his lips when he was so bad for her?

"What do you want? I thought you were going to take a few days to look into what the Witch Doctor might be doing."

"I am looking into it, as I told you I would. I just wanted to make sure that you got home safely last night and had… a good sleep."

"Home safely, yes. A good sleep, no."

He chuckled. "I expect not. Did you get any?"

"I slept, but too many dreams and my mind was going in circles all the time. I can't understand… whether the man I saw was the Witch Doctor or just reminded me of him."

Corvin grunted in agreement. "It's difficult to wrap your mind around. What happened to you years ago and miles away… it seems so unlikely that it is related, and yet…"

"You don't think it is, do you? It wasn't the Witch Doctor that I saw when I was little. I'm just… superimposing his face over whoever it was that I saw. Someone who reminded me of him."

"It's possible, Reg, but I don't think so. You have been keeping those memories in a vault for so long… it isn't like you have touched them and contaminated them over the years with other ideas and faces. The memories that came out last night are pristine. They may not stay that way; you need to remember what you saw and heard. Write it down or draw a picture or whatever is your chosen way to record things."

"You think that it really was the Witch Doctor."

"I think… that seeing the Witch Doctor in Warren's memories helped to jar it loose. Seeing him again, after all of these years, made you go back and search your memories."

Reg argued, not wanting to hear that from him. She wanted to hear the opposite. That obviously it couldn't have been the same person. "He wouldn't still look the same. That means that I didn't really see him. I just took the way he looks now, and popped him into my memory, for some reason…"

"Do you think that's what happened?"

"Yes."

"Damon isn't still with you, is he?"

Reg was surprised at the suggestion. Was he jealous?

"No, of course not. He didn't come in."

"I just wondered what his face would look like when you said that."

"I'm telling the truth!" Reg insisted.

"You will say anything to protect yourself, won't you?"

"No!" It sounded just like the gobbledygook that had come out of her therapists' mouths over the years. And what her foster moms had said. Regina would say and do whatever it took to get what she wanted.

Foster parents insisted on full, uncompromising honesty, and Reg had done her best to convince them that she was truthful. That was pretty hard for a little girl who saw and talked with spirits. Those strictly honest foster parents had forced her to lie to satisfy their own consciences. Ironic.

"I want to help you, Reg. You aren't doing yourself any favors by lying to me about it. You and I know the truth. Are you ready to talk about what the Witch Doctor did to your mother? What it was he wanted?"

Reg had refused to go into any details the night before. She had been reeling with the realization that her mother had been murdered. Wasn't that enough revelation for the night? And for the next week. Or decade.

"I didn't see. I don't know what he wanted."

"You did see. You wouldn't be able to tell me that she was tortured if you hadn't seen anything of that. You would have just said that she was killed. Murdered, even. But you would not have said she was tortured. No one told you that as a little girl. You knew that because that was what you saw."

"I... can't."

"What did he want? I think that is more important than what it was he did. Why he did it. What did he want from her?"

"Who knows? He's this big, scary-looking dude. You think I listened to him? I was hiding. I wanted to hide from all of it."

"I believe that he was scary, that you were afraid of him. But I don't believe that you saw and heard nothing. You hid somewhere you could still see him. Where were you hiding?"

"I'm not sure. In a kitchen cupboard, I think. Under the sink."

"And he didn't look for you? He didn't know that you were there?"

Reg closed her eyes. She could see him searching through the apartment. Looking through her mother's closet, under the bed, in the broom closet in the kitchen. She couldn't see him opening the cupboard where she was hiding. Had it looked too small to hold a person? Had he not seen it? Why would he look in the other closets and not there?

"I think... he looked around, but he must not have known about me. Maybe he was looking for someone bigger. Older."

"Your father?" Corvin suggested.

"My father?" The idea was absurd. "I didn't even know who my father was. He didn't live with us. I don't know if my mother knew who he was."

"Did your mother have powers? Did she hide you?"

"I told you before that no one in my family had powers. Certainly not her."

"You might not have known. She might not have known. She might have suppressed them, like you. She might have been forced to act normal to survive. But that doesn't mean that she didn't have innate powers that even she didn't know about."

"No."

"Was she the one who hid you in the cupboard? Or did you hide yourself?"

Reg focused on the scenes she could see in her mind. A lot of it was still inaccessible. There were blanks. And what she could remember was not in the right order, but all a jumble of thoughts and feelings. Had she sneaked into the cupboard? Crawled in there, afraid of being discovered by the big scary dude with the dreads? Or had her mother pushed her in there, hiding her from sight when the Witch Doctor knocked on her door? Maybe that was something that happened with regularity, her mother wanting her out of the way whenever she had company.

Neither scenario rang true, and Reg didn't know what the other options were. Either she had gone there on her own or her mother had put her there.

"I don't know. I can't reach it."

"You need to try, Regina. We need to know what happened so we can see how it connects up with the present. If we know what he was doing back then, maybe it will help us to figure out what he is doing now."

Reg pushed the memories away, frustrated. "I can't do this," she snapped. "My head hurts and you're just making it more muddled. I don't want to do this."

"Fine." His voice was gritty. She supposed he was just as frustrated as she was. But he didn't have as much at stake. He wasn't the one that they were after. He wasn't the one with the memories. He was only concerned because he could feel the movements of the Witch Doctor. He wouldn't suffer more from the effects of a smuggling ring than anyone else in the town. There might be an increase in violent crime generally, making the streets less safe to walk on late at night. But Corvin was a big man, a powerful warlock, and he could increase his powers at will, as long as he had a source to feed on.

"Can you get power from other things too?" Reg asked.

Corvin seemed confused by the segue. "Can I… you know that I can. I can get something from magical artifacts and powerful objects. Not as much; it won't fill me up. But incrementally, yes."

"So if the Witch Doctor is starting up his business again, that might be good for you. He'll be bringing more magical artifacts into Black Sands, and that will make them available to you."

"Not unless I were to join him," Corvin pointed out dryly. "We're not exactly buddies."

Sarah said that the only reason Corvin was meeting with her and encouraging her to tell him about the Witch Doctor was to get her alone and steal her powers. But was it possible that he was looking for an opportunity to gain access to the Witch Doctor's artifacts as well? When they had busted the ring previously, he had only been given a few items as compensation for his help. The rest had gone… Reg wasn't sure where. Into the police evidence locker? If the Witch Doctor were back, maybe Corvin was hoping to get in on the action without police intervention this time.

"Reg?"

"Yeah, I'm still here."

"Can you reach out to him? Without alerting him to your presence?"

Reg shook her head at the suggestion. "It's not so easy with living people. I think… I would need to be closer to him, at least. I could reach out to Warren because he had already connected with me once. But the Witch Doctor… I don't have any way to reach him."

"You've been aware of his activities. You thought he was close to you in the parking lot, maybe even coming after you. So you have been connecting with him."

"No, it's not the same." Reg tried to explain the difference. "I haven't been connecting with his mind, just… feeling his influence. It isn't the same."

"I think it's close enough. Can you try? You've exercised some pretty sophisticated powers in the past."

"No. I don't want to. What if I get stuck? What if he knows I'm there? He could… he could bind me or something, couldn't he?"

She could tell by Corvin's silence that he was trying to form an answer that was not a lie, but would convince her to do what he asked.

"I'm not doing it, Corvin."

"Marta said that you did a call. You called Calliopia."

"Detective Jessup told you that?" Reg couldn't think of a way it would have come into casual conversation. And Jessup always acted like she didn't want anything to do with Corvin. Until she decided she needed him for something. Wasn't there any magical confidentiality? Some kind of rule that you didn't tell about the magic that other people were performing without their consent? Damon wouldn't even tell her what gifts he had; he considered it a personal matter. So what gave Jessup the right to share that kind of information about Reg?

"It came up in conversation," Corvin said casually.

"Did you talk to her this morning? Did she tell you anything else? Like maybe what happened at the cemetery last night?"

"No, not today. What happened at the cemetery?"

"I don't know. She wouldn't say."

"How do you know something happened at the cemetery?"

"When we went by there last night, it was blocked off and the police were detouring traffic around it. They were investigating something. Sarah said they've had trouble with vandalism. Teenagers, she thought."

"Hmm. If it was just some minor vandalism, I wouldn't have expected the police to be there late at night. They would leave it until the next business day. Did Sarah know something about it, or was she speculating?"

"It seemed like she knew. She said that headstones had been broken and… vaults opened. I don't know what else. I don't know how she found out, since Jessup wouldn't say anything about it."

"Marta's on probation. She's got to be pretty careful not to step out of line. But another cop might not have been so careful about it."

"I suppose. Well, you could call Sarah and see what she knows about it. I'm sure she'd be happy to tell you."

Corvin chuckled. "I wouldn't be so sure. You would think she would be grateful for my part in bringing her back from the brink of death, but she is remarkably stubborn. Keeps insinuating that I'm trying to do something underhanded. Can you imagine?"

"No," Reg said dryly, "really?"

"It would be different if I could see her face-to-face. But she seems to be keeping herself busy these days. I'll pop by The Crystal Bowl for supper tonight and see if I can have a chat with her."

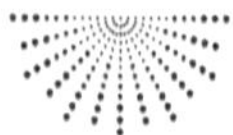

# CHAPTER FOURTEEN

*R*eg was surprised at how much time had passed when she looked at the face of her phone. She had talked with Corvin longer than she had thought, and the day was slipping away. She needed to eat. And make her bed. She was dressed, but she hadn't accomplished anything other than changing.

Starlight meowed from the other room.

And she had fed the cat. He would never let her forget to do that.

She wandered over to the fridge to see if there were something that appealed to her. With a knot in her stomach from the spiritual disruption in Black Sands, she didn't have much appetite.

There was a knock at the door, which made Reg jump and nearly drop the bowl in her hand. It hadn't been loud or violent, just unexpected. She picked up her phone and tiptoed over to the door to look out the peephole. It was a young woman, probably around her age. Reg opened the door and smiled at her, not sure what to expect. Had Sarah made another appointment for Reg that hadn't ended up in her appointment book? Or had it been there and she hadn't seen it?

"Hello," Reg greeted, giving a dramatic flip of her skirt. "I'm glad you came."

Even if it wasn't someone she should have expected, Reg figured she could get away with acting as if she knew the visitor. After all, she was a psychic. She could easily pretend that she had predicted the woman's arrival.

She was a pretty girl, slim, rose-cheeked, long, spiraling blond hair. She looked like a child's doll. One of the fancy ones that was supposed to represent the traditional dress in a particular country or place. Not that the woman was dressed in anything special. Just blue jeans and a blouse.

"I am Francesca," the woman said, holding out one slim, white hand. "But I guess you figured that out!"

Reg flipped through her mental contact list, trying to remember who Francesca was. There was a meow behind her, and she turned to look at Starlight, who was coming over to greet the new visitor as if he knew why she was there. Reg remembered in a flash. Nicole's owner. The woman looking for her missing cat.

"Yes, of course. Why don't you come in for some tea?"

Francesca gave her a smile full of even white teeth, and she entered the cottage. "What a sweet little house!" she commented, looking around. "I thought you said you had not been in Black Sands long, but you have made it very nice."

"Thank you. But I can't take the credit. It came furnished. All I had to do was unpack my clothes. It's my landlord who deserves the compliments."

"I see. You are fortunate to have found such a nice place, then. The house I am in..." she rolled her eyes. "Well, it is so old and dark. I looked around at other places, but I cannot afford much, and it was the best deal. I thought that once I painted and put up new curtains, it would be better, but so far... I cannot say it has done much."

"That's too bad." Reg wondered who had owned the house before Francesca. Maybe a dark witch or warlock who had left a spiritual impression on it? Or perhaps Francesca was also attuned to the oppressive atmosphere in Black Sands, only she attributed it to the house rather than the town. "You know... I know someone who might be able to do something about that, make it feel a bit better." Corvin blessed houses and removed old curses. If there were a magical residue in Francesca's house, maybe he could help with that.

"Oh? Is she a decorator?"

"He. No…" Reg wasn't sure what to say about it. Francesca so far hadn't given any indication that she knew about the existence of the magical community, and Reg didn't want to reveal anything she shouldn't or to make Francesca think she was a nut. "He is just good at… making spaces feel welcoming."

"Oh, like Feng Shui?"

"Yes, something like that."

Francesca shrugged. "I do not believe in stuff like that. I do not mean to bash anyone else's beliefs; there might be something to arranging your house in a way that makes you feel good, but all of the stuff about facing east or west, I cannot believe that."

"Sure." Reg nodded. So, magical or not? Did she not believe in any kind of spiritual energy, or just not in arranging objects according to a specific pattern?

Francesca sat down on one of the wicker chairs. Reg started the kettle heating again.

"And tell me about this little fellow," Francesca said, looking at Starlight, who was sitting up tall on his haunches and watching her intently. "He does look very wise, does he not?"

"He always looks like he knows better than I do." Reg laughed. "And sometimes I think he does. He saw Nicole out the window a few times, and he keeps sitting there looking for her now, yowling at me when she doesn't show up. I don't think he's too happy about Sarah chasing her out of the garden. If it is Nicole and not one of the Nicoys." Reg chuckled at the nickname.

"I hope it is her. I am getting quite worried, with her not coming back, and not being able to find her again. I hope that nothing has happened to her."

"There are a lot of dangers out there for an outside cat," Reg pointed out as she prepared the tray of tea things. "Cars and predators."

"Or people who might steal them," Francesca acknowledged, "use them for medical research." She gave a shudder. "I cannot bear to think of her in a cage in a lab somewhere. My poor Nicole."

"Well, hopefully, someone just thought she was cute and took her in. They wouldn't have any way of knowing that she had an owner when she's spending so much time outside and doesn't have any identification."

Francesca nodded. Reg took the tea tray over to the coffee table and set it down. She and Francesca were silent for a few minutes as they poured their tea. Francesca sipped hers while Reg was sure it was still too hot to drink.

"It is amazing how many black cats there are around here," Francesca said. "I am getting calls from all over Black Sands. But Nicole obviously cannot be all over town. I see these other cats, and they are too big to be Nicole, or they are the wrong shape, and they look at me with their cold, disdainful eyes. Nicole never looked at me like that. She is very friendly. She loves to cuddle and is a very nice cat. These other cats are just so… not Nicole."

Reg nodded. Maybe Francesca had psychic powers without realizing it. She could feel her own cat's affection for her and recognized that she didn't get the same feeling from other cats.

There was another knock on the door. Reg looked toward it in irritation. Francesca looked at the slim gold watch on her wrist. "You have other callers. I should be on my way."

"I don't have any appointments," Reg said, getting up to see who it was. She knew as she neared the door who it was going to be. She felt his presence like a pulsing heat on the other side of the door.

Reg opened the door a few inches to verify who it was and to talk to him without having to shout.

Corvin leaned toward her. "Invite me in," he said impatiently.

"I have company. And you're not coming in."

He tried to see who it was through the gap in the door. "Who? Damon again?"

"A client," Reg fibbed, not wanting to have to explain about the black cats. "What do you want?"

"We need to talk. How long will you be?"

There was a movement behind Reg. She glanced back and saw Francesca hovering behind her.

"I am just leaving," Francesca offered. "You go ahead and meet with your friend. I was just visiting."

Reg stepped aside, opening the door farther for Francesca to exit. Francesca looked curiously at Corvin but didn't stop to talk to him or seem unusually attracted to him. Corvin did, however, follow Francesca's progress with his eyes, swiveling to watch her walk across the yard toward the front of the property. Reg had to admit that Francesca was a very attractive woman and it would have been strange if Corvin had not shown some interest in her.

Corvin turned his eyes back to Reg. "A client?"

She shrugged. "Missing cat. You don't know her?"

"No. Haven't seen her before."

"She said she was new in town. I can't figure out if she knows about the magical community or not. I don't want to put my foot in my mouth or make her think that I'm loony toons. Isn't there some way to tell if someone is magical without actually asking her if she is a witch?"

He grimaced. "Not always. Especially if it is a fairly low level of powers. When someone has very strong gifts, I can feel it. But with someone like her... she might or might not be; I don't know."

"And with me?"

He gave a close-lipped smile and didn't answer aloud.

Reg took that to mean that he could sense her powers, and not just because he'd held them before. He'd shown interest in her from the start.

"So what do you want?"

"Invite me in."

"No. What's up? What are you doing here?"

"We need to talk."

"Not here."

"Regina," he growled impatiently.

"No. And don't give me any hurt-puppy look, either, because I'm not buying it. You know very well why you can't come in here. I'm not letting you charm me again."

"I'm not here for that. This is much bigger than your gifts."

"What is it, then?"

He stood there stubbornly. Reg folded her arms across her chest. "If you want to tell me about it, you can tell me about it. If you don't want to, then why don't you get off of my doorstep?"

"Not here. Not out in the open where we could be overheard. We don't know who might be out here listening."

"Then where? It's going to have to be around people who can overhear, because I'm not going to agree to be alone with you. You want me to call Damon, and we'll meet at your club again? Or head over to The Crystal Bowl?" After she said it, Reg realized that even that wouldn't be much of a protection. He had influenced her when she was around other people. She had to have someone who was there specifically to help her, not just bystanders who might not notice or know what to do. And she needed someone to make sure that she got home safely, without a warlock tagging along with her. When Corvin had stolen her powers, she'd thought that she was safe going out to eat with him, but by the end of the night, he had charmed her sufficiently that she had invited him in willingly. She'd thought that he was interested in her romantically; she hadn't realized that he was after her powers.

Corvin scowled at her suggestions. "We don't need anyone else around."

"I do. I'll call Damon."

"He's probably working."

"Then I guess you'll have to wait until he's not. Maybe you should get back to work and come back when it's a better time."

"This is important. This affects everyone in Black Sands. We can't just put it off for another time when it is more convenient."

"If it's that important, then you won't mind if we have company." Reg looked toward the big house. "Maybe I should get Sarah too. And I could bring Starlight along."

"You don't need to bring your damn cat!"

"I happen to know that he has the ability to interfere with your magic. If nothing else, he can bite your ankles."

She could feel Starlight behind her, keeping a close eye on what was going on, making sure that Corvin didn't enter. She should have had enough sense to listen to her cat the first time, but she hadn't; she'd locked him in the spare room, howling and crashing around when she wouldn't release him.

"I'm not charming you," Corvin said reasonably. "That much should be obvious. I'm not going to get distracted from my goal, and you're not going to be ensorcelled. So let's be grown adults here, and sit down and talk."

"Just because you're not charming me now, that doesn't mean that you won't. Even at the club last night, you still tried to get away with connecting with me, and that could have turned out very badly. I'm not going to risk it. You're too dangerous."

"I won't do anything."

"And you lie. So why would I trust you?"

"I don't lie."

Reg cocked her head at him. "What, you just shade the truth? I've heard you tell bald-faced lies. Don't tell me you don't."

He leaned against the doorframe. In his eyes was grudging respect. Reg hadn't broken down. She was being strong, and she wasn't going to let him talk her into anything. No compromises. He did things her way, or not at all.

"Call Damon, then. We can meet here. Call whoever you like to come and make sure you are safe, though I think he did a fine job last night. You are getting distracted from the importance of this case. It isn't just a matter of the Witch Doctor smuggling a few animal bones. That wouldn't be a big deal. This is far worse than that, and you know it, or you wouldn't be so disturbed by his aura. So call Damon. Call Sarah. Call Marta Jessup. Just don't delay."

Reg studied his face. She could hear the urgency in his voice as he tried to convince her that she needed to be concerned about it and act immediately. But she still wasn't sure. He had fooled her enough times before that she wasn't going to let it happen again.

"We're not going to meet here."

"Quit stalling."

"We're not. You're not coming into my house again. I don't know how all of the rules work about inviting you in and warding against you and all that, so I'm not even going to deal with it. You are not coming inside." She nodded toward the garden. "We can meet on the patio over there. Outside."

"I told you we can't meet outside." His eyes flashed around as if he thought someone were spying on him. "You don't know who might be eavesdropping. I can't secure an area like this."

"Where, then?"

"Maybe Sarah would agree...?" He nodded toward the big house.

"I don't know. Why don't you go over there and ask? Then you can let me know before I call Damon, so I'm not sending him all over town."

Corvin huffed impatiently and turned around, marching over to Sarah's back door. He rapped on it sharply, and Reg hoped that it didn't startle Sarah as much as Francesca's unexpected knock had surprised her. Reg closed her own door and turned to look at Starlight, worried that he would make a break for the outdoors now that Corvin wasn't blocking his path. Starlight paced back and forth, looking for an opportunity, then sat back when she wouldn't let him out. He stared at her with his blue and green eyes.

"Sorry," Reg said. "I know you want to go out looking for Nicole," she pronounced it as Francesca had, "but I don't want you going out and getting lost when all of this… spiritual unrest is going on. It's not fit out there for a domestic cat."

He stared at her crossly, tail switching back and forth.

Corvin returned a couple of minutes later. Reg opened the door partway.

"She won't let us have it in her house either," Corvin snapped. "What's with you women? I've been in your houses before. Especially Sarah's. You're shunning me now too?"

"If I was shunning you, then I wouldn't be talking to you now," Reg pointed out. "Where, then? You want to go to The Crystal Bowl? To some other meeting place? Back to your club?"

"The Crystal Bowl is close, that will have to do," Corvin said. "I'll go over and see if I can get a private room. You get Damon and meet me there."

"What if he is working and can't get off until later?"

"Impress upon him how important this is." Corvin met Reg's eyes, intense. "You both need to understand that I'm not joking around. This isn't just a prank. My coven may have shunned me, but they didn't take my powers away, and they are considerable. I'm not just a beginner. This is serious magic."

"You really think anyone is in danger? Other than me?"

"Yes, I do."

Reg sighed. "Okay."

"And so does Marta."

"She said that? I thought she was on probation and she wouldn't talk to anyone."

"I don't need her to explicitly tell me to know that she is concerned. I may not have your psychic powers, but I have some ability to read people. She is very worried."

"Okay. Should I call her too? I don't want to involve her in this, especially since…"

Corvin waited, but Reg decided not to finish.

"Since she's on probation?" Corvin suggested.

Reg nodded. "Yeah. That."

She could tell he knew that he had guessed wrong, but she

wasn't about to tell him how she still felt about having been the prime suspect in the theft of Sarah's emerald. She was already going against her better judgment by agreeing to meet with Corvin again to find out what he had learned. She didn't need to attract the attention of the police force again too.

"I had them bring you your car back," Corvin said, nodding toward the front of the house. "Since you apparently rode back with Damon yesterday."

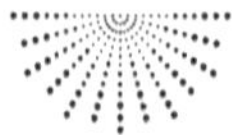

# CHAPTER FIFTEEN

*D*amon was waiting for Reg in the parking lot of The Crystal Bowl, a restaurant that catered to the magical community, when she arrived. They both got out of their cars, and Damon approached Reg. He gave her a cursory hug around the shoulders and a peck on the temple. She pulled away slightly, not sure how she felt about the physical affection. They had only been on one date, and that hadn't even gone very well. But it was the second time that he had come at a moment's notice to help her out with Corvin, so maybe she did owe him something.

Reg shook her head in irritation. She didn't *owe* him anything. He might *think* that she owed him something in return for the favors that he had done for her, but she didn't owe him physical affection because he had agreed to sit in on a couple of meetings with her. If she owed him anything, it was cash payment for the hours that he had spent acting as her personal security officer.

Damon did not comment on her pulling away. Reg gratefully headed for the glass front doors of The Crystal Bowl.

"So, what is this all about?" Damon questioned.

"I don't know yet. Corvin is supposed to be telling me. I don't know whether he's really found anything more than he knew last night, or if it's just a bluff." She considered, thinking about the way he had been behaving. "If I had to guess, though, he does have something."

"Okay, well, let's see what it is."

They entered and looked around for Corvin. He wasn't in the main dining room or at the bar. Reg motioned to Bill, one of the bartenders that she knew. "Do you know where Corvin is? I thought he was supposed to be here."

"Got a private room. Just grab one of the waiters." Bill motioned to one of the nearby waiters and whistled to attract his attention. "Hey, take Miss Rawlins and her guest to the back. Room booked for Corvin Hunter."

The waiter looked at Reg, and then his eyes went to Damon. "I thought his coven wasn't supposed to have anything to do with him."

"I'm not in his coven," Damon corrected. "And I'm not sure who appointed you to the council. It's up to the coven to police him, not you."

The waiter turned a bit pink and didn't argue the point. Black Sands was not a big town, and Reg was always a little surprised when she found two people who didn't know each other. The waiter and Damon obviously didn't know each other well, or the waiter would have known Damon was not in Corvin's coven. It just seemed strange to Reg that in such a small place, everyone didn't know everyone else. She misjudged how people would run into each other everywhere they went.

They followed the waiter back to a hall with several unmarked doors. He knocked on one, then opened it to peer inside. "Yeah, this is the one." He motioned them in. Reg let Damon lead the way. Not that it mattered. Corvin wasn't going to do anything to her in the split second it took for her to walk into the room ahead of Damon.

The two warlocks nodded at each other and didn't exchange greetings. Corvin looked at Reg and motioned her to sit down. The waiter closed the door when he left.

The room was small and only dimly lit when the door was

shut. Reg looked at the ceiling to see if the lights were burned out, but it seemed like they just weren't turned on. There was a small grouping of candles in the middle of the table. Reg leaned over to look at the flickering flames and saw that they were electric lights. Cheap dollar-store candle lights. She shook her head. Atmosphere. Window dressing.

She sat down in the chair opposite the one Corvin had indicated, and Damon sat in the other. She took pleasure in seeing Corvin grind his teeth over this little demonstration of her independence, but he didn't complain.

"Let's get down to business, then."

"Okay." Reg opened her arms. "Lay it on me."

"The activity at the cemetery wasn't just teenagers fooling around and desecrating graves."

"Did they… plunder them, then? Were they looking for valuables?"

Corvin shook his head. "No. It was a good lead. The police are doing their best to keep it quiet and out of public hearing. It wasn't just teenagers. They weren't stealing valuables from graves. They were stealing bodies."

Reg swallowed. She looked over at Damon to see what he thought about this. Was that something that happened regularly at Black Sands, and she was just naive? Maybe practitioners of black arts needed human body parts to produce their magic spells. Human hair or fingernails. Maybe even teeth. Reg didn't want to think of anything more graphic than that. She didn't need more nightmares.

She looked back at Corvin. "Why would they steal bodies?" she asked in as calm a voice as she could manage.

# CHAPTER SIXTEEN

There was silence around the table for what seemed like a long time. Reg waited for Corvin to explain, or for Damon to jump in with questions or an explanation of his own. But Damon didn't seem to know what to do with this news any more than Reg did. So it wasn't something common.

"There are a few reasons that someone might want to steal human remains," Corvin said slowly. "None of them good, as you can well imagine."

"And that's why you said that Detective Jessup was worried. Because it isn't just vandalism or kids messing around. She knew that they were stealing bodies."

Corvin nodded.

Reg shifted in her seat. She looked around the room. Her eyes were more used to the dimness of the room, but she felt closed in. There was some kind of magic in the room that was making her itch. She looked toward the door.

"We are safe from being overheard here," Corvin said, misjudging her look.

"Yeah, I already figured that. But this room... can't we meet somewhere else? This is creepy."

"We could turn the light on," Damon pointed out the obvious, indicating the wall switch.

Reg nodded. "Yeah. Why don't you turn them on? I'm getting creeped out here."

Corvin shook his head. "It's easier for me to maintain the integrity of the room in the dark. It's going to take a lot more energy in bright light, and I need to be able to focus on you, not just on the room."

"Maintain the integrity of the room?" Reg lifted an eyebrow. Was he teasing her?

"If we want to be somewhere that we cannot be overheard, no matter who is trying to spy on us through magical means, then I need to cast a spell to seal the room from any eavesdroppers. Like I said to you earlier, I can't do that outside. I need an enclosed space. And it helps me if it is by candlelight, or at least not too bright. There is a reason most of us do magic at night rather than in the daylight. Moonlight or candlelight makes it a lot easier to focus and maintain the spell. With sunlight or bright overhead lights—I can't do that and carry on a conversation."

Reg looked over at Damon for confirmation. He was, at least, a warlock, and would know if it were just all crap Corvin was hoping she would swallow. Damon gave a nod. "Night is easier."

Reg shook her head. "We could have waited until tonight, then, and met somewhere else instead of this tiny room. It's claustrophobic."

"You're feeling the spell," Corvin said. "Not the closeness of the room."

"Why does it feel like that? If it's a protective spell, then shouldn't it feel warm and comforting? This feels… itchy and restless and irritating."

Corvin's smile was somewhat strained. "You're just going to have to put up with it, Regina, because I don't want to risk him overhearing us."

"Him? Who?" A second or two ticked by before Reg understood. "The Witch Doctor?" She looked around. "How would he be able to hear us here? Is he in the restaurant? I didn't feel him that close!" She half-rose out of her seat.

Corvin made a calming gesture with his hands, motioning her back to her chair. "No, he's not here. But his spies could be close by, and he has powerful magic, as you and I both felt. You know you can connect to people with your mind even when they are not in the same room. I don't know how far his remote capabilities are, but I don't want to take the chance that he can reach us. I don't want him to know that we know anything about him."

Reg sighed, letting as much air out of her lungs as she could in an effort to calm her breathing and slow her heart. As Corvin said, she was going to have to put up with the uncomfortably prickly feeling. She didn't want the Witch Doctor to be able to hear or see them remotely either. She closed her eyes and felt for the spell, trying to visualize it as a warm blanket around them instead of a force field. The itchiness eased a little. She rolled her shoulders and looked back at Corvin.

"So are you avoiding telling me exactly what he is doing for a reason? If you wanted me to come here and listen to you so badly, why don't you get on with it? Why does the Witch Doctor need bodies?"

Corvin's voice took on a professorial tone, like he was lecturing to a class. She knew that he did a lot of historical studies, and wondered if he lectured at some magical university about his topics. "In almost all cultures around the world, there are stories of the dead being reanimated through one method or another. Occasionally, such as in Christian resurrection, the resulting beings are seen as good, but in most cases, they are not. It is almost always believed to be the result of dark magic, creating malevolent beings that terrorize the living."

"Reanimated?" Reg repeated. She tried to wrap her mind around what he was saying. "Are you talking about... zombies?"

"They have many different names in many different cultures. That is... one of them."

"Zombies. The Witch Doctor is creating zombies. That's why he needs dead bodies."

"That is the only explanation I can find. Of course, other kinds of magic might use parts of the bodies, but he isn't taking parts. He is taking the whole bodies, and they are recently deceased. That tells me that he is… reanimating them."

Reg shook her head, feeling sick. "Zombies aren't real. Come on."

"If a myth persists across all cultures… you have to assume that it is real in some form. Maybe each culture gets it a little bit wrong, but myths that span the globe… they have at least a kernel of truth."

"And you want me to believe that zombies are one of those things. That they are real."

"I have studied this kind of magic in some detail. The mythos that I believe is the closest to the truth is the Viking draugr."

"A drow-ger? What is that?"

"The Vikings believed that any corpse could be reanimated into a draugr, a sort of a large, shapeshifting monster that has an animus toward the living. It usually takes a human form, which can grow to double its usual size. Unlike your shuffling TV zombie, it can look just like a regular human. One of the only ways to tell that it is a draugr is that it doesn't bleed. It can sometimes talk, quote poetry, or prophesy of the future. It can only be controlled by a powerful sorcerer."

"Like the Witch Doctor."

"Yes."

"I thought that zombies were created by… some drug that made people look like they were dead, and then controlled their minds so that they didn't have a will of their own." Reg tried to remember what she had seen about this on TV. "Like… pufferfish toxin…?"

"According to Wade Davis," Corvin said, rolling his eyes. "He claimed to have infiltrated a group of bokors in Haiti and learned all of the secrets of zombie conjuring. His claims were… sensational and widely-questioned. But what do you think everybody remembers? Pufferfish toxin." He sighed and shook his head.

Reg shrugged. "It sounds just as likely as what you're talking about. A powerful wizard that can raise the dead? That can't really happen."

"You're judging something that you know nothing about. What makes you an expert on the dead?"

Reg raised an eyebrow. "Well… talking to them."

"That's the spirit of the dead. I'm talking about the body of the dead. Two different things. The ghosts that you have talked to don't know anything about reanimation, because spirits are not reanimated. Bodies are. Have any of them told you any details about what has happened to their bodies after they died?"

Reg frowned. She shook her head. "No. Why would they talk about something like that? Once they've been separated from their bodies, they don't have any more sense of it. Except for Warren, but that was different. Because he wasn't dead, just bound."

"So how could they tell you about draugar? Most spirits wouldn't have any idea about them. You don't suddenly gain all knowledge about death just because you've experienced it. Do you know everything there is to know about what cold viruses look like and how they work in the body? And how many colds have you had? Experiencing something doesn't make you an expert in it. Even if one of your spirit friends had been turned into a living zombie by a bokor using puffer fish toxin, they wouldn't be able to tell you that was what had happened. Because they wouldn't have been aware of the fact of it."

Reg's brain was whirling. She looked aside at Damon for his take on the conversation, then looked back at Corvin again. "So how is a zombie made, then?"

"A draugr," he corrected. "I don't want you getting these creatures confused with the reanimated corpses you see in popular media. Thanks to *Night of the Living Dead*, everybody has a completely skewed idea of what a zombie is."

"Whatever. How is a draugr made?"

"I have studied the literature rather than the dark art itself, so I can't give you a detailed recipe or conjure. Whatever so-called experts might have said in popular media, you can't turn someone into a zombie just with drugs. You can keep a living person under your control, but you can't use a drugged person for your own means like you could use a draugr. Drugged people are not great at taking commands or fighting off attacks."

"Do you know for sure that the Witch Doctor is making draugrs? Couldn't he be using the bodies for something else? Or couldn't it be someone completely different stealing bodies?"

"Like medical students?" Corvin said dryly. "This isn't the dark ages. Could someone be using them for something else? Cannibalism or other bodily appetites? Ingredients needed for spell-casting? It's possible, but why would they need more than one or two bodies for such a venture? This was not a quiet operation. This wasn't one person sneaking into the graveyard at night to surreptitiously steal a body. You saw the police operation. They wouldn't have been out there for a simple disturbing the peace or suspicious behavior charge."

There had been a lot of police, Reg had to admit. And they had set up roadblocks and not allowed anyone close to the cemetery. Not just a simple case of vandalism. Something big and bad.

"How many bodies are missing?" Damon asked.

He had been quiet up until then, just serving in his role as Reg's protector. Reg had not expected him to take part in the conversation. She looked at him and then looked at Corvin for his answer.

"I don't have a handle on that yet," Corvin said. "But there were a number of them. My sources are not clear on how many. It is still under investigation, so maybe the police don't have a number either."

"They would know how many graves had been dug up," Reg protested.

"Not all graves contain bodies. Sometimes it is an empty casket or just a marker. Or there may be the remains of more than one person, which could also skew the numbers. The police have to investigate each one to find out how many bodies were taken. This just happened last night. They haven't had time yet to investigate fully. Or, they hadn't when I talked to my source."

"And that source wasn't Detective Jessup?" Reg challenged.

He looked at her and didn't answer.

Reg wasn't quite sure why she was so angry at the thought that Jessup would talk to Corvin but not her. Jessup and Corvin had a past. They had known each other for much longer than either had known Reg, who was a newcomer on the scene. Why would Jessup trust Reg with confidential information when she knew that Reg was a con?

"Did your source have a ballpark figure?" Damon asked.

Reg tried to suppress her irritation at him involving himself in the conversation. But she wasn't paying for him to be there. He had come as a friend, which she supposed entitled him to ask questions if he wanted to. But she didn't like to have a man speaking up for her, as if she couldn't ask questions on her own. She was more than capable of getting the facts out of Corvin. Just as capable as Damon. He might have a gift as a human polygraph, but he wasn't an expert interrogator.

"Somewhere between five and ten," Corvin said.

Reg's mind went into overdrive. Between five and ten of the zombie creatures, the Frankenstein's monsters that Corvin was talking about? Ten of them? She had imagined two or three, and that was horrific enough. But a larger number? She pictured them all walking down the street, dark shapes shuffling toward her out of the night—despite what Corvin had said, she still couldn't help thinking of them shuffling—and the feeling of horror and dread grew inside her, strangling her breathing.

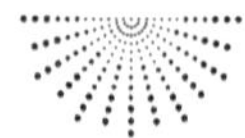

# CHAPTER SEVENTEEN

"I have to get out of here." She rose to her feet. She didn't know where she was going, but she needed to get out of there. She didn't want to know anything else. She didn't want to hear any more horrors.

"Reg," Corvin was quickly on his feet as well, reaching out to grab her by the arm. "You need to stay here so we can talk. We can't talk about this openly outside this room."

"No." Reg jerked back, avoiding his touch. Damon was slower, but he was on his feet as well, edging closer to Reg to try to get between her and Corvin.

"Leave her be. If she wants to leave this room, she can."

"I'm not looking for your opinion on this matter. How is your experience in fighting draugar? You think you can do something about this plague? This is up to Reg and me. It's got nothing to do with you; you're just here as her guard dog."

Damon pushed past Reg at that, making her knock her hip hard into the table. The two warlocks were shoving each other, getting in each other's faces, acting like a couple of teenage boys in a schoolyard fight. Reg rubbed her hip and grabbed at Damon.

"Cut it out, both of you. Go to your own corners!"

They eventually broke apart. Reg grabbed Damon's arm and tried to direct him back to his seat. "Quit acting like a couple of twelve-year-olds. You think Bill wants a fist fight back here? Control yourselves."

They ended up on opposite sides of the table. Reg didn't know whether to make them sit down again. She really wanted to be out the door. She didn't want to stay there anymore, and she certainly didn't need to be schooling a couple of testosterone-driven adolescents when Black Sands was on the verge of a zombie apocalypse. The three of them stood there, eyeing each other, trying to formulate their next step.

"Reg, you need to stay here. We need to work out a plan."

"What kind of plan? What are you talking about?"

"We have to find a way to stop the Witch Doctor."

"You and me? Why? Can't you call in… Zombie Busters or something? There must be people a lot more qualified than I am…"

"Curiously, there are very few people who are equipped to fight draugar."

"Well, what makes it our job? What makes it mine? I don't care if you want to go fight the draugrs. But I'm not trained in zombie warfare. I have no idea how to deal with any of this."

"It is our job because we are the only two who are aware of what is going on. You and I can feel the Witch Doctor and no one else can. You have a connection with him, no matter how much you try to deny it. And that makes you uniquely qualified to fight him."

"Why?"

"Because you have insight into his mind that no one else has."

"I'm not getting inside his head."

Corvin huffed out his breath in frustration. "Can we please sit down and discuss this? Running away is not going to solve anything."

"I could leave Black Sands. That seems like the only logical thing to do at this point. If I want to stay safe, I should get as far as possible away from this lunatic. What the rest of you do is up to you. But like you say, I have a history with this guy." Reg didn't know if it was true or not, but she would use his own argument against him. "I know how dangerous he is. I'm not sticking around to face him down like some stupid woman in a horror movie."

"Please sit," Corvin repeated through gritted teeth.

Reg fought back against the urge to run. She could run after the meeting was over. She could hear Corvin out, agree with everything he said, and then bolt as soon as she was out of his sight. She didn't even have to go back to her cottage to pack; she could just get in her car and hit the road. There was Starlight, of course, but Sarah would make sure that he didn't starve. She could call and have Starlight taken back to the animal shelter.

But Reg hated to think of him back inside one of those little cages, depressed and thinking that she didn't care about him anymore. He had chosen her. Out of all of the people who had gone to the shelter and who had tried to engage with him and get him out of his grief for his previous owner, she was the only person that he had responded to. She was his choice as much as he was hers. More so.

So she'd have to go back to the cottage, but only for long enough to coax Starlight into the cat carrier. Then she was leaving. She would put Black Sands behind her and she would never have to worry about the Witch Doctor or warlocks like Corvin again. She could go to California. She hadn't explored the West Coast yet. She would be unknown there. She could take on a new name. She could leave all of the magic behind and go back to cold reading people and inventing stories. She was good at that. It had worked for her before she had arrived in Black Sands.

So she sat down. She would let Corvin say his piece. She would agree with everything he said. Then she would run.

Corvin smiled thinly and nodded, also sitting. Damon stayed

on his feet for a few more seconds, letting Corvin know that he wasn't doing it just because Corvin had said to, but because he was there for Reg. Corvin paid him no attention.

"You and I are the only ones who even know that the Witch Doctor is back in operation," he told Reg, "So it's up to us to deal with him."

"Why not just tell Jessup where he is and have the cops deal with him? Why should we have to?"

"How are the police going to deal with him? Think about it, Regina. They have no idea what he is or how to deal with him. Someone like that isn't going to be caught by the police. You need someone who understands the paranormal and has some insight into his mind. If we sent the police, he would slip through their fingers. He'd be laughing. You've dealt with him before, remember?"

Reg fought back against the memories. She didn't want to remember anything about the Witch Doctor. She'd rather think that he wasn't the same man as she had seen torturing her mother. She didn't want to face that evil man. She had been a little girl, scared out of her mind. He had been so big and strong and horrible.

Reg was suddenly overcome by the sounds of her mother screaming. She swayed with vertigo and gripped the table, trying to stay in her seat when every muscle in her body was turning to jelly. Damon was there, his strong hands on her, trying to steady her. Corvin was there, the warmth of his energy flowing into her, but even in the state she was in, she could tell that it wasn't the same as usual. His energy seemed weak and slow, not flowing freely like it usually did.

"Just leave her alone," Damon snapped. "Don't you think you've done enough already? It's too much for her. And if you think she's going to be joining you hunting down this Witch Doctor and his draugrs, you'd better think again. She's not going to have anything to do with you."

"I'm trying to help her," Corvin argued, as he always did. He always had a way to justify himself, whether what he was doing was right or wrong.

"Stop. Give her a few minutes to recover on her own."

The warmth and energy faded. Reg felt like he had let go of the rope that was keeping her from drifting out to sea. She held on to Damon's arm but, while he was strong, none of that strength flowed into her. He couldn't hold her and anchor her like Corvin could.

"It's okay, Reg," Damon said quietly. "Just breathe. You're okay. Do you want me to get you some water? Something stronger?"

"No." Reg shook her head. If they left the room, it would mean breaking the spell that Corvin had woven to keep them from eavesdroppers. And she did not want the Witch Doctor to see her or feel her and to know how vulnerable she was. She didn't want to be that little girl anymore. And she didn't want to be her mother.

"You don't have to connect with his mind," Corvin conceded. "We can use what we know about him already to track him down and try to bring him down. But I need you. I can't do this on my own. You are the one who knows him."

"I don't know him. I've seen him in action, and that means I want to stay as far away from him as possible."

"I understand that. But we need to think about the other people in Black Sands. What about your other friends here? There are people you care about. People you don't want to get hurt."

"What makes you think anyone in Black Sands is in danger? So he's smuggling. So he has these draugrs to… I don't know, to help him. Aren't they just slave labor? How does that put anyone else in Black Sands at risk?"

"Draugar are difficult to control when you only have one or two. I can't imagine someone controlling five or more. That means that the ones that he isn't in control of are free to roam around Black Sands doing whatever they want to. And what they want to do is terrorize and kill people. It isn't clear from the mythologies whether they consume people or not, but I think that's beside the point, don't you? Would you want one going after Sarah? After Damon? Anyone else here in Black Sands that you've gotten to know?"

"You, maybe," Reg muttered.

"Then I would think that you'd want to join up with me so that you could happen to push me toward one of them." The corner of Corvin's mouth quirked up in a sardonic smile.

"Exactly."

"I don't know why the Witch Doctor created so many. Maybe he is doing some experiment and needs to test it on several different subjects. But I hate to think about what kind of experiment he would be performing on draugar. What would he want them to do?"

"I don't care. Why don't you just tell people what he's up to and let them decide? They can leave if they don't want to face zombies. I don't know why anyone would choose to stay."

"Because most of the population, even the magical community, are not going to believe that what he's doing is possible. They're just going to roll their eyes and go on with their lives."

"Then that's their choice. Why do I have to put myself in danger for anyone who's too stupid to listen?"

Corvin was silent. Reg thought about Sarah, who had already told her that she didn't think there was anything to Reg's feelings of doom and the presence of the Witch Doctor. So was Reg willing to leave her behind to face the living dead? Reg pounded her forehead with her fist.

"Fine, okay! Tell me what you want from me. What's your plan?"

Corvin's expression was frozen. Reg looked at him, waiting. It slowly dawned on her that he didn't have a plan. He had no idea what to do. She looked over at Damon and then back at Corvin in disbelief.

"You don't know?"

Corvin cleared his throat. "Err…"

"You want me to hunt draugrs with you, and you don't even know what you're going to do when you find them?"

"I was hoping you and I could work through that and come up with a plan."

# CHAPTER EIGHTEEN

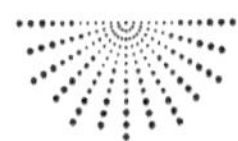

Reg ran her fingers through her braids, massaging her scalp like she did when she woke up in the morning and was trying to get her brain running.

"I don't know anything about draugrs. How am I supposed to come up with something?"

"I probably know more about draugar than anyone other than the Witch Doctor, and you know all about the Witch Doctor. The two of us together should be able to come up with something. And the plural form is actually draugar, not draugrs—"

"I don't care! Do you think they're going to be correcting my grammar?"

Corvin fell silent, tucking his chin and looking down at the table.

"Tell me what you know about them," Reg snapped.

He licked his lips. "Distilling everything I know about them into a short conversation is not going to be easy."

"We're not getting any closer while you stall."

He nodded his acknowledgment. "As I said, there are myths in most cultures about undead or reanimated corpses. Zombies, draugar, vampires, barrow-wights, revenants; even the Asian cultures have jiang shi, ganshi, kyonshi, and ro-langs. There are remarkable similarities between all of them—"

"I'm sure."

Corvin heeded her impatient tone and moved on in his lecture. "The Vikings and other cultures started putting large stones over graves to prevent the dead from rising again. That is where our tradition of marking the graves with slabs of stone comes from, only now we stand them up instead of laying them over the body to keep it there."

"So that's what we need to do? Pin them down with something heavy?"

"Well, as it turned out, the Vikings found that the stones were not enough to prevent dead bodies from being raised as draugar. If men were able to move the stones onto the grave, they were able to remove them off again in the night. Or else the bodies were reanimated in the grave, and the draugar were big and strong enough to move them themselves."

"So, no stones."

"No." Corvin licked his lips again. He focused for a moment on the room, and Reg could feel the spell he had cast to guard against spies. She rubbed her arms, trying to rub away the itchy, uncomfortable goosebumps.

"So is there any way to defeat the draugrs?"

"The Vikings decided that the only way to prevent bodies from being reanimated was to burn them or bury them at sea."

"But we're not trying to stop bodies from being reanimated. They already have been, right?"

"The same principles apply. Bear with me. Remains have been discovered in Syria that show that stone age man had disinterred bodies that had previously been buried and crushed the skulls and separated them from the bodies. And of course, the Egyptians frequently destroyed the brains in their mummies during their burial rituals—"

"I thought they saved them. In jars."

"Not the brains. And the latest studies show that they—"

Corvin stopped himself. He held up his hands. "Let's just say they were not preserved. No need to get any more graphic than that."

"Right. Zombies are bad enough."

"Suffice to say that in ancient mythologies as well as in the modern fairy tales we call TV, destroying or removing the brain or head is a sure-fire way to kill a draugr."

"So you suggest that we go out and find six to ten super-human giant zombies and cut off their heads."

"That's a bit of an oversimplification," Corvin grumbled.

Reg looked at Damon. "That's what I heard. Isn't that what you heard?"

Damon nodded.

Reg put her hands on the table and pushed herself to her feet. "Okay, I'm ready to leave. Is that everything?"

Corvin jumped up, his face flushing red with fury. Damon was also up in an instant, shoving past Reg and putting himself between them. Corvin swiped the electric candles off of the table, and they went pinging around the room, making it almost impossible to see.

"Do you think this is a joke?" Corvin roared. "Do you think this is just a fairy tale that I made up to entertain you? We are in danger. *You*, in particular, are in danger! Do you not understand that?"

Reg stood up. "Yes!" Her heart pounded in her throat, making it difficult for her to speak. "That's why I want to get out of town!"

"You can't just leave them here. Everybody else in Black Sands will then have to deal with them, with no idea what they are or how to handle them. The population could be decimated! These creatures are vicious and have no human feelings, none at all. They must be stopped before they can get a foothold."

Reg's hands were clenched into fists. "And what am I supposed to do about it? I am one person. Why does it have to have anything to do with me?"

"Because you can feel them."

"So can you."

"I can feel *him*. The Witch Doctor. I cannot feel the draugar."

Reg stared at Corvin. It was just one revelation after another. "You can't feel them?"

"You said that the feeling was growing and getting stronger. I haven't felt that. If the Witch Doctor is reanimating corpses, that would explain why your feeling is increasing. He is marshaling his forces. He will only continue to get stronger."

"How is he going to get any more bodies now? The police will be guarding the cemetery now, watching for him."

Corvin didn't answer. But he didn't need to.

The draugar could kill, and their victims could be reanimated.

* * *

Reg felt a sudden whoosh as if the door had opened. She looked toward it, startled, but it was still closed. She realized that the feeling wasn't air on her body, but feelings rushing into her, filling her back up with that dread that had been plaguing her—the Witch Doctor. For a few minutes, she had found some relief from it. Corvin must have blocked the influence of the Witch Doctor with his anti-spying magic, but then it all suddenly rushed back, and it was stronger than ever. Reg gasped and held her breath, trying to straighten her body and steel herself so it didn't crush her. Corvin and Damon were both looking at her, suddenly concerned.

"What just happened to your spell?" Reg gasped.

The angry flush left Corvin's face, leaving him pale and gray looking. He swore. "I was… distracted from it."

Reg pressed her fingers to her temples.

It was more than just the feeling of dread-filled expectation. Now that she knew what the Witch Doctor was doing, she could feel the individual forces. The draugrs he had created. Each was a little spot of darkness in Black Sands, like a miniature black hole. And they were only going to get bigger and stronger, drawing all of the light and goodness into themselves. The draugrs were strong. Picturing them in her mind, Reg saw their dark shapes as they moved around, following the instructions of the Witch Doctor.

"I can feel them."

"I know. I'm sorry. But I don't think I can repair the spell." Corvin moved around the room, gathering up the lights that were not broken and putting them in a group in the middle of the table again. "I shouldn't have lost my temper."

He might have said that he was sorry, and he was acting like his tantrum was over, but Reg could still feel the anger radiating off of him. If Damon could detect lies, then he undoubtedly knew it too. She glanced over at him, and he gave her a grim look. He knew, alright. He wanted to communicate to her that she should be on the alert and not let down her guard. Just because Corvin was pretending that his fit of pique had blown over, that didn't make it true. He was still seething beneath the surface, and it wouldn't take much to set him off again.

In her mind, Reg had a sudden vision of him raging. Not just the momentary loss of control that he'd just displayed, but a raging meltdown, destroying everything around him. She pretended to herself that she was safe from him as long as she had someone there to guard her and that the only danger came from his charming her again. But that wasn't the only danger. He was a powerful warlock, one of the most powerful in Black Sands, and if he lost it, he could do some real damage. He wasn't that soothing, warm, calming presence that he affected when he was solicitous of her. That was just one side of him. A thin veneer. One of the tricks that he had learned to do to gain women's trust.

Reg pushed the images away. Fearing him now would only make things worse. She needed to focus on the more imminent danger, which was the Witch Doctor and his undead minions.

"What do we do now?" Reg asked.

"Can you tell me where he is, what he's doing right now?"

Reg closed her eyes, focusing on the man with the dreadlocks. She hated to do it. She didn't want to see or feel him again. Every instinct screamed at her to run away, not to poke and prod and try to figure out what he was up to. She swallowed and breathed slowly in and out. She wished that Starlight were there. He was good at helping her to focus and acting as an antenna for her psychic powers. He helped her to feel calm and safe, which was not what she was feeling presently.

"I don't know the town well enough," she said, trying to pinpoint where he was. "It's… not that far from the other warehouse. The one that he trapped us in. Close to there…"

"Close to the waterfront," Corvin said. "Makes perfect sense if he's smuggling again. He needs somewhere to store his goods and access to the water so he can ship them out."

"Yeah." Standing there, opening herself up to feeling him, Reg could feel the motion of the ocean waves. The ocean was a deep well of power itself, and distracted her for a moment from the man. He stood on a dock, looking out at the waves, and she felt what he felt, the power of the water. The magnetism between the moon and the ocean, pulling out the tides. "He has… a connection with the natural world… a strong one…"

"I would think that he would need it if he's going to animate the dead. They don't have spirits of their own; each one is an extension of him. They can only operate independently to an extent. He needs to keep his thoughts on them regularly."

"He isn't right now. Right now, he's… resting. Gathering strength."

She opened her eyes and saw Corvin's nod of understanding. "Is he going to make more draugar, or is he done?"

"I don't know. How am I supposed to know what his intentions are?"

"You don't have to," he soothed her immediately. "I was only curious. Our job will be to stop him from making more and to destroy the ones he has already made. Then maybe we can drive him out of here if he doesn't have any more automatons to protect him."

"He's so strong," Reg protested. "How are we going to drive him out? He's much stronger than you or me."

"You are stronger than you know. And both of us together… and whoever else we can convince to help out…" Corvin's eyes went to Damon, but the other warlock did not jump in with an offer to help with hunting and slaying draugrs or the Witch Doctor. "We will gather together whatever powers we can. I can boost my powers… I still have some artifacts that I have not used."

And how else would he boost his powers? What if he didn't plan to use Reg, but only her powers? If he stripped them from her, then he could use them himself and focus them the way he wished. He wouldn't need Reg's help.

Corvin looked at her, his eyes narrow, as if he guessed what she was thinking. But he didn't tell her that she was wrong.

Reg felt a shift in the Witch Doctor's consciousness, and then what she had feared, happened. He felt her presence and reached out to touch her. Reg fought back against the intrusion, trying to wall herself off and to push him away.

When she had been a little girl, she had been able to, hadn't she? He had searched the apartment and never found her. He hadn't been able to feel her presence there or to hear her screams. She had been walled off from him as if sealed in an invisible box so that he didn't even know she was there.

Reg clutched at her heart, looking for extra strength, trying to channel all of her powers into making that wall around her so that he couldn't even tell she was there, but her efforts were feeble and she knew she wasn't succeeding. He knew she was there, and the curiosity he felt was palpable.

"Who are you and what are you doing here?"

And then worse.

"I remember you. I know who you are, little girl."

She swallowed back a scream. She clawed at the air, looking for something to hold on to. Damon and Corvin both closed in, asking questions and offering support, trying to get her back into her chair and to find out what was going on. Reg couldn't help crying out as the consciousness probed and pulsed, thick black laughter building up around her.

"I remember you, little girl. You are not going to escape me again."

"He sees me," she choked out to Corvin, trying to explain what was going on. "He knows!"

"He can't know who or where you are," Corvin soothed. His hands hovered above her, directing extra strength into her. He was trying to weave his spell again, to wrap that protective web around her, but he was too depleted from maintaining it for as long as he had. She didn't know whether he needed physical sustenance, or more ingredients or potions, but whatever he needed, he didn't have it in him. He couldn't protect her from the Witch Doctor.

Corvin's reassuring words were nonsense. Of course, if she could feel the Witch Doctor and tell Corvin where he was, he could do the same and know where Reg was. His powers were far greater than hers.

"You do not have a guardian this time," the Witch Doctor's thoughts came to her. "This time, you are all on your own."

A guardian. Reg grabbed hold of Corvin's arm and held it tightly, trying to draw the strength out of him faster than he was imparting it. She tried to find a way to use it, to build that wall up so that the Witch Doctor could no longer see her and threaten her.

Corvin's eyes were wide. He jerked back from her, breaking his connection, and abandoned his attempt to protect her. Reg looked at Damon.

"We've got to get out of here," she told him urgently. "Before he comes. I need to get out of here. Get out of town. I can't stay here now that he knows I'm here."

"He doesn't know you," Corvin protested.

But Reg already knew the truth. Corvin couldn't hear the Witch Doctor's words. He was trying to calm her with empty platitudes, acting like he knew what he was talking about when he had no idea at all. She looked at Damon insistently, widening her eyes. "Now!"

"Come on." Damon reached out to her and helped her to her feet and directed her to the door. As he reached for the door handle, Reg was terrified that when it opened, all of the evil would pour in on her and she would be lost. He jerked it open, but it did not open a pathway straight to hell as she had feared. He looked out into the hallway and nodded. "All clear. Let's get you out of here."

He went out of the door first. Reg followed close behind him. Corvin was behind her, slower, reluctant, not believing that she was in imminent danger and that she needed to get out of there to preserve her life.

Damon rounded the corner ahead of her and stopped. Reg ran directly into his back, her nose taking the impact and driving consciousness of the Witch Doctor out of her head with the burst of pain.

Another man was waiting in the hallway. He leaned against the wall casually, arms folded as if he'd been waiting there for them for some time. He gave Reg a broad smile.

"Hello, darling. Long time, no see."

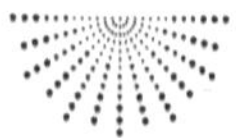

# CHAPTER NINETEEN

The man looked like some kind of circus performer. He had a black and white striped shirt and a large, curling mustache. He had long limbs and a casual manner. Reg stared at him. He was strangely familiar, and even in her state of panic, she searched her memory for how she might know him. It was a long time since she had seen him. She tried to remember his name, or at least what she had called him. Reg turned to look at Corvin.

"Is he... can you see him?"

She already knew the answer. Damon wouldn't have stopped so abruptly if he couldn't see the man. The man had to be real, corporeal, visible to the physical eye. He wasn't just a spiritual manifestation.

"I can see him," Corvin said, his voice low. He stared at the stranger, scrutinizing him.

"I'm disappointed, Regina," the smiling man said. "Is it so easy to forget me?"

"No... I... where did you come from?"

"I still check in on you now and then. This time, things seemed to be getting a little dicey, so I thought I should stop for a chat."

As he stood there, Reg felt a force enveloping her. Not like

Corvin's spell, which had been uncomfortable and itchy, but like a soft, warm blanket. Something familiar and comforting. The Witch Doctor's voice was gone. The feeling of dread was swept away, like the air escaping a balloon. The familiar sensations and the release of the tension helped her to focus on the memories.

"Uncle Harrison?"

His grin grew even wider, and he nodded. "I knew you couldn't forget completely," he approved.

"You know this man? I thought you said you didn't have any magical relatives," Corvin accused.

"I don't. But I don't think he's a real uncle. Are you?" she appealed to Harrison. "It was so long ago."

"No, you're right," he agreed. "Just a friend of the family. A sort of a… godfather, if you like."

"How did you do that?" Reg looked around. She couldn't see any hint of his spell, no aura or shimmer in the air, just the warm feeling and the silence so that she could hear her own thoughts again and the Witch Doctor could not see her. Corvin had said how hard it was to cast his spell in an open area. He'd needed the small, dark room to keep their conversation private. Harrison seemed to be able to do it effortlessly.

"That? A little trick I learned a long time ago. You used to get anxious when I did it. I guess that as a child it was disconcerting because it would block out the other voices and you didn't know how to deal with that. But we had to practice so that you would not disrupt the spell if you were in danger."

"I don't understand."

He cocked his head, studying her. "How do you think I kept Destine from finding you that day?"

Reg swallowed. The day her mother had been killed. Destine had to be the Witch Doctor's name.

"*You* kept him from finding me?"

"Yes." He looked at her steadily. His eyes were clear and bright. She pictured herself hidden in the cupboard. Remembered how the scary man had searched through the apartment, but had not found her. She had screamed, and he had not heard her. If the Witch Doctor was the powerful force that she had just felt, then he should have been able to sense her in the apartment even if he couldn't see or hear her. So Harrison had blocked her thoughts and had used his magic to hide her.

"Yes. I am sorry that you had to go through what you did." His smile disappeared and he shook his head, eyes sad. "No child should have to go through such a traumatic experience. We did our best to keep you safe. To keep you alive and away from Destine."

"We? Who is we? And how did you know—and why would he want to find me? What was he looking for that day? Why did he... why did he do that to my mother?"

He continued to look at her. His eyes were warm and brown, and she felt like she had known him for a long, long time. "So many questions. I suppose there is no way you could know what was happening back then. We tried to stay out of your life and not to have any contact while you were growing up, to give you a chance at a normal life without Destine trying to find you. But you were so lonely, and no one in the mortal world could understand what you had gone through. So we had to help a little, here and there."

"Who exactly are you?" Corvin demanded. Reg looked at him, irritated. She was doing just fine talking to Harrison and she didn't need him butting in to her business. He was there only by chance. If she'd had a choice, he wouldn't be. She would be alone with Harrison and be able to ask all about everything she could remember and not remember. He could tell her all of the things that she didn't know. But she didn't want to share it with Corvin and Damon. She needed to talk to him in private.

"I am a friend," Harrison said simply. "You do not need to know anything else, warlock."

Reg examined Harrison closely. Was he a fairy? He didn't look like any of the fairies that she had seen. Nor was he a pixie. Too tall and long-limbed to be one of their kind. But the world was filled with all kind of folk that Reg had no idea of. By addressing Corvin as *warlock*, he gave the impression that he was not humankind.

"Can you get us out of here?" Reg asked. Standing in a hallway was not exactly the most comfortable or safe environment. Someone from the restaurant could walk in on them at any moment.

Harrison nodded. "Where would you like to go?"

Reg's mouth was dry. She held up her hands, having no desire to be magically transported somewhere else. "Let's just walk out of here normally, okay? As long as you can keep the protection in place, I mean."

"Of course." He gestured toward the door back to the main room of the restaurant, directing her to go ahead of him. Reg exited, followed by the two warlocks. While they did so, she was wondering where she did want to go. She didn't want to take everyone back to her cottage, even though she was pretty sure that Harrison could keep her safe from both the Witch Doctor and Corvin. But she didn't want Corvin entering her house, even under the protection of some other powerful being. The wards that had been set in place to protect her would be broken, and she would be vulnerable to him coming back at a later time if Sarah didn't have time to put them back in place. Reg didn't think she could create wards herself. She didn't know any real magic, just how to do a few mind tricks.

"You would like to talk here?" Harrison suggested, motioning to the restaurant, half-filled with witches and warlocks and others there for lunch or on breaks.

"No, we need privacy," Corvin advised. "We can't take the chance of anyone overhearing us."

"They can't overhear us while I am blocking them out," Harrison said in apparent amusement.

"You can protect a place as big as this?"

"I only need to protect us, not the whole room. That takes hardly any effort at all. We are not under active attack."

The three of them looked at each other, trying to guess whether the dining room would be safe. Eventually, Corvin nodded, just a slight twitch of his chin. Reg looked at Damon, who raised an eyebrow and shrugged, giving no opinion whether he thought it was safe or not.

"Well, okay then," Reg agreed. "Let's be seated and then we can talk."

She tried to catch the eye of one of the waiters to get a table, but Harrison just herded her toward an empty one in the corner and they all sat down. Reg slid into the booth first and Damon sat beside her. Corvin and Harrison sat on the other side. Reg looked around, still afraid that someone might overhear them. But no one was looking in their direction, not even the waiter who should be concerned with serving them.

"You were very young, and it is understandable that you would not remember much," Harrison said without preamble. "You were such a wee thing. It was our job to try to keep you safe, knowing that Destine would be interested in finding you, using you as leverage."

Reg frowned, trying to take it all in. The Witch Doctor would want to use her as leverage for what? Against her mother? So that her mother would give them whatever it was they wanted?

Somehow, that didn't seem likely. She could remember her mother's screams, her promises that she would tell if she only knew the answers they were looking for. She screamed and swore and insisted she would help them if she could. She would find out. She would do whatever they wanted her to.

"My mother..." she started awkwardly.

Harrison nodded. "Norma Jean. She couldn't protect you. And she did not understand what she was dealing with. We knew she would not be able to keep you safe if he came."

"She said... she would tell them if she knew..." Reg struggled for words. "She would have... she would have given me to him."

Harrison's smile dimmed again. He nodded. "You cannot judge her for that. Anyone would have broken under the torture.

Even if she had loved you… she would still have given him what he wanted if she could. But he had not the magic to see you or free you from the protective spell."

"Even if she had loved me?" Reg repeated.

He shifted uncomfortably. "She was there for many years after she died. Do you remember?"

"She talked to me; I know that. I remember. And she's… she's talked to me a couple of times lately. Even though I don't want to hear from her."

"She tried to make up for the way she had been in life. Many spirits… they find themselves unable to depart or to find peace after they leave the mortal world. When they have regrets, it is very hard for them to rest."

Reg nodded slowly. She could remember very little about her mother or about life when her mother was still alive. But she knew that she did not associate her mother with a feeling of love and safety, no matter how sweetly Norma Jean talked. She associated her mother with fear and hunger and pain. Reg had only been four when her mother had died, but in those early years, she had not come to expect love and tenderness from the person who had borne her.

"She should go on anyway," she told Harrison. "She's never going to find any peace here. I don't have any intention of forgiving her."

Harrison shrugged. "The past is in the past, and no mortal can change it. You were in danger, and your mother was not able to protect you, so we did instead. Or we did our best. We were not as successful as I would have liked."

"What were you trying to do?"

He gazed off into empty air. "Simply trying to protect the innocent. Sometimes, innocent lives are threatened in the battles between the forces of the world."

"Why did the Witch Doctor want to find me?"

"Some entities are predators," Harrison offered obliquely. "And predators prey on those who are weaker."

Reg's eyes drifted over to Corvin. She had come to accept that he was a predator by nature, even if he said that he didn't want to hurt her. Even when he promised not to do anything to harm her, she had to assume that, given the opportunity, he would. Like the story that one of her teachers had taught about the scorpion getting a ride across the river on the back of a frog. The frog was worried about being stung but agreed to help when the scorpion pointed out that if he stung the frog, they would both die. Halfway across, the scorpion had stung the frog, and as they were both doomed to sink and drown, the frog demanded to know why the scorpion had stung.

"You knew my nature when you agreed," the scorpion had replied.

Even knowing stinging would result in his death, the scorpion had not been able to deny its nature.

And that was Corvin. He probably wouldn't do anything to her while she was helping him. He would probably wait until he had everything he needed from her, at least. But he was still a predator and, in the end, he would act on his instinct.

"This is all very well and good," Corvin said impatiently. "But we are not getting any nearer to the immediate question of the day, which is how we're are going to get the better of the Witch Doctor and his draugar. He is very powerful. Is it within your ability to defeat him?"

"He is one of my kind," Harrison said. "I am not permitted to harm him."

"Then this little rap session isn't likely to get us anywhere, is it? Reg has agreed to help me. If you are not going to help her, even though you claim to have her best interests in mind, then we're just wasting our time here."

Reg stared at Corvin coldly. "Since you're not getting anything out of this discussion, why don't you just leave?"

He looked back at her for a moment. She could still feel the anger bubbling under the surface, but she wasn't cowed by his anger. She had a new protector—one whose magic was stronger than Corvin's or Damon's. Corvin stood up.

"I will be in touch, Reg. I still expect you to help me."

He stalked away from her, whirling his coat dramatically as he made his exit. One of the waiters nearly walked into him, then took a step back, eyes widening at Corvin's demeanor. Reg watched him leave The Crystal Bowl.

"I never told him I would help him."

Laughter bubbled from Harrison. "Ah," he said, "but in the end, you will."

* * *

"Did you want to go?" Reg asked Damon. "I don't need you here with Corvin gone, so if you have something else to do, I won't keep you."

Damon looked at Harrison thoughtfully. "I get that you want to connect with this guy because he knows something about your past. But you don't really know who he is, so I would be careful if I was you."

"Certainly," Harrison agreed, "your friend is absolutely right."

Reg shrugged. "Harrison is not going to do anything in public. And if he did… I don't think you or I could do anything about it anyway. So… if you want to go, you can."

"Besides which, you don't want anyone to hear about your past."

There was no point in trying to lie to a diviner, so she didn't. "No. I don't."

"Okay. Call me later. I'd like to… do something less stressful one of these days. A real date. Where we both go home feeling good and don't have to battle any forces of darkness on the way."

Reg smiled. "Yeah. Sounds good to me. I'll call you."

Damon got up. He put his hand on her back for a moment in an intimate gesture. But unlike Corvin, no warmth and energy radiated from him. There was no electrical charge when they touched. His hand was just warm and strong and friendly. She closed her eyes for a moment and could see the two of them wandering along a beach somewhere, carefree, arms around each other, just feeling the sun and hearing the surf and picking up the occasional seashell to examine and throw back into the water. It was a pleasant daydream. She breathed out a little sigh.

"See you later."

He walked away. Harrison watched him go, then turned his attention back to Reg. "They are both attracted to you."

"No kidding."

"You know that the first is a magic drinker?"

"Yes. Would have been nice to know back when I first met him. We've had… some interesting times together."

Harrison's lips pressed together as he thought about that. "Most women would not stay around him if they knew what he could do. Women with powers, anyway. You have a lot to lose."

"He took my powers once. And then he chose to give them back. But having held them… he's kind of obsessed with me. Now there's all of this stuff with the draugrs, and I don't know what to do. He's talking about hunting them down and killing them, and I can't figure out why he would want to. I don't think he's altruistic."

"No. That kind will always be on the alert for chances to feed his hunger. Perhaps he thinks that he will be able to imbibe power from the draugar."

"Can he? Or is that impossible?"

"Who is to say what is impossible? Many things in this world are not known, even now."

"So you don't know."

He gave her a mischievous grin. "You must be psychic."

His words brought her back to the reality of the danger. She couldn't stay with Harrison forever. He couldn't protect her all of the time any more than he had been able to when she was a little girl. Sooner or later, she was going to have to face the Witch Doctor.

"What do you know about him? This Witch Doctor? You know his name."

"Destine. Samyr Destine. He is powerful. He has grown in his skill over many years. He is a formidable foe indeed."

"He remembers me. And wants me."

Harrison considered. He tapped the table like he was playing a musical instrument to music only he could hear. "I do not think he will come hunting you. I believe you are safe if you do not make contact with him."

"I didn't mean to. Corvin wanted to know where he was and what he was doing, and I thought I could find that out without him being aware of it."

"Anyone with experience will know when you are seeking them. It was not as bad as it could have been. You did not join with his mind. But you need to understand the danger in what you did."

"I do now. But it doesn't seem like I find these things out until after I do them. It would be nice if someone could tell me what not to do before I do it!"

"Ah, but how would you learn then? We must experience life, drink it in deeply. Yes, we will make mistakes. Maybe fatal ones. But is it better not to try?"

"Uh... well... I'm going to say yes. I'd rather not lose my powers, be consumed by a draugr or a prisoner of some Witch Doctor or other dark force. I'd rather not die trying."

Harrison gave a philosophical shrug. "To each her own."

# CHAPTER TWENTY

$\mathcal{H}$arrison was curiously difficult to get any information out of. He answered questions with questions of his own, answered vaguely or couched his replies in terms that she didn't understand. He was generally obstructive, leaving her with a feeling that she hadn't gotten any further ahead than she had been before he had appeared.

But the man could weave a protective spell.

Even though it was still afternoon, Reg was exhausted. Being in that little protective bubble, unable to feel the Witch Doctor and the dark foreboding that he brought Reg made her realize how tired she was. If she could stay in that protective spell, she would be able to sleep. Maybe for days.

"Time to get you home," Harrison observed. He rose and stood at her side, encouraging her to get to her feet. She must have been nodding off right there at the table, the first chance that she'd had to relax in days. In a few minutes, they were in her car, and without Reg asking or giving permission, Harrison was in the driver's seat. She didn't remember him asking her which car was hers or giving him her keys. He didn't ask for her address or directions.

Her cottage wasn't very far from The Crystal Bowl, so it only took a few minutes to get there. Harrison escorted her to the door of the cottage.

"Here we go. Let's get you settled in."

He still had her keys, which he inserted into the lock. He opened the door and motioned her in ahead of him.

He didn't seem to be constrained by Sarah's wards and didn't need to be invited in. He just walked in as if he owned the place. Reg wasn't upset about his being there, but she was a little concerned that Sarah's protective spells had so little effect.

Harrison shut and locked the door and took a look around, as if making sure there was no one else there. She half expected him to look under the beds for monsters and thought that he might have done that once or twice when she was young. Because there really could be monsters under her bed, or just to calm a child's imaginary fears?

Starlight must have been sitting in the windowsill again watching for Nicole. Reg heard him jump down. He came out of the bedroom at a trot, obviously sensing an unfamiliar presence.

He stopped and looked at Harrison, his ears pricked forward curiously. Reg watched him to see if he would hiss or growl at Harrison like he did at Corvin. Starlight and Corvin did not like each other.

Starlight didn't hiss at Harrison, but instead headed straight for him and rubbed against his legs. Harrison made a pleased noise and bent down to pick Starlight up. Reg was going to warn him about getting scratched, but before she could, Harrison had picked Starlight up and was holding him close.

"I didn't know you had a cat. What a wonderful surprise!"

"I guess you're a cat lover."

"Oh, yes. They are such interesting people."

Starlight was purring a loud, rumbly purr, and Harrison diligently scratched and rubbed all of his special cat places. Starlight was obviously in heaven with all of the attention. Reg shook her head slightly. They both seemed to have forgotten about her and were completely wrapped up in each other's company. There were waves of pleasurable feelings radiating off of Starlight. Reg laughed.

"Well. Glad you're having a good time. I'm going to bed."

"You should have something to eat," Harrison suggested, not looking up from Starlight. "You're going to sleep for a long time, and you need to have something to boost your blood sugar, so you feel better when you get up."

Reg raised an eyebrow. "I'm going to sleep for a long time?"

"Yes."

"Is that a promise or a prophecy?"

He finally looked at her instead of Starlight. "What's the difference?"

Reg conceded the point. She went to the fridge and checked through some unidentified fast food containers before finding something that looked appetizing and putting it in the microwave. Starlight didn't even abandon Harrison at the idea of food being warmed.

"You really do love cats," Reg repeated.

"Yes, I do. And Starlight is an exceptional cat. Very wise." He pressed his nose into the top of Starlight's velvety head, the same as Reg often did. She didn't think she had told him Starlight's name. He obviously had some pretty good psychic gifts himself to be able to pick that out of her brain without her saying anything aloud.

"Wise," Reg repeated. "What's he telling you? If he tells you that I don't feed him enough, he's lying. And about Nicole…"

Harrison stroked Starlight's fur. "He is rather concerned about Nicole," he agreed.

"I've been looking for her. And her owner came by the other day. Nicole will probably show up sooner or later; it's just that Sarah scared her away, back when she was sick."

"You haven't seen Nicole lately?"

"No. I've been watching. There have been a lot of other black cats around, but I don't think any of them have been Nicole. They don't look at me when I call her name."

He shrugged with one shoulder. "Cats are notorious for not responding to their human names."

"I suppose so. Maybe she doesn't like the name. But I don't think any of them have been her. I had… a different feeling about her than I have had for the other cats I have seen. It was… I don't know… warm and lonely. These other cats I feel… nothing."

"Hmm." Harrison nodded. "Well, hopefully, she will show up before long."

Reg thought he was speaking to Starlight rather than to her and didn't bother replying. The microwave beeped, and she took her chicken sandwich out and started to eat. It wasn't the best food reheated, but it was better than having to make something fresh herself. She didn't have the energy to pull anything together. She wasn't even sure if she could finish the sandwich before falling asleep. It was a good thing she was standing up. If she were sitting down, she would probably end up face-down on top of her sandwich.

Starlight made a few chirping meows, and Harrison put him down. Starlight approached Reg and rubbed against her legs. She looked down at him while she chewed her chicken.

"Took you long enough. You have deigned to acknowledge my presence now?"

Harrison chuckled. "He was just being polite by acknowledging my presence first," he advised. "I will get him something to eat now. When you are finished eating that, you will take yourself to bed."

"And what are you going to do? Are you going to stay here or are you going away?"

"I will make sure you get settled, and then I will leave. You do not need me here in your house while you are asleep."

"You're right about that. And you're not going to try to steal my powers from me?"

His mouth turned into a straight line. "Certainly not," he said haughtily. "We are not that kind!"

"I'm sorry," she realized that she had truly offended him. "It was only meant as a joke. I know that you're not going to do that. You're not like Corvin. Not in any way that I can see."

"No," he agreed. "Other than taking on a male form, we are nothing alike."

"Right. Sorry. It was only a joke."

His mouth released into a cheerful smile. "No harm done. Your human jokes are always so entertaining."

Reg wasn't sure whether he was being sarcastic or sincere. She only had a couple of bites left of her sandwich, so she started toward her room, chewing as she went. She didn't even care if she got crumbs in the bed; she just wanted to get there before she passed out.

Her bed was still unmade, rumpled from when she had gotten up that morning after a frustratingly restless night. Reg slid into her place between the sheets and pulled the bedclothes up over her, popping the last bite of sandwich into her mouth.

She was barely conscious of Harrison coming into the room to check on her.

"You'd better swallow that before you choke."

Reg swallowed. She felt her consciousness drifting away.

"I leave you in peace. Have your long sleep. Don't worry about anything else. The world will not end before tomorrow."

"Okay," Reg mumbled.

Starlight jumped up on the bed beside her. Harrison petted him. "Keep watch over her tonight. I will be close by, but I don't think she is in any danger now. The wards will keep Destine away for a while, as long as she does not reach out to him."

Starlight began to wash noisily. Harrison laughed and moved away from the bed.

And then Reg was asleep.

* * *

In the beginning, Reg slept soundly and sweetly, without the sense of doom hanging over her. But eventually, whether because her body started to catch up on sleep or because Harrison's influence began to fade, she started to toss and turn restlessly.

She dreamed about Francesca and the Witch Doctor, and somehow their stories became interwoven, and it was the Witch Doctor who had a black cat and Francesca who was a witch. She was definitely a witch. No pointy black hat, but her pretty blond hair was twisted into stringy masses, her nose was bigger, and she was stirring something steaming on the stove in a big black cauldron.

"My kitty, my precious kitty," the Witch Doctor crooned in Francesca's lilting accent. He picked up a black cat and cuddled and stroked it as Harrison had, lavishing it with attention.

There was a rock in the pit of Reg's stomach.

"He's a witch," she tried to tell Francesca. "The man with the dreads. He isn't a cat lover; he is a witch!"

"We are all witches, dear," Francesca replied, smiling cheerfully. "You have nothing to fear from witches."

"Nothing? Corvin said it would be the end of the world. He said that we have to kill them all or it will be the end of existence as we know it!"

"No," Francesca assured her. "Just the end of your existence, Regina."

The Witch Doctor put the black cat down on Reg's chest as she lay on the bed. "Just watch my little kitty for a while," he encouraged.

Reg stared into the face of the unfamiliar cat. It was not Nicole; she was quite sure of that. Its aura was very different from the feelings she got from Nicole. He was… menacing. Just like the Witch Doctor himself. Reg tried to remember what Harrison had called him. If she named him, she took away part of his power.

Destiny?

Was Reg's destiny somehow wrapped up in his? Reg wondered fleetingly if his name was Destiny to everyone, or just to her. Maybe Harrison, her guardian angel, was only there to protect Reg, and similarly, Destiny was put on the earth solely for the purpose of killing her. Two opposing forces. As long as they remained balanced, Reg survived, but as soon as Destiny overpowered Harrison, as Destiny must always do eventually, she would die. It would be the end of her time on earth.

The cat continued to stare down at her, his cat-breath in her face. He was much heavier than Starlight. His solidity was like that of a well-muscled man rather than the softness of a cat. And he seemed to be growing heavier with each breath. He weighed down on her, compressing her chest until she could barely breathe. She struggled, trying at last to push him off, but he wouldn't budge. He was like a rock. Like the tombstone that Corvin had spoken of, weighing down on her so heavily that she would never be able to rise.

There was a snarling cry, the rising notes of two cats facing each other, fighting over territory—a howl followed by snarls and screams.

And then Reg was awake. She breathed in the warm, sweet air in gasps. There were flashes of color in front of her eyes like she was on the edge of passing out, but she told herself that it was just her brain's reaction to the dream. She wasn't really smothering.

They said that if you died in your sleep, you died in real life. If the cat had stayed there any longer, would she have died?

Then there was a familiar furry, whiskered face nudging at her, Starlight's concern for her almost palpable. Reg tried to slow her gasps and convince herself that she was okay. She wasn't going to die because of a dream. People didn't die from dreams, no matter how scary they were.

It was just her brain's way of telling her that she'd had enough sleep and it was time to get up.

She petted Starlight, murmuring to him, telling him that she was going to be okay. There was nothing for him to worry about. She was just fine.

He started to purr, rubbing against her hand and then her face, lavishing her with love and attention, just as Harrison had given the cat attention a few hours earlier. Reg rubbed her eyes, even though she knew that she'd end up getting cat dander in them and would have bloodshot eyes the rest of the day.

She sat up and looked around.

It was still light out, so maybe she hadn't slept for as long as she thought she had. It seemed like it had been hours, but with the bedroom still brightly lit, it was probably only a couple. She looked at her phone. After eight o'clock. She frowned. It should have been starting to get dark.

Then she realized that it was eight in the morning, not eight at night. She had slept away the afternoon and the night, and it was morning again. She double-checked the date on her phone to make sure she hadn't slept for even longer, two days or a week. She felt like she had been asleep for a very long time.

But it had only been an afternoon and a night. Still a long sleep, especially after the problems she had been having recently.

Reg sat up and looked around. She looked toward the window.

"Were there cats fighting out there? I thought I heard a cat fight when I was dreaming."

Starlight rubbed against her, making little purring meows. He licked her hand, and Reg pulled back.

"Yuck! No licking! I don't slobber on you, do I?"

For once, it was easy to get out of bed. She didn't have to stumble like a zombie into the bathroom and splash water on her face to wake herself up. Starlight met her in the kitchen and Reg looked for something to eat and something to feed to Starlight. It was going to be a good morning. She felt rejuvenated and refreshed and ready to face whatever life had to offer.

Except for the Witch Doctor.

She didn't want to face the Witch Doctor.

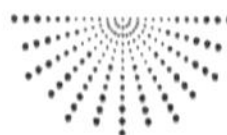

She knew Corvin was there before he banged on the door. She could feel the warmth of his presence as he approached the cottage. So she was already on her way over to the door when he knocked, a sharp, impatient rap.

Reg turned the bolts and opened the door a few inches to talk to him.

"Long time, no see," she told him.

"I tried to get ahold of you last night. Where have you been all this time? Out with your new best friend?" The rage had left, but there was still anger simmering below the surface. And maybe jealousy too? Did he even like her? Or was it jealousy at another magical man being in her life, worry that Harrison would remove her beyond Corvin's reach so that his dream of acquiring her powers would be dead?

"I was sleeping."

"I called you several times."

"I was sleeping," Reg repeated. She had looked at her call log and seen that he had called her several times. Damon had called too, and even Francesca. Francesca hadn't left a message, and Reg wondered idly why she would call. Maybe to say that she had found Nicole and Reg didn't have to watch for her anymore? That would be good news. Reg could use a little bit of good news.

Corvin's anger abated a little. "You weren't out with Uncle Harrison?"

"No. We talked for a bit, but he wasn't very forthcoming about anything I couldn't already remember. I came home—" she didn't tell him the part about Harrison coming home with her, "—and I went to sleep. I just got up. I really needed a good sleep."

"Well, now that you're nice and well-rested…"

"I never said that I would help you. You said that I had agreed to help. But I never did. That was a lie."

Corvin looked taken aback. "Regina, you know that you're the only person who can help me to bring down the Witch Doctor and his draugar."

"I don't know that. You've said that, but you have magical friends. Recruit some of them. Tell them the stories that you've been telling me. See if they'll help you. I'm sure they're a lot more powerful than I am. I'm just a psychic. I see and hear things in my head. That's all."

"You do a lot more than that. You've been showing psychokinesis, affecting things in the corporeal world with your mind. You were able to call Calliopia from halfway across the country. Those are more than *simple* psychic powers."

"Telekinesis is still a psychic power," she maintained. "It's not magic. And the call… that was just because Calliopia and I were joined. I couldn't have done it with anyone else. Now that our connection is severed, I wouldn't be able to do it again."

"Have you tried?"

"No, and I don't want to. It's very disconcerting, moving through space like that. I don't want to do it again."

"I still maintain that your powers are much greater than a simple psychic."

"That's all I am. And even that… I wonder about sometimes. So I'm good at reading people's faces and body language. I'm good at guessing and imagining things. That doesn't mean that I'm actually psychic. It's just… intuition. That's all it is."

"And seeking? And moving objects? Breaking glasses and lighting my cloak on fire? Those are all just imagination? Intuition?"

"You don't know that I was the one that did those things. It could have been someone else. Who would know the difference? I never intentionally did any of those things."

"And seeking?"

"I haven't been able to seek," Reg reminded him. "I wasn't able to find the knife or the emerald, remember? Sure, I've always been good at finding lost objects, but that's just logic and imagination. Thinking about where they should be and about where they could be. It's not magic and it's not going to have any effect against the Witch Doctor. I don't *want* to seek him!"

"You don't need to seek him to find him. You are already psychically connected to him, so all you have to do is feel that connection and tell me what he's doing. I'll… I'll do the rest."

"After yesterday? What happened when I felt for him yesterday? He talked to me and knew who I was. I am never going to do that again!"

Corvin studied her. Reg could feel him thinking things through. She hadn't been able to tell them what had happened the day before. She had been too panicked by his reaching back to her, and then in finding safety in Harrison; she had not had that conversation with Corvin or Damon. They didn't know what had happened in those dreadful few moments.

"The Witch Doctor spoke to you?"

"Yes! And he knows who I am and he wants to kill me. So why would I reach out to him again? That would be like shooting myself in the foot. Worse than that. Picking up a fully-loaded gun and holding it to my head. Why would I do that?"

Corvin ignored her histrionics. She could sense that was actually how he thought of them. *Histrionics.*

"What did he say to you? What do you mean, he knew who you were?"

Reg was impatient. He should have picked up at least some of those clues from her conversation with Harrison the day before. He'd been right there.

"Because he was the one who killed my mother. He knew about me then, and he knows who I am now. He recognized me."

"How could he do that? He's never seen you."

"He doesn't have to see me. He just has to… he recognizes my presence, my being, just like he would recognize my face. Probably better. He felt me and he knew who I was. So I don't want to have anything to do with him. I really don't. I don't want him to seek me out because I reached out to him. Someone else is going to have to defeat him. It's not going to be me."

She remembered Harrison's laughter the day before, and his comment that she would help Corvin eventually. She didn't want it to be true. She wasn't going to help him with anything.

"Regina. I'm not asking you to put your life in danger. Can I come in? We can look at a map. You can tell me where he is operating, where you can feel the draugar, and then I can formulate a plan…"

"You're not asking me to put my life in danger? How exactly are you planning on cutting off draugr heads without putting our lives in danger?"

"What I mean is… you don't have to face the Witch Doctor directly. And you don't have to reach out to him again if you don't want to. You can just give me a little detail about what you felt yesterday. Okay?"

"Not okay."

"Reg… let me in. Invite me for a cup of tea. We'll talk it through, and that's all you have to do. That's reasonable, isn't it?"

Reg could smell the scent of roses. She could feel the warmth and attraction radiating out from him, making her want to crawl into his arms and do whatever he said.

But she had been there once before, and having her powers stripped from her had been one of the most traumatic things that had ever happened to her. Up there even with seeing her mother tortured and killed. He had taken away something basic from her; he had stolen what made her Regina Rawlins and left her naked and vulnerable without them. Reg took a deep breath, even though she knew she was breathing in the rose-scented air and it went directly to her head. She focused the heat he was radiating into one sharp point and reflected it back at him, like focusing the sun through a magnifying glass into one hot spot of light strong enough to light a fire.

"Hey!" Corvin took a step back, not liking the taste of his own medicine. He pulled back on the charm enough that Reg could breathe without the dizzying intoxication. "What are you doing?"

"Quit trying to charm me."

"I wasn't."

"You told me that you don't lie. What exactly do you call that?"

"I was… it was an unconscious reflex. It's just part of who I am, Regina. I can't always control it. I want to come in. I want to discuss this with you, two grown adults on an equal basis. You don't have to tell me anything you don't want to. Yesterday you said the Witch Doctor was down at the wharf. Can you be any more specific? Can you tell what dock or building he is using? What ship or plane he is loading his goods onto? Just solid, practical stuff like that."

"You are not coming in."

"What danger is there in it if you can resist me?" There was a bitter edge to his voice. He hated it when she withstood him. When she had worn Sarah's ward, so he hadn't been able to be with her. When she had told him that she wouldn't dance with him unless he agreed not to ensorcel her. And when she used the heat of his charm as a weapon against him.

Reg couldn't help but feel some sense of accomplishment. Since she had first met Corvin, she had been attracted to him. She had been unable to resist his pull. But she was standing on her own two feet. It meant that she had power over him instead of the other way around.

"So much for not having anything more than intuition," Corvin growled.

"I still don't think it's a good idea for you to come in here. Besides, Starlight is here and you don't want to have to be in the same room as him, do you?"

"I'll put up with the animal if you will just hear me out."

"There's nothing else to say. To answer your questions… no, I'm not sure what dock or building he is in. Since you can feel him too, why don't you go down to the wharf and wander around until you can pinpoint it? Like a psychic game of warmer and colder. Then you'll know where he is, and you can sit there and watch his operations. Wouldn't that give you more information than some vague psychic mumbo-jumbo?"

"That's also more dangerous," he pointed out grumpily. "To watch him with my physical eyes, I have to expose myself."

Reg stared at him and waited for him to make the connection. That might be more dangerous to him, but it was less risky to her. Which was worse, for him to expose himself to the Witch Doctor's or one of his minion's sight, or for Reg to risk the Witch Doctor getting inside of her head and being able to control or kill her? It would be a lot worse for her if the Witch Doctor felt her than it would be for Corvin to walk past their operations on some dock somewhere.

"I suppose if that's all you can give me, that's what I'll have to do," he said grudgingly.

"I can't give you information I don't have. And I can't risk letting him inside my head. Harrison said that if I leave the Witch Doctor alone, he won't come after me. He has other things to do —his smuggling agenda or taking over the world or whatever it is he is hoping to accomplish. I'm just a little blip on his screen, and if I stay quiet, I'll be safe."

A crease appeared between Corvin's brows. "Did it ever occur to you that this Harrison could be working *with* the Witch

Doctor? He makes an appearance immediately after you make contact with him? He tells you to stay away and not interfere? It sounds to me like he's trying to protect the Witch Doctor, not you."

Reg's jaw dropped. It was such a ridiculous idea she didn't even know where to start.

"Didn't you feel it?" she demanded. "His spell? He was *protecting* me. He was keeping the Witch Doctor out. You couldn't even feel that?"

"Or keeping you from reaching out to the Witch Doctor. It would be the same thing, wouldn't it? He puts a magical barrier there so that you can't feel the Witch Doctor. You feel like you are safe, but really, he's just suppressing your powers. You have the power to feel the Witch Doctor. That gives you a warning if he is near or if he is a danger to you. If dear old Uncle Harrison suppresses that power, then you are vulnerable. You don't know if the Witch Doctor can still feel you or not. You only know that *you* can't feel *him*."

Reg shook her head adamantly. "No. I know him. I trust him. He's not working with the Witch Doctor. That's ridiculous."

"How do you know him? You know him from back when the Witch Doctor was threatening your family. Why didn't he protect your mother? If he could protect you, why couldn't he protect her? Why did he let her die? Maybe he was working with the Witch Doctor back then. His job was to keep you out of the way so that the Witch Doctor could pursue his own nefarious plans."

"How was I going to do anything to stop him? I was four years old! I didn't have any powers to speak of. Sure, I could hear the ghosts, but that was all. I couldn't fight someone like the Witch Doctor. I couldn't have prevented him from doing anything."

"Why didn't he protect your mother?" Corvin pressed.

"Maybe he couldn't. Maybe he could only put a protective spell on me, not on both of us or the entire apartment. You don't know what powers he has or had then. You don't know what his limitations were." She felt the stirrings of anger against Corvin.

She knew that Harrison was her friend. Her protector. He had always been there during her worse times.

She hated Corvin for the doubts that started to creep in. *Why* had Harrison always been there during her worst times? Did the bad times come *because* he was there?

He hadn't been the one who had victimized her. She couldn't remember him ever doing anything that had caused her any harm. She could remember times when she had felt that protective blanket of power envelop her and protect her from the evil men and women who had wanted to hurt her or take advantage of her.

There had been other times when he hadn't been there. Plenty of times when she'd had to fight opposition all on her own. But the worst times, facing the strongest and most vile predators, Harrison had been there to help her.

Except with Corvin.

Where had Harrison been when Corvin had stolen her powers? Had it been such a small thing that he didn't think it mattered? Her gifts were weak when compared with Harrison's; maybe he felt that they were insignificant. Perhaps he thought that she was willingly giving them away, as Corvin had said she was.

She had agreed, after all. She had yielded to Corvin.

But she hadn't known what she was doing. She hadn't understood that she was letting him take something so precious from her.

So where had Harrison been then? Why hadn't he been there to guide and protect her?

"I know he's not working with the Witch Doctor," Reg said with certainty. "There's no way he is."

Corvin studied her for a long time, trying to read something in her face. Did he think that she was lying? Or that she didn't understand? He didn't try to probe into her mind, but he was too close. She could feel him trying to decide how far he could push it. She took a step back and closed the door a quarter of an inch.

"Reg!" He put up his hand to stop her.

"Don't try to mess with me, Corvin. I'm tired of your games."

"No games." He still held his hand up, but she couldn't detect any power or changes in his energy.

"What, then? I've answered your questions. I can't tell you any more specifics about the Witch Doctor. Harrison didn't tell me anything that might be helpful, but he wasn't blocking me. He's not working with the Witch Doctor."

"Someone is. I'm sure of it. If it's not him, then who? I don't believe he just recognized you from when you were four. That's a long time ago, and you've grown and matured and increased in your powers since then. People don't stay the same forever; they're always growing and changing."

"So… if you don't think he recognized me, then what?"

"I think someone we know is working with him. Someone who has been around here and knows that you've been feeling the changes in the spiritual structure of Black Sands."

"Well… that's pretty much everybody I've talked to."

"But you don't know a lot of people. Your circle of friends is still pretty small. So who could it be?" His eyes narrowed. "Personally, I favor Damon."

"Damon? You think he's working with the Witch Doctor? No." Reg shook her head, frowning. "No, he wouldn't do that. Besides… what powers does he have that the Witch Doctor would want?"

"It may not be powers; it may just be information. Keeping an eye on you, reporting back your activities. Letting him know your suspicions and your progress."

"Damon wouldn't do that."

"Did you ever feel the Witch Doctor before Damon came into the picture?"

"Yes."

Corvin waited, frowning, for her to think it through. Reg shook her head. "We just went on our first date this week."

"So you must have met before. That wasn't the first time you met him."

"No. He was at your hearing. He was one of the security guards there."

"Was he?" Corvin's voice was low and meditative. Reg wondered what he was thinking. There wasn't any way that Damon had anything to do with the Witch Doctor. There was no connection between the two of them.

"You still claim that you were not the one who lit my cloak on fire," Corvin said.

Reg blinked at the non sequitur. "Uh… no. I don't know how to do that. I've never lit anything on fire before."

"And Damon was there. He's sweet on you. Maybe he was the one."

"You're just paranoid. Why would he do that?"

"Because he liked you. Wanted to protect you. Wanted to punish me. Make me stop talking about you."

"I suppose." Reg shook her head. "But I really don't think it could have been him… does he have that ability? Wouldn't you know? He's been in the community a lot longer than I have been. He grew up here."

"Magical persons don't always reveal their powers. Sometimes they keep secrets. It's personal and private. He could have a power like that without anyone knowing."

"But when we were at the hearing, his hair started to smoke. It lit on fire, and he put it out. So it must have been someone else causing the fires."

He cocked his head at her. "Why? What does that prove?"

"If someone lit his hair on fire, well it wouldn't have been him, would it? He wouldn't have done it himself."

"Why not?"

"Because…" Reg fumbled. She couldn't find a reason. Because it was dangerous? Not if he was the one lighting the fire, managing it, and extinguishing it. Because it would draw attention to him? But it hadn't. Reg was the only one who had seen, while Corvin was taking the attention of the rest of the room. "I don't think it was him. What do you know about his powers? All I know is that he can discern the truth. And you're the one who told me that."

Corvin smiled a little. "He has another interesting ability. He is able to put visions into people's minds. Sometimes with such clarity that they think that something actually happened when it didn't."

"You think he's the one putting these feelings of dread into me?" Reg challenged. "You feel them too, so you know it's the Witch Doctor."

"I know that he is here and that he is disrupting the forces of the town. But you have had several experiences that I have not, feeling the force close by you, possibly even about to attack. That is the sort of thing I wouldn't put past Damon the Dreamer."

# CHAPTER TWENTY-TWO

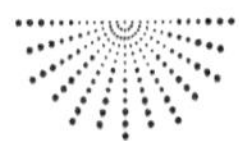

*R*eg thought about the vision that she'd had at the bowling alley about rolling the ball directly down the middle of the lane and getting a strike. That had given her the confidence to try again and to actually roll the ball down the middle and hit a couple of pins. Not a strike, but not a gutter ball. It had seemed very real at the time. And she remembered the vision that she'd had when he put his hand on her back the night before, of the two of them wandering on the beach.

Reg frowned. "Is that what was going on?"

Corvin nodded eagerly. "It is Damon, isn't it? You can see it now. He's been manipulating you."

"No… at least, not about the Witch Doctor and the Draugrs. But maybe some other things…"

"Are you sure? Are you really sure that he's not making you see these things?"

"Like what? Like Harrison? You saw him too. I didn't just see a vision of him."

"No, but these early memories, and feeling the draugar around you… he's been there. It could be him."

"Why would he want me to think there were draugrs? Wouldn't the Witch Doctor want to keep them a secret?"

Corvin's forehead creased. "Uh… maybe. I suppose it depends on whether he wants to terrorize people or whether he has another goal."

"I thought it was all about his smuggling business. Isn't he just using them for slave labor? Isn't that why witch doctors make zombies? I thought they were all about working sugar plantations."

"Traditionally, at least in Haiti. But draugar are used all over the world, not just in Haiti. He could be using them for some other dark purpose."

"You've been saying that everyone is in danger. Why would the Witch Doctor want Damon to warn anyone of that?"

Corvin's mouth was a straight line. "Maybe it's not Damon, then," he admitted. "But someone must have told him about you."

Reg didn't see it. She knew that the Witch Doctor had recognized her. Corvin was wrong about that.

"I don't think so. Now I've got some calls to make, so you should get on your way."

He looked at her phone as she took it out.

"Who do you have to call?" he asked suspiciously.

"Not that it is any of your business, but I was going to call this lady who lost her cat. I'm not sure why she called me again. Maybe she found it. Her."

"Cats," Corvin said with distaste. "She should be happy not to be burdened with it."

Reg glared at him. "Harrison loves cats."

"He *would*."

"You saw her here the other day," Reg reminded him. "You were here when she left."

He was still, thinking about it.

"I dreamt about her last night," Reg said. "Or this morning, whichever it was. She and the Witch Doctor were all mixed up. He was speaking with her accent."

"What kind of an accent?"

"I don't know for sure. French, I think. It sounds French. She says Nee-cole instead of Nih-cole."

"Could it be Creole?"

"I… don't know. What does Creole sound like?"

"It was a French pidgin. So it sounds something like French."

"Well then, yeah, I guess it could be." She shrugged. "Why?"

"She's white, so I wouldn't have taken her for Haitian. But of course there are white people living on and born in Haiti."

"Where the Witch Doctor is from?" He'd never explicitly said that the Witch Doctor was Haitian. But she assumed that he was. She didn't know of any other culture in the modern world that had the knowledge to make zombies.

"If she's from Haiti…" Corvin mused.

"You think she's the leak? She's the reason he knew who I was?"

"You talked to her before you reached out to the Witch Doctor. So she could have told him details about you."

"I suppose," Reg said reluctantly. Why was she so hesitant to accept that maybe the Witch Doctor hadn't really known her when she connected with him psychically, but had only been told about her? Wouldn't it be more comforting to believe that he was oblivious and her chance encounter with him when she was a child had not stuck in his memory? For some reason, though, it was not. And Reg didn't want Francesca to be involved in it.

But she didn't know Francesca or anything about her, other than the fact that she had a cat that she didn't appear to care for properly and she had only recently moved to Black Sands. Everything else was speculation.

"And then there's also…" Corvin trailed off.

"What?"

He shook his head. "I have to think about it. Read some of my research."

"So do you think… I shouldn't call her back?"

Corvin rubbed his chin, thinking about it. Finally, he shook his head. "No, I don't think you should. If there's any possibility that she's passing information on to the Witch Doctor, it's too risky. It's not like it was something important anyway, is it?"

"Just about her cat. That's the only thing I know about her." Reg raised an eyebrow. "That is important to some people, you know. Their cats are like their children."

He wrinkled his nose and shook his head. "People never cease to amaze me. Children are bad enough. Spoiling your pet because you don't have any children… you should celebrate the fact, not turn to zookeeping."

"Don't you have a familiar? Sarah doesn't like cats either, but she has a parrot."

"No, I have never seen the need for a familiar."

"Do you just not like animals?"

"I don't like cats. There's a difference."

"Cats are animals."

"Cats are just one kind of animal. Other animals are not so… offensive."

"Offensive?" Reg shook her head, smiling. "It's not like they smell. Now mice or guinea pigs… I don't have the super sensitive sense of smelling that my foster-sister has, but ugh—I hate the smell of rodents. And then there are dogs. They poop all over the place indiscriminately. At least cats are tidy."

"It isn't their cleanliness habits that offend me."

Reg raised an eyebrow, waiting for further explanation, but he didn't elaborate. Reg shrugged. "So, I guess you're going over to the wharf to dowse for the Witch Doctor or off to do your research."

"Yes…" He looked past her into the interior of her cottage for a moment before nodding. His shoulders relaxed, dipping down. "I will be back."

"Just call me," Reg urged. "There's no point in coming here to talk on the doorstep."

"But maybe next time, you'll invite me in."

"No. I won't," she said with certainty.

"Is your uncle coming back today?"

"My uncle? Oh, Harrison. I don't know. I don't understand who he is or what he's doing here… But he told me I would be safe if I stay out of the Witch Doctor's business, so… that's my plan. Stay out of the way."

"You think it's better to turn your back on this business and let the chips fall where they may?"

"Yes. If he is busy enough not to come after me, then why should I do anything to get his attention? I don't want to be targeted."

"I thought you were one of those people who put the common good ahead of herself. I guess I was mistaken."

Personal survival had always been more critical to Reg than the common good. Maybe that was what came from being hungry and endangered as a child. She had learned to look after herself when no one else did. The altruistic people were the ones who had been raised with safety and security and everything they needed. They didn't have a sense of mortal danger because their mortality had never been at stake.

"I put myself first," Reg told Corvin, shutting the door on him. "Just like you do."

He said her name, but nothing else, and he was soon gone without any cajoling. He did have other things to do, and he must have decided it was in his best interest to go and do them.

She was thinking about him and about what exactly he was hoping to get out of the Witch Doctor situation as she sat down to look at her phone and check her email. He had received some of the Witch Doctor's smuggled goods before, and she had to assume that that was what he was after again. Except for maybe more this time.

The phone rang when it was in Reg's hand and, not having expected the call, she startled violently and was distracted from what she had been doing. She looked at the screen, but the caller

ID was blocked. She wondered if it were Francesca again, calling from one of her other numbers this time. Corvin had said it was best not to talk to her, but Reg thought she might be able to get information from Francesca. If Francesca were working with the Witch Doctor, which Reg doubted, despite her disturbing dream, then maybe Reg could find out what the Witch Doctor's plans and motivations were. She picked it up.

"Hello?"

"It's Detective Jessup, Reg."

"Oh, it's 'Reg' again instead of 'Miss Rawlins,' is it?" Reg asked, allowing the bite to enter her voice.

There was silence for a moment from Jessup. "Uh… do I do that?" she asked uncertainly. "Switch between the two?"

"Your cop persona calls me Miss Rawlins when I'm a suspect. I mean, I'm glad that I'm not anymore, but I'm not sure I'm ready for us to go back to Reg."

"Okay, then, Miss Rawlins," Jessup said in a stilted manner. "I'm sorry to disturb you…"

"What is it you want?"

"I would like to know… if you happen to know where Corvin Hunter is. I've tried to reach him a couple of times, but his phone must be turned off. I don't know if he's in contact with you, or whether you decided not to have anything to do with him. But I thought it was worth a try. In case he was hanging around your door."

"No. He was here earlier, but he's gone now."

"Do you happen to know where?"

"Not for sure." Reg wasn't sure she wanted to share any details with Jessup. Or whether Corvin would want her to. Since Corvin wasn't exactly working with the police on the case, they would undoubtedly not approve of him sneaking around the wharf trying to find out where the Witch Doctor was working in order to steal from him.

"Okay. I was hoping… I had something to discuss with him. Some… unusual reports."

"More draugrs?" Reg asked.

"Oh. Hunter told you about that, did he? I don't know if I believe in the whole thing, but we've had some strange things going on, and I hoped that he might have some insight."

"What kind of things? You may as well talk to me since he's not the one who can feel them. But I can."

"Can you? Could you come in so we could talk about it? I'm just not sure how to handle the situation, but if you could give me some direction…"

"Come in?" Reg repeated.

"Uh… to the police station. I know you're going to say no, but I could use your help."

"Then it will have to be somewhere else. Somewhere neutral. I am not going to the police station."

Jessup hummed and hawed uncertainly. Reg knew that she was delaying in hopes that Reg would just agree to come to the station. But Reg knew from experience that she didn't have to go to the police station if she wasn't under arrest. They could ask her for her thoughts on the draugrs and the Witch Doctor anywhere.

Maybe Jessup too wanted to secure a room against eavesdroppers, but then she could do just like Corvin and meet in a small room somewhere else. Maybe it was Corvin who had told Jessup to call Reg. If he couldn't get the information he wanted to out of Reg, maybe he thought Jessup could give it a try.

Reg didn't have any trouble waiting Jessup out. There was no benefit to her rushing in to make suggestions. She wasn't the one who wanted to consult with Jessup.

"I'm on probation," Jessup said. "I'm not really supposed to be out of the office interviewing subjects."

"Okay."

"So you'll come in?" Jessup asked, confused.

"No. If you can't interview me, then you can't interview me. Just tell them that I refused to come in."

"But Reg, it would really help me out if you could…"

"Uh-huh."

"Can't you help a friend out?"

"You've gone back to Reg again. And I don't remember you being willing to bend when I was a suspect and asking for your help."

"I helped you whenever I could," Jessup protested, "but my hands were tied. There is only so much that I can do."

"Yeah. That's too bad. I'll talk to you later, then. See you around…"

"Reg—"

Reg tapped the hang-up icon on the screen. She sat there, feeling self-satisfied for about ten seconds before the guilt hit. She probably shouldn't have been so rude to Jessup.

The phone rang again. It was, again, a blocked number. Reg considered. It hadn't been long enough for Jessup to go to her boss and get permission to leave the police station.

Reg answered the call. "Hello?"

"It's Detective Jessup."

"Oh, hi. I thought we were done."

"I can meet you somewhere. I'll get it approved. You want me to come there?"

"That depends."

"Depends on what?" Jessup asked with a sigh.

"Depends on whether you are coming over to talk or to make accusations. I'm not letting you in here to perform a search. I don't want my privacy invaded."

"I'm not coming to invade your privacy; I'm coming because you didn't want to meet at the police station. If you have somewhere else in mind, let me know now before my head explodes."

Reg couldn't help laughing. "Last time you were here, it was with a warrant," she reminded Jessup.

"Yes. I admit that. And you know I was required to pursue all leads. People were pointing at you and your cat, and I didn't have any choice but to follow up."

"So, no warrant this time?"

"No. Can I come over?"

"I suppose."

"Okay. I'll be maybe half an hour. Does that work for you?"

"Sure. I'll put on some tea."

"Thanks. I'll see you then."

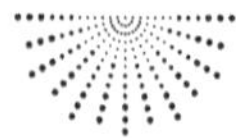

# CHAPTER TWENTY-THREE

Reg searched through the cupboards, thinking it would be nice to have something to go with the tea. She found half a bag of cookies, and when she tested them, they were still crisp and sweet, not stale, so she added some to the tea tray. When Jessup got there, everything was arranged, and the tea was steeping. Despite the knot in her stomach, Reg was feeling as calm and peaceful as she could at the prospect of talking to a police officer about zombies.

"This is nice," Jessup approved as she sat down and looked over the tea service. She stretched her legs out in front of her and massaged her neck and shoulders. "I'm just feeling so cooped up having to be at the police station all the time. When I'm not out directing traffic or paired with someone else on an investigation."

"They let you come over here without another officer?"

"I told them that I knew you and you wouldn't talk if there were someone else with me. They didn't like it, but I've been behaving myself, so they decided to throw me a bone."

Reg picked up her teacup and had a sip. She looked around for Starlight and saw him sleeping in a warm sunbeam.

"So what do you know about these draugrs?" Jessup asked.

"Well, it depends on what you want to know. Corvin is the

one with the historical knowledge. I haven't spent my whole life studying zombie culture. But he can't feel them. Corvin is sure that's what the Witch Doctor is doing with the bodies he disinterred, but he can't feel them himself."

"And you can."

"Yes. They don't feel good; I'll tell you that."

"I don't know if you've turned the TV on today, but we've had more trouble. Not with more body-snatching, but..." She let out a deep sigh. "We have some strange and suspicious deaths. And I think... it matches up with what Hunter was saying about draugrs."

The knot in Reg's stomach became tighter and heavier. Up until then, they had only been talking about the Witch Doctor using already-interred bodies. Corvin had said repeatedly that Black Sands was in danger, but Reg had hoped he was wrong and that they didn't have to worry about anything if they just left the Witch Doctor alone. But now the Witch Doctor had taken it a step further.

"What's happened?" she asked, not sure she wanted the details. Of course she didn't want the details. She just wanted to live in peace in her own happy little bubble and not have to worry about what a powerful magical being was doing in her town.

"They look like asphyxiation and crush injuries." Jessup seemed just as reluctant to give the details as Reg was to hear them. "There were four last night."

"And... did he turn them into draugrs too?"

Jessup gave Reg a puzzled look. "No. If he had, we wouldn't have found them, they would be missing. These victims were left behind after they were killed."

"Oh. Right."

"If he's planning on making them into draugrs, maybe he ran out of zombie powder. He'll have to steal them back from the morgue or the cemetery if he wants to use them."

"And you're sure that draugrs caused the deaths? Or the Witch Doctor?"

"They were killed at night, most of them in their own beds. But it is as if they were pinned down by something very heavy until they died. It just doesn't make any sense. They weren't strangled, and it wasn't a car accident or construction injury. They died in their beds while they slept. And that suggests something supernatural like the draugrs. If it wasn't, then I don't know what it was. Aliens from another planet, maybe." She rolled her eyes, signaling that she didn't really think it was aliens. Reg was relieved. She'd had to accept enough other inhuman races lately; she didn't want to believe that as well as the magical folk she struggled to accept now that she was also going to have to come to terms with extraterrestrials.

"So what do you want from me?"

"If you can feel them... do you know where in town he is keeping them? Or how he is keeping so many of them under control? Corvin said there were half a dozen or more. I've never heard of a bokor who could control more than a couple at a time. He could put them to work like automatons, but after a while, they would decelerate... sort of fall out of orbit until they were started again. But he seems to be actively controlling all of them. I don't even know if that is possible."

Reg took a deep breath in and let it out again. "Okay. I can do this. As long as you're not asking me to tell you anything about the Witch Doctor. I'm not reaching out to him again."

"Oh...?" Jessup obviously hadn't heard from Corvin what had happened the night before. Reg just shook her head. She didn't have the time or energy to explain. Not if she were going to focus on the draugrs to try to give Jessup the information she needed.

"The Witch Doctor has been operating down at the docks. Corvin was going to head over there to see if he could figure out exactly which warehouse the Witch Doctor is operating out of or what ship or plane he is using."

She reached over and placed her crystal ball in front of her. It wasn't just a prop, even though that was what she had initially purchased it for. She had been able to see things in it quite clearly a couple of times. And even when she couldn't see anything in it, she found that it helped her to calm her brain to focus on something physical.

Jessup saw that she was preparing herself and was respectfully quiet. Starlight, stretched out in his patch of sunlight, lifted his head to look at Reg. She met his eyes. "Do you want to help?"

He rolled onto his feet and got up, stretched, and gave his head a shake so rapid it made his ears flap. He marched over to where Reg was sitting and assumed a regal posture in front of her chair.

"Do you want me to pick you up, or are you going to jump up here yourself, Your Highness?"

Starlight snorted and jumped up into her lap. He extended his claws just to remind her who was boss. He quickly settled in, tucking his feet under him, wrapping his tail around his body, and closing his eyes. Reg could feel the sharpening of her senses.

She gazed into the crystal ball. She didn't want to see them. She hated movies with rotting, peeling zombies. She didn't want to see the dead bodies. She just wanted to know where the draugrs were and what they were doing. Anything further would have to wait, until she was sure she wasn't going to attract the Witch Doctor by asking the universe to give her more information.

She could see Black Sands as if it were a map, stretched out in front of her. Hovering above the image were several small, dark clouds. Reg focused on them. They seemed to have a single heartbeat, throbbing a slow, steady rhythm as she watched, just barely discernible.

It was much more clear than her previous attempt. Reg did a quick scan of the black clouds. "There are nine of them."

"Can you tell me where they are?"

"They're not all in the same place." Reg studied the scene, trying to visualize where they all were. It was easier than a street map, more like a satellite picture, but she still had trouble placing everything and assigning place names to each. "Uh... most are along the waterfront, I guess, which is what we figured because that's where the Witch Doctor is operating." She thought about Corvin being over there. She squinted, wondering if she could tell where he was and bring him into focus, but she didn't want to release the vision of the draugrs to find out. "There are some… one over near the cemetery still. I don't know what he's doing. Keeping watch? Scouting out more bodies?" She let her eyes drift along the streets, trying to imagine driving down them to place them on her mental map of the community. "There are a couple…" She swallowed. "A couple that are pretty close to here."

"How close?" Jessup asked, her voice sounding far away. Reg shook her head. "Um… I guess they like dark, sheltered places while it's still daylight. There's a wooded area," she gestured toward the back of the cottage, "a few blocks that way."

"Centennial Park?"

"Yeah, maybe. I don't think I've ever been there. And there's one over this way," Reg made another gesture, focusing on the picture in her head. "I don't know what it's doing. Would it be inside a house?" She looked up away from the crystal ball, and the picture evaporated. "I never thought about them being in houses, just… you know… wandering through the streets."

"Corvin said that they can look just like regular people. They're not like the zombies on TV. So I guess they could come and go anywhere that people would normally go. Inside stores or other buildings. And if it was someone that no one knew had been turned into a draugr… then he could go back into his own house. No one would know, except that he'd be acting funny."

"And he wouldn't bleed. Corvin said they don't bleed either, that's how you can tell."

"We can't exactly go stabbing people wherever we go to make sure that they're human. We're going to need more than that to go on."

"Yeah."

"The one that's in a house… can you tell whose house? Can you tell me the address or what it looks like?"

Starlight's claws dug into Reg's leg. She winced and tried to detach him. "Come on. Nice kitty."

He snuggled and purred, so she let him stay on her lap and didn't push him off onto the floor. Reg stroked him, trying to absorb all of the comfortable, happy feelings that he exuded. He wanted her to feel good, not to continually have to feel the Witch Doctor's wicked aura.

"I can't do any more today," Reg apologized. Though she probably could have, she was willing to accept Starlight's warning and not look more closely. Did she really want to know which of her neighbors was now a zombie? How could she sleep at night if she knew that Old Mr. Kurtz down the street had been killed and was now inhabited by an evil presence, waiting to follow the instructions of the Witch Doctor?

Then again, how could she sleep not knowing who it was?

"Nine draugrs," Jessup said. "I do not like this at all."

"Did you like it before you knew there were nine?"

Jessup made a face at her. "No, smarty-pants. I didn't like it before I came here. But knowing the details… I like it even less. And Hunter is out looking for them? Or looking for the Witch Doctor?"

"I'm not sure, I think he's looking for the Witch Doctor and hoping to avoid the draugrs, but I can't figure out exactly why he's so interested in defeating the Witch Doctor. I would have thought he would just leave town. That's what I want to do. Get out of here and leave it all behind."

"For what it's worth, I'm glad you didn't. I really need every bit of information you can provide me with."

"You're welcome. I'm just not sure how much longer I'll be able to hold out. It's one thing if he's smuggling and doesn't bother anyone. But if he's killing or reanimating random people—or if he's trying to kill me—I'm not so good with that."

"I can understand that."

Reg petted Starlight and scratched his ears. "What about

Corvin?" she asked him softly. "I think we should try to see him and what he's doing. Make sure he's not in danger."

Starlight dug his claws into her leg again and put his ears back. But he retracted his claws and waited, seeing what she was going to do. Reg looked over at Jessup. "I'm a little worried about Corvin being over there with the Witch Doctor and all of the draugrs around… I told him that if he wanted to find the Witch Doctor, he could go himself, but now I'm worried he's going to get himself in trouble."

"Well, he is not well-known for keeping himself out of trouble, unfortunately."

Reg nodded, thinking about the last couple of times that she and Corvin had walked right into a trap together, in too much of a hurry to remember to check for hazards. While she didn't like to compare herself to Corvin, she had to admit that they had impulsivity in common. Jump in first, figure out how to get back out of trouble later.

Reg burrowed her fingers into Starlight's short fur, closing her eyes to focus. "I just want to know where he is… and if he's okay. That's all."

She reached out with her mind, tentative because she didn't want to risk the Witch Doctor feeling her and following her back. Corvin wasn't exactly a friend. She wasn't sure why she didn't just leave him to his fate. But she couldn't.

She had been in his head before. He had held her powers. They had a strong connection, one that shouldn't be hard to reestablish. She didn't want to read his mind or communicate with him. She just wanted to see where he was.

She didn't see the overhead view again. Her fickle brain was determined not to make things too easy. She saw instead what she assumed was Corvin's viewpoint. A street, warehouses, gulls wheeling overhead. It was quiet other than the calls of the gulls and the lapping of the waves. Like he was the only person on the planet.

"He's outside," Reg said. "At least he's not a prisoner. I don't think there's anyone else around, so the Witch Doctor shouldn't know that he's there. He's not strong enough to reach out and connect with the Witch Doctor."

"Don't assume you know what his powers are," Jessup warned. "They can change as he takes strength… elsewhere."

Reg hadn't even thought of that. He hadn't taken her powers, so she just assumed that he hadn't taken anyone else's either. But that wasn't necessarily true. She nudged herself a little closer to his consciousness, curious about whether his powers had increased or had another gift added to them.

There was immediate resistance. He knew she was there. Or knew someone was there. She withdrew. He looked around. A glance back over his shoulder this time to make sure he wasn't being followed. Reg remained on the backward view, even though he had only spared a glance back. She searched the shadows and hiding places behind him. She strained to separate all of the shadows, to match them with the objects that were casting them. They seemed too thick and indistinguishable beside a dumpster, but she needed to get closer to see if there were anything there or not.

"I think there might be something…"

"What is it?" Jessup prompted after a minute of silence.

"I don't like it… he needs to pay attention. He needs to look again."

"Can you tell him to?"

"No, I…" It was difficult to communicate with a conscious person. Especially one like Corvin, who would have stronger defenses. If she did communicate with him, they would become even more inextricably linked, and she was discovering that magical links caused a lot of problems.

She worked on making out the shadows behind Corvin while he moved forward. Then one of the shadows finally separated and, for the first time, she saw the vaguely man-shaped form following him.

"Corvin!" Reg shouted a warning.

He whipped around, startled, and after a split-second of not understanding what he saw, he knew it was one of the draugrs. He ran. There were long rows of warehouses and other kinds of storage units with roads intersecting around them in a never-ending gridwork of streets. He put on a burst of speed, turning into one of the cross streets, and then as soon as he could, turning again. He didn't look behind him, so Reg had no way of knowing whether the draugr was in pursuit.

On TV, zombies could only shuffle, but Corvin had said that they weren't limited that way in real life. That meant that they should be able to move at least as quickly as a man, and had a good chance of catching up to Corvin. She wanted desperately for him to look back. He didn't, focusing on the road ahead and on making his way through a maze of streets. Reg was reminded of her move from one foster family to another, always with the feeling of dread behind her, until after many moves over several years, she had finally been able to settle into a foster home without the sense that he might find her at any moment.

How long had it taken? Much longer than it would take Corvin to lose the draugr. It was a much faster-paced game.

She encouraged him in her head, trying to hurry him ahead, to impress upon him that he needed to stay ahead of it. But he knew more about draugrs than she did. He knew what was at stake. He wouldn't want to be killed and turned into one of them.

If he were changed into a draugr, would she still be able to see through his eyes and communicate with whatever was in his head? Would he be gone from his body? A ghost? Or trapped in it forever?

"Regina!"

She was pulled suddenly out of Corvin's head by Jessup's cry. She was on the floor, Jessup feeling for a pulse and at the same time trying to raise a response from her. She didn't know what had happened to Starlight. Hopefully, he'd had the sense to jump free before she had fallen and she hadn't landed on top of him. She grasped Jessup's arm. "It's okay. I'm here."

"Sheesh!" Jessup sat back onto her heels. "Don't do that!"

"I didn't exactly mean to!"

"What did you see? Is Corvin okay?"

"One of them saw him. It was following him. He's running, trying to get away."

"Can you tell me where he is? I can send a car over there on a disturbance call."

"I… I'm not sure, and he won't be in exactly the same place for long, because he's running, trying to get away from it. He could be blocks away by the time a car gets there."

"I'm going to anyway. Can you give me some location? Two cross streets? A landmark?"

"Everything looks the same… uh… there was a number on a door. Sixteen-oh-two?"

Jessup frowned. It wasn't much to go on, but at least it was a start. She clicked the mic button on the radio mounted on her uniform and made a call. Reg was in a fog, having a hard time focusing on what was going on around her. Starlight came over and started to nose at her.

"Oh, there you are," Reg said in relief. "Are you okay? I'm sorry about that."

He didn't seem to be upset with her, rubbing against her and purring and snuffling at her face and neck, making sure that she was okay.

"I'm fine. It was just Corvin. I guess… I got carried away."

Jessup talked to her dispatcher for a while, then finally signed off. "Okay, I'd better get over there too, or I'm going to have a hard time explaining how I knew something was going on. Are you going to be okay?"

"Yeah. Really. Everything is okay."

"Everything? Corvin too?"

"I don't know… I'm okay."

"Let's at least get you up on the couch, okay? You can keep resting, but at least you won't be on the floor. Do you want me to see if Sarah is in and send her over?"

"No, I don't need anyone to baby me. Nothing to worry about."

Jessup helped Reg get to her knees and then up onto the couch.

"I don't need to lie down."

"Well, it's not going to hurt you. Just placate me and do it for a few minutes until you're not… dizzy or anything."

Reg let Jessup stretch her out on the couch, which was too short to accommodate her full height but, as Jessup said, it was better than being on the floor. Maybe she would have just a little nap while she got her strength back again. Communicating telepathically took a lot of energy. She was always surprised at how physically exhausted she was afterward.

"Okay. I'll call you in a few minutes to make sure you're okay and let you know what's going on. Have you got your phone? Can you get at it when it starts to ring?"

"Yeah. Right here." Reg patted the pocket of her skirt. Hopefully, the screen hadn't broken when she had fallen.

Jessup left quietly. Reg sat there, remembering how one of her foster families had investigated her "fits" to see if she had epilepsy, but, of course, the doctor had instead concluded that she was faking it for attention. That had gone over really well.

* * *

Reg was starting to doze off when her phone rang. She blinked sticky eyelids and fished her phone out of her pocket. It certainly hadn't taken long for Jessup to get to the scene and see what was happening. Or maybe time had passed faster than Reg had realized. Worse yet, maybe Jessup hadn't been able to find Corvin and was calling in the hopes of getting more details and tracking him down.

Or something might have happened to Corvin.

She was horrified by the idea that the draugr might have caught up to Corvin. It might have killed him. Maybe the Witch

Doctor had even turned him into draugr number ten. How would Reg feel knowing that her enemy was permanently gone and he would never try to charm her again?

She didn't even glance at the ID on the face of the phone before answering it and putting it up to her face.

"Hello?"

"Reg!" It wasn't Jessup's voice, but Corvin's, harsh and out of breath.

"Corvin, are you okay?"

"How did you know that thing was coming after me? I thought I was a goner!"

"You're okay? You lost it?"

"Yes." He made a disgusted noise in the back of his throat. "You have no idea how big and dangerous those things are. How... disgusting!"

"You said they were just like normal people. That they weren't like the zombies on TV. It wasn't... rotting, was it?"

"Not visibly, no. But the stench...!"

"They smell?"

He swore and made a noise like he was snorting and blowing his nose at the same time. "You've never smelled anything so foul! Maybe not everyone can smell it, but I don't think anyone could think that that thing was anything but a rotting corpse."

"Yuck. I'm glad I couldn't smell it."

"Yes, you are," he agreed. He blew his nose again. "So are you coming here to help me? I don't really feel like running into another one of those creatures unaware. I need you with me so that I have some warning."

"No. I already told you I don't want to get close to the Witch Doctor."

"If he wasn't tipped off by you spotting one of the draugar and yelling at me telepathically, then I don't think he's going to know you're there just by proximity. As long as you keep it low-key and just tell me where the draugar are..."

"Corvin, I can't. Really."

"You're just going to spy on me telepathically? That's a little intrusive."

"I can't do that, either. I used up too much energy already. It's too hard to maintain at this distance and with your natural barriers."

"Reg, do you want me to get killed? Why bother warning me if you're going to back off again and refuse to be involved? You have to make a decision. Get off the fence; you can't stay balanced up there."

"I'm not hunting draugrs."

"Reg, just come!" he insisted angrily.

She was unnerved by his demand. Like a father who was at the end of his rope and tired of cajoling a recalcitrant child, he was serious now. She was to get over there and help him, or *else*.

Harrison had said that sooner or later, she would help Corvin. So why was she fighting fate? Corvin couldn't see the draugrs. Reg could. The logical conclusion was that it was her fate to help him, however afraid she was.

Reg pulled the phone away from her ear and stared at it for a minute, not sure what to do. She didn't have the words to argue with him. She couldn't keep resisting.

She hung up the call and closed her eyes, breathing slowly and trying to figure out what to do.

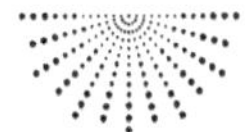

# CHAPTER TWENTY-FOUR

Reg could see the police car lights flashing, so she pulled in behind them and parked her car. Jessup hadn't called her back yet, so Reg could only assume that they hadn't yet been able to sort the situation out. She climbed out of the car and looked at the little knot of people, trying to discern what was going on.

Jessup peeled away from the group and walked up to Reg, frowning.

"I thought you were going to stay at your house? What's going on?"

"Corvin called. I… I had to come."

"Hunter called you? Where is he? We haven't been able to find him or any sign of the… party who was stalking him."

"He's okay. He escaped. But he wanted me to come down to… I don't even know what I'm supposed to do. Be his early warning system, I guess."

"How about he stays away from here? Wouldn't that be safer? Leave it to the police to investigate."

"You know he's not going to do that. Why even bother suggesting it?"

Jessup gave a low chuckle. "You sound like an experienced

mother."

"And Corvin is my child?" Reg wrinkled her nose and shook her head. "Heaven forbid."

"I wouldn't want to lay claim to him either."

"Besides which, you said he's… really old."

"I prefer to go with appearance rather than actual years. It just gets too complicated otherwise."

Reg's face warmed. This was not the conversation that she needed in the middle of a crisis. She was there to help Corvin stay alive, not to discuss whether their ages were compatible.

"I need to go find him."

"How are you going to do that? Did he tell you where he is? Are you going to use your powers?"

"I'm going to call him on the phone."

"Such secret superpowers."

Reg tried not to be pulled in by Jessup's sarcasm. She appreciated the dry humor and could easily be pulled into thinking that they were friends because they had an easy repartee. But it wasn't the same as being friends. Reg had learned the difference between friends and easy acquaintances over the years. Actual friends were few and far between. People like Erin. People who cared about her and wanted to share experiences. Not people who just wanted to use her for her powers, or as a scapegoat, or for some other use. Reg did not like being used.

She took out her phone and tapped the last number in the history to call Corvin back. He answered almost immediately. His voice was low and he was no longer out of breath.

"Hello?"

"I'm here. So, where are you?"

"You can't find me?"

"I don't want to exhaust my energy. Especially if you want me to keep you from draugrs. So tell me where you are."

Corvin was quiet for a few seconds, while Reg assumed he got his bearings and checked the nearest cross streets. Eventually, he gave her his coordinates.

"Hang on a sec," Reg told him. She repeated the streets to Jessup. "Where is that?"

Jessup looked around, orienting herself, then motioned. "Over there. Follow me."

"You just come with me," Reg suggested. "We don't want to attract attention."

"Then you can come in my car. Just leave yours here. It will be safe."

"No, I'm not going in a police car. Just get in my car or give me directions."

"Do you need to be so stubborn, Reg? I'd rather have access to my equipment."

"Get whatever you need out of your car and come in mine."

Jessup shook her head, frustrated, but she went to Reg's passenger door and got in. She didn't get anything out of her squad car. So much for needing her equipment. Reg got into the driver's seat.

"This way?" she pointed.

Jessup nodded. "Yeah. Head back down this aisle and turn right."

Reg twisted anxiously as they got closer to Corvin. He might have thought that he had lost the draugr, but Reg had a feeling that he hadn't. Or the draugr was on his trail a second time. Perhaps it had lost him for a few minutes, but it had been able to pick up his scent. Corvin probably smelled just as bad to the draugr as it smelled to him. Just following the stench, he would find Corvin again.

"Are you okay?" Jessup asked, noticing Reg's discomfort. She probably thought Reg needed to pee, the way she kept twisting around.

"I don't like being down here. Everything is... darker here. It's like walking through a forest at midnight."

"It looks just the same to me."

"It isn't the way it looks... it's the way it feels. I can feel how close the Witch Doctor is. The evil he is spreading. The draugrs..."

and one of them is really close. I don't know if we can find Corvin without tipping it off."

"Do you want me to call Hunter and warn him?"

"No. I don't want anything buzzing around the airwaves. Let's just keep quiet." Reg swallowed. "Keep your gun ready."

Jessup readjusted the gear in her heavy duty belt. "Can you kill them with guns? Do you need a silver bullet? Because I left my only silver bullet at home."

Reg didn't know if a simple gunshot was enough to kill a draugr, but at least it was a start, and hopefully, it would at least slow one down for a few minutes.

"I'm… not entirely sure. Aim for the head."

Reg slowed the car and crept along, her eyes open for any unusual shadows or an increase in the feelings of fear and anxiety. She didn't see anything, but she could certainly feel that it was close by. She remembered how it had been behind Corvin before, and he hadn't even known it was there because he only took quick looks behind him and didn't take the time to separate it out of the shadows or to watch it when he was on the move.

It was like a lightning strike to the heart. Like an explosion right beside her. Reg swerved and Jessup was forced to grab onto the door to keep herself upright.

"What the—"

"Look out!" Reg warned, hitting the gas and trying to avoid hitting the draugr. Why would she want to avoid hitting it? Didn't they want to kill it? A car could be a deadly weapon, one that the Vikings hadn't had on hand. If they had, maybe their draugr-killing instructions would have included running them down with a car. Reg corrected her steering to aim back toward the draugr instead of away from it.

Jessup held on to the door handle on one side and the parking brake on the other, taken off-guard by Reg's decision to go on the offensive. "Be careful! Watch out for the…"

Reg plowed straight into the draugr. There was a sickening thump and crunch as Reg plowed into it.

"Whoa!" Jessup exclaimed, reaching for the handle on her door to get out and see. "Hell, Reg, you just ran into—"

Reg grabbed her arm to keep her from opening the door. "It's one of the draugrs. Don't get out."

"It's a man—"

"Trust me; it's one of the draugrs. I know you don't believe it, but remember what Corvin said—they look just like regular people. You can't tell."

"Reg, you're barely functioning after your psychic contact. You don't know what's going on—"

"I know what's going on better than you do. Look, is it bleeding? Can't you smell it?"

As Corvin had said, the stench was something indescribable. Reg couldn't believe that anyone could not smell it.

"Smell what?" Jessup challenged. She again reached for the door handle. "I at least have to look, Reg. I can't just leave a body on the ground and not even take a look at it. I have a duty as a police officer—"

"You are doing your duty as a police officer. You're supposed to be protecting people. You can't do that if you're going to get out of the car every time we hit one of them. I don't know if I've killed it or just disabled it, so unless you're planning on cutting off its head or putting a bullet into its brains, stay put."

Jessup hesitated, her hand still on the handle, not sure whether to believe Reg or whether to think she was off her rocker.

"You need to listen," Reg insisted. "Do you see it bleeding?"

Jessup craned her neck this way and that, trying to get a good view of the fallen draugr. Her lips tightened. "I don't see any. But..."

"Then you know it's a draugr. Come on; we still have to find Corvin."

Jessup sighed. She let go of the door handle. "Okay, but we have to come back here after and make sure that..."

"That I didn't just kill an innocent bystander? Don't you trust me any more than that?"

Jessup didn't answer, which was in itself an answer. She stared out the window as Reg reversed the car and backed away from the draugr. She wiggled the steering wheel to try to dislodge the draugr from where it was caught on the bumper. Eventually, it fell away. Reg didn't feel the need to get a better look at it, but Jessup leaned into the window, looking down at it.

Reg continued down the road, scanning mentally for any more of them. One down, eight to go. Or one temporarily disabled, anyway. Reg wasn't sure how long it would actually stay out of business.

Jessup gave her directions and they eventually pulled into the road where Corvin was standing, trying to blend in with the dumpster and the detritus in the alley.

At the sight of the car, he approached the passenger side, then realized that Detective Jessup already occupied the front seat.

"What's going on?" he demanded, opening the back door. "Why is she here?"

"I'm here to find you and see if you're okay," Jessup snapped. "Since Reg was pretty wiped out after warning you. I don't know how you convinced her to come here when she's already too tired to do anything."

"I'm not too tired to do anything," Reg argued. "I did just run over the draugr that was on your trail again."

Corvin looked at her. "You killed it?"

"I don't know. I hit it. Left it back there."

"If it was a draugr," Jessup amended.

"Of course it was a draugr. I told you it was."

Jessup shrugged helplessly at Corvin, appealing to him. Corvin looked behind himself, making sure there wasn't another one following him, before addressing Jessup.

"Well, did you smell it?"

"I didn't smell anything. Reg said that it stank, but I didn't notice anything unusual."

"Did it bleed?"

"I didn't see any blood."

Reg nodded at Corvin. "Draugr," she said firmly.

"Okay. So you've taken care of the one that was following me. That's a good first step. Even if it isn't completely dead…"

"Aren't they all dead? That's the whole point, isn't it?"

"I meant dead as in… not a draugr or capable of being a draugr anymore."

"Then you should have said that."

"Are there any other ones close by?"

Reg took a deep breath, closing her eyes and feeling the atmosphere for the rest. "There are too many of them close by," she said. "Explain why we have to be here, right in the middle of everything?"

"Because this is where the Witch Doctor is operating and we want to be able to track him."

"There's no way we can beat him. He's too powerful."

Corvin gave a slight smile. "If we can find his warehouse, I can beat him."

"How?"

Corvin just shrugged, like he had a big surprise for her. Like it was her birthday and all of her friends were coming for a surprise party.

Reg had never actually had a surprise party. She'd had few enough birthday parties as a child, and of course, as an adult, she didn't bother to observe them. What exactly was the point in celebrating the day she had come into the world? Like that was such a great accomplishment? Sure, surviving another year was a good thing, but she could think of a lot of better things to celebrate in her life.

"Hunter," Jessup said seriously. "I hope you're not planning what I think you are."

He just gave her what Reg assumed was supposed to be an enigmatic smile. He looked around. "So? Are there any others close?"

"Yes."

Corvin climbed into the back seat. "Okay. Let me know where

you see them. Is there a larger cluster? Somewhere they are gathering and working together?"

Reg was starting to get overwhelmed by the dark feeling. It was becoming less distinct, harder to separate into separate beings. They seemed to all be coalescing into one large dark force.

"I don't know if I can. This is… getting complicated."

"Just try," Corvin instructed. "You can do it. If you're getting low on energy, I can help you with that."

Reg knew that he could. But she worried about what else he might do if he knew she was too low on energy. It would be the perfect time to breach her defenses and to take instead of giving.

She inched the car forward, trying to drive to the area where the darkness was the densest. That meant more draugrs. As long as it didn't indicate the presence of the Witch Doctor. How was she going to separate the Witch Doctor's aura from the rest of the evil creatures?

A cat cut across in front of the car, making Reg jump and hit the brakes. Everyone was thrown forward. Corvin wasn't buckled in, and his face hit the back of Jessup's headrest with a thump. Reg glanced over at him. His lip had split and started to well up with blood.

"Sorry. There was a cat. I didn't want to hit it,"

Corvin was patting his pockets, looking for a tissue for his bleeding lip, and stopped suddenly. "A cat?"

"Yeah, sorry."

"Describe it."

Reg rolled her eyes. "Describe it? A black cat. That's all. Just like all of the other black cats in Black Sands. It seems like everyone has one these days."

"Was it a draugr?"

Reg frowned at him. He had hit his face pretty hard. Was he concussed?

"A *cat*," she said distinctly.

"A black cat. That thing that I said I had to look up… the Vikings believed that the draugrs were shapeshifters. As well as being able to grow in size to attack, they were also able to turn into *kattakyn*."

"Cats?" Reg demanded.

"I know. I never really thought anything of it. There are shapeshifters in many cultures, from werewolves to—"

"Shut up. Cats? Black cats?"

"Yes. And they could kill in their cat form, by sitting on your chest, and increasing in weight until—"

"Why didn't you tell me that?" Jessup interrupted, her lips white. "We've had several suspicious deaths, and they were all—"

"Asphyxiation?"

Reg felt again the sensation she'd had in her dream of the black cat sitting on her chest, getting heavier and heavier, until she wasn't able to breathe. It had been Starlight who had banished the draugr-cat, if it had really existed and not just been part of her wild dreams.

"Why didn't you tell me that?" Jessup demanded. "I've been running around trying to find out what was happening, and you knew all along—"

"I didn't know about any suspicious deaths. You didn't tell me."

"Asphyxiation and crush injuries. That certainly sounds like one of your cat draugrs sitting on someone's chest, doesn't it?"

"Yes. It does. Do you have names? Who are these people who were killed? If you don't give me the information, I don't know how I'm supposed to figure anything out."

Jessup pulled out her duty notebook and flipped through the pages.

She read the names out. Reg couldn't believe that Jessup would give Corvin the names without objection when she wouldn't tell Reg anything. What exactly was the relationship between the two of them? Was Corvin an official informant? She knew that he consulted with the police department, but she really didn't understand what he did for them.

Corvin considered. The names obviously didn't trigger immediate recognition for him. But his expression suggested he might be able to do something with them, given enough time. He looked at Reg, frowning.

"I don't know them," Reg said, putting up her hands defensively.

"I didn't think you did. I'm just trying to focus. I'm hoping that the two of us together can sort this out…"

"How?"

"If I could get just a little bit of your powers, not even enough for you to notice, I bet I can find a connection. You may think that you don't have much that would be useful, but you do."

"I can't control how much of my powers you take, and I don't think you could control it once you started. You'd suck me dry."

"What makes you think that? I returned your powers to you once before. What if I retake them, temporarily, on the promise that I'll return them, just as I did the first time…?"

"Who do you think you're kidding, Hunter?" Jessup asked in disbelief. "No one is going to lend you their powers voluntarily for just a little while. Reg knows that you wouldn't ever return her powers. After how hard you've been working to take them away from her?"

Corvin scowled at her. "If I promise to do a thing, I will. A promise is a promise. I'm a man of honor," he said pompously.

"With your track record? You are clearly not a man of honor. You would never return them."

Corvin's face suddenly lit up. "Check the ownership records of the warehouses around here," he said suddenly, switching tracks in an instant. "I'll bet that one of your draugr victims is the owner of the warehouse the Witch Doctor is using."

"Yes," Reg agreed, as it suddenly crystallized for her too. "The warehouse… the boat… everybody who had something to do with the Witch Doctor setting his business up here. That must be who he is killing. I couldn't figure out why he would be killing anyone without turning them into zombies. But that must be it."

"I'm sure he has plenty of people who he would like to kill,"

Jessup said. "All he has to do is tell his draugrs to kill them. I'll check the ownership records, see if there are any obvious connections. But the warehouse and boat could be rented rather than owned. He could be using a holding company. We can't just search every single company that owns something in the area."

"Where did the cat go?"

Reg pointed. "That way."

Corvin followed her finger to a building. "Did he go inside, or just in that area?"

"I didn't see. I was too busy making sure everyone was okay…" She indicated his lip as he dabbed at it with a white handkerchief. Seriously? Who carried fabric hankies?

"Can't you feel him?" Corvin suggested, still looking at the building in question.

"I can't separate them all right now. And with the cats… I've seen a lot of black cats lately, but I haven't had that dark sense from any of them. I would have noticed that."

"What have you felt? You said earlier that they didn't feel the same as the lost cat. Whatever her nonsense name was."

"Nicole."

"*Nicole.* She's a cat, not a soap opera character! What you felt from her was different from what you felt from the other black cats. That's why you didn't think they were her."

"Yeah. I don't know… I just felt emptiness when I saw them. It wasn't anything evil, just like… a shell."

"Well, that's a pretty good explanation of what they are. So maybe when they are in their feline form, they don't give off the same aura as when they are in human form."

Reg nodded slowly.

"Can you check the ownership of this building?" Corvin asked Jessup, indicating the one that the cat might have gone into.

"I guess that's how they get around without anyone noticing them," Reg mused. "I thought that if there were that many draugrs around town, it was weird that no one had noticed them. Unless they can become invisible. Or maybe if they just killed any witnesses. Could the people who were killed have just been people who happened to have seen them?"

Jessup shook her head as she dialed a number on her phone. "I doubt it. They weren't killed out on the street where they might have seen a draugr; they were killed in their beds. They didn't report any suspicious activity before they were killed."

"If they were killed in their beds… were the houses broken into?"

Jessup motioned for her to be quiet and spoke on the phone, giving the person who had answered her call the address of the warehouse.

Reg looked around restlessly. Her mind was going a mile a minute. "If this was the warehouse with all of the smuggled goods in it, couldn't you sense it? I thought you could feel the power of magical objects."

"He could be blocking it with a blocking spell similar to the one Harrison put around you. You can't tell if this is where the Witch Doctor's activities are centered?"

Reg moved around restlessly. She shifted the car into park and revved the engine, keyed up and unable to be still. She didn't want to reach out to the Witch Doctor. It was too dangerous. But she still wanted to do something, not just sit there waiting for more information. What difference did it make if they knew it was the Witch Doctor's warehouse? Were they going to attack him?

She wished that she had Starlight with her. Starlight had been a big bonus when they had fought the pixies, and she thought that if the draugrs could take cat form, he might be able to fight them too. He'd driven away the one who had come in her dream, hadn't he?

Jessup was nodding and ending her phone call. She tapped to hang it up. "They'll have to do a search," she said, "it's not exactly instant, because they have to match up the municipal address with a legal address and then if a corporation holds it, they'll have to see who is associated with that, and if it is rented, that will be another complication. But they'll call back when they know something."

"How did the draugrs get into the victims' houses?" Reg demanded. "Did they break down the doors when they were in their giant form?"

She really wanted to hear an affirmative answer, not wanting to know how close she had come to death herself.

Jessup didn't answer right away, considering carefully. It made Reg grind her teeth. If Jessup were going to be so reluctant to share information with her, then how was Reg supposed to help? What did she think Reg was going to do with the information about how the draugrs got into people's houses? How was she going to use that to her advantage? Take over the draugrs from the Witch Doctor and use them to break into houses and steal? Cat burglars? Did they really think she had that kind of ability?

Jessup glanced back at Corvin.

Corvin raised an eyebrow. "If you know, then spit it out, Marta. What are we supposed to do? Guess? Reg already did. Either they broke the doors down or they got in some other way. Which is it?"

"There was no sign of forced entry. No sign that anyone had broken into the houses or had picked a lock or entered through an unlocked door."

Reg looked at Jessup and then at Corvin.

"A locked-room murder?" Corvin asked. "Really? There must have been some sign of how they got in. Did they have keys? Charm the locks? Were the victims practitioners or not? Were there wards?"

Jessup shrugged. "It's under investigation, Hunter. I haven't had a lot of time to work with this, and the police force doesn't look for things like charms and wards. They work with physical evidence. All I can tell you is that they were locked room murders."

Reg sighed. "I know how they do it."

# CHAPTER TWENTY-FIVE

They both looked at her. Reg couldn't help smiling at their shocked expressions. They had not expected any insight into the police work from Reg Rawlins. She was nice to have around if they needed someone with psychic powers, but they had not expected her to be able to help with the investigation.

"You know how they got in?" Jessup repeated.

"They were all killed while they were asleep?"

"Yes."

Reg looked at Corvin. "And you don't know? There isn't anything in the mythology about how they could get into a locked room?"

He looked baffled. Pressing the hankie against his lip, he wrinkled his forehead as he considered the possibilities. Reg was pleased that she was the only one who knew.

"The draugrs came into their dreams."

Corvin's face cleared. "Of course," he agreed. "I should have figured that out. The Vikings believed that the draugar could come into their dreams and that they could leave physical evidence of their presence. Sometimes they left objects behind to signify that they had been there. I don't remember ever reading that they could kill a person in their dreams, but it follows, doesn't it? It makes perfect sense."

Reg nodded.

"How did you know that?" Jessup asked, head cocked slightly.

"Because… one of them came to me last night."

Jessup and Corvin both gaped at her.

"One of them came to you?" Corvin echoed.

Reg nodded. "It was sitting on my chest, just like you said, getting heavier and heavier until I couldn't breathe." She thought about the mysterious deaths and how close she had come to being another statistic. "But then Starlight attacked it and scared it off."

"Are you sure?" Jessup shook her head, eyes wide in disbelief.

"Am I sure? Are you really going to ask me that? Do you think I could be mistaken about something like that?"

"No, I'm sorry. It's just an automatic reaction. I never thought… it never occurred to me that they could come after you like that. In your dreams? It's like something out of a horror movie."

"So is the rest of the stuff about reanimating corpses," Reg pointed out.

"I guess it is. It's just getting bigger and bigger… we need to recruit some more help, figure out how to get rid of these things. They're already killing at will. We need to figure something out."

"That's what I've been saying," Corvin agreed. "We can't just let them run rampant. We have a responsibility to try to defeat them."

Reg narrowed her eyes at him. "We're having a hard time believing that's really why you want to get involved here. Wouldn't it be safer to turn tail and run?"

"I may not normally be altruistic," he admitted, "but I do have friends in Black Sands, and I wouldn't want to leave them to the Witch Doctor and his draugar."

"So what are we going to do?" Jessup asked practically. "Are we going to get some help? Go in there and check things out? What's the plan?"

They both looked at Corvin. He smiled. "Can you get a search warrant? Or do we need to get in there without one?"

"We'll find out what the results of the ownership search are in the next few minutes. If it's one of the dead men, then I think we have enough to get a warrant."

"How is that going to help?" Reg demanded. "If you sent a bunch of policemen in there to search the place, aren't they just going to be killed? They're going up against draugrs, not illegal aliens."

"I want to get in there," Corvin reiterated. "If I can get in there, either with a warrant or by some other method, then I can access the power of the smuggled items. That may give me enough strength to tackle a few of the draugar on my own."

"And then what? If you can't take on all nine of them and the Witch Doctor, then we're right back where we started."

"I can at least try. What's your suggestion?"

Reg didn't have one.

"What about the guy that Corvin was telling me about?" Jessup prompted.

"Damon?"

Corvin rolled his eyes. "No, not Damon. What kind of help would he be? She's talking about Harrison."

"Actually, Damon might be helpful…"

"Not Damon," Corvin repeated. "Do you know how to get ahold of Harrison? He has a vast store of power. I don't know what he is, but he could have what it takes to fight the Witch Doctor."

"He already said he wouldn't. He is prevented from killing someone of… his own kind, or something like that."

"He might change his mind if he thought you were in danger. He seems to be committed to protecting you. Can you call him?"

"I don't… have his number. I don't even know if he has a phone, he's sort of… I don't know… I don't think he's exactly… human."

"He's pretty obviously not human," Corvin agreed. "But that doesn't mean he can't use a phone." He sighed. "A lot of the more ancients won't have anything to do with technology. Can you just… reach out to him? You have some connection with him."

Reg wasn't sure why she hesitated. Harrison was a friend and protector. She wasn't afraid of him. But maybe she was afraid of calling him when she didn't need him, in case he might not be there the next time she did.

"Just try," Corvin coaxed. "What is it going to hurt?"

"Okay… but don't expect any help."

She closed her eyes and thought about Harrison, told him in her mind that she needed his help.

Rather than Harrison appearing, Reg was suddenly flooded with the memories of her mother and the Witch Doctor, while at the same time, Norma Jean's voice filled her head. Reg held her head with both hands, trying to steady herself and take back control of her brain. But instead, Norma Jean's voice just got more insistent, impossible to block out.

"Leave me alone!" Reg insisted.

"Listen to me," Norma Jean told her. "Tell him you know where Weston is."

"What?"

"Are you listening to me? Sam will want to know. You can stop him."

Reg pulled at her hair. "Get out of my head. I need Harrison. Not you!"

"Reg, are you okay?"

Reg waved off their concerned inquiries. She kept focused on an image of Harrison, his wide grin and mustache and his striped shirt, remembering how he had protected her from the Witch Doctor before.

She banged her head on the steering wheel in frustration. "Come on, Harrison, I need you!"

"Reg, maybe you shouldn't—" Jessup started, putting a hand on Reg's arm.

Reg shook herself free. "Don't touch me when I'm concentrating," she snapped.

"Okay, sorry, but I think…"

There was a knocking on the window. Reg startled, opened her eyes, and looked to see who it was.

Harrison, of course. He had on a royal purple silk shirt this time, but it was still unmistakably him. Reg rolled her window down.

"No need to beat yourself up," Harrison chided.

"Look, I know you said you couldn't do anything to harm the Witch Doctor, but is there something you can do to help us out? We can't go after the Wi—after Destine and nine draugrs by ourselves. We're not strong enough."

"You have the tools at hand."

"The tools? What are you talking about? What do we need? What are we supposed to do?"

"You need to use your brain, Reg, and your powers. You're right; I can't do anything to harm Destine. If you want to stop him and his draugar from devastating this town, then you need to do something, and it needs to be soon. He already grows stronger."

"What are we supposed to do? We can't fight him physically. If we go up against someone so powerful with just the three of us…" Reg gestured at herself and her friends. "I mean, I'm just a psychic. And Jessup…"

Jessup shook her head. Reg knew that she had some powers, but they were relatively minor. Reg had never asked her for details or what her background was.

"Then there is the spirit-eater," Harrison pointed out.

Reg glanced over at Corvin, still dabbing at his split lip. Yeah, he looked really powerful.

"That's not enough," Reg protested.

"Then you need to get more. Where is that nice boy who was with you the other day? The visionary."

"Damon?"

"We don't need Damon," Corvin growled.

"He's better than nothing. Shouldn't we have all of the power we can get on our side? And what about Sarah?"

"She won't have anything to contribute here," Corvin said, shaking his head. "She is not a warrior."

"Who, then? Who else can we get?"

"What about the charmer?" Harrison suggested.

"Who? Do you mean Corvin?"

He was the only one Reg knew who had special charms. But Harrison wasn't looking at Corvin, and Corvin shook his head, indicating that it wasn't him.

"The charmer," Harrison repeated. "The guardian of the other cat."

"Other cat…? Do you mean Nicole?"

"Nicole… that is a human name. I don't know."

"Starlight's lady friend."

Harrison smiled, his eyes dancing. "Yes, her. What about her guardian?"

"I don't know who her guardian is. Do you mean a guardian like you? I don't know anyone else like you."

"The human who cares for her."

"Francesca."

"You should call her. And Damon. Then you have a chance."

Reg looked at Jessup and Corvin for their reactions. They both seemed just as disconcerted by the suggestions as she was. She turned back to Harrison to ask him for further help, but he was gone again. Reg looked in front of and behind the car, hoping that he had just wandered off, but he was nowhere in sight.

"Thanks a lot, Harrison."

"Do you think those two will be of any help?" Corvin challenged.

"Well, I know that they can do more than I can by myself. What about you? Are you going to turn down Harrison's suggestions just because you don't know how they're going to work out? Didn't we ask for help? You're the one who said to call him."

"I was looking for power, not advice."

"Well, advice is what we got. So do we call them?"

"Go ahead. It's not likely to make anything worse. Though I warn you… I'm not protecting Damon if he gets himself into trouble. Ditto the cat lady."

"You don't even know the cat lady."

"I've seen her. And she's a lovely girl, but I don't trust her. Not if she's Haitian. If they're coming, it's to help us in the fight, not vice versa. I don't want to be pulled ten different directions. We're going to need to be focused when we get in there, and I can't do that if I have to protect anyone else."

"Fine. It's understood, you're only in there for your own purposes. Just like always."

Corvin pulled his hankie away from his lip, scowling at Reg. "Didn't I help you when Hawthorne-Rose was torturing you? And didn't I help you fight the pixies? I didn't have to do those things. I didn't do them for my own well-being. That was for you."

Reg's face got hot. She covered her cheek with her hand, not wanting him to see her flush. With the other hand, she took out her phone and found Damon's number.

# CHAPTER TWENTY-SIX

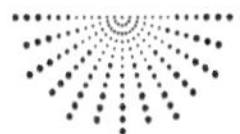

Damon arrived before Francesca. Reg got out of the car to talk to him, looking back at Corvin anxiously as she did so. She hated to tell Damon that she was now working with Corvin. Again. Even though she kept saying that she needed to be protected from him. Damon looked into the car and saw Corvin sitting there.

"Again?"

"Uh… well, it's a long story."

"And do I take it you punched him in the face? Because that would make my day."

He had seen Corvin's split and swelling lip. Reg suppressed a smile at this.

"Actually, no, just hit the brakes too hard when he wasn't wearing a seatbelt."

"Well, at least that gives you plausible deniability," Damon approved. "So, what's going on? Why are we meeting here, out in the open, when I thought he was trying to avoid detection?"

"Yeah… well, we've been detected. The Witch Doctor tried to kill me last night, or this morning. And we're… trying to formulate a plan. We're just waiting for one more party, so maybe I could hold off on explaining until everyone is here."

Damon nodded. "Fine. We'll wait."

He leaned back against his car, arms folded, looking both casual and wary at the same time. Reg took a deep breath and let out a sigh.

"So what's this I hear about you being able to put visions into other people's heads?"

"What?" Damon's eyes went to Corvin again. "Did he tell you that?"

"Is it true?"

"Well, that is one of my talents, yes."

"So how many times have you done that to me?"

Damon shifted his stance, no longer looking quite so casual. He obviously sensed that Reg wasn't happy about being the target of his gifts any more than she was of Corvin's.

"You make it sound like it's some kind of assault. But it's not… it isn't like that at all. It's just… part of my way of communicating."

"Your way of communicating."

"Well, yes. How often have you had to describe something that is difficult to put into words? Wouldn't it be easier to just… put that image directly into someone else's mind?"

"Sure, but entering someone else's mind is against the rules. It's impolite. Right?"

"I'm not entering into your mind when I do it. No more than I am by talking to you. I'm just communicating in a different way."

"And how am I supposed to know whether I'm really experiencing something, or whether I am making it up or visualizing it, or whether you are putting it there? Why didn't you tell me you could do this?"

"It never really came up. It isn't something that's always conscious; it's often just… the natural way for me to communicate. It just comes out in visions instead of words."

"So you're saying it's like a speech impediment. A stammer."

He chuckled. "It isn't always something I can control. I do my best, but sometimes it does just kind of slip out."

"And when you put visions into my head while we were bowling? And that whole walk-on-the-beach vision the other day? Those were unintentional?"

"Uh…" Damon scratched his chin. "Well, not exactly."

"So you did intentionally put thoughts into my head."

"I suppose. But like I say… it's not like that. It isn't something I'm forcing onto you. We're just on the same wavelength, and I happen to…"

Reg frowned. "So do you have to be on the same wavelength to give someone a vision? You couldn't do it… by force? Say, against an opponent, someone you were fighting?"

Damon tilted his head toward Corvin. "Him?"

"No. Not Corvin. Worse than that."

"I could still do it. It would be more difficult if it was someone who wasn't… sharing a moment with me. But I could still do it if I had to. That would be… more of an assault, though. I wouldn't want to be censured for doing it."

"You're not in a coven, though. So you wouldn't be subject to discipline by them. And the non-magical police force wouldn't have anything to do with it. So how is a lone wolf censured? On a pillory in the public square?"

"There are methods for dealing with even lone wolves. I still have a job that I wouldn't want to lose. And I wouldn't want to be known in the community as someone who was breaking magical rules. People can be quite… hostile."

"I would imagine so."

Another car pulled up close. Reg watched Francesca climb out, her slim, graceful form attracting Damon's attention. Reg wondered what visions he might be putting into Francesca's head as she walked up to them. Corvin and Jessup got out of the car, and they formed themselves into a loose circle to discuss what was going on.

Reg looked around at everyone and waited for Corvin to begin the discussion. But Corvin looked at her and raised his eyebrows, inviting her to start. She didn't know whether that was because she was the only one there who knew everyone, or just because he didn't want to expose himself to criticism. Reg took a deep breath and looked down at her feet.

"So… here's what we're dealing with. A guy is operating out of this warehouse that we call the Witch Doctor. His name is…" She tried to dredge it up from her memory. "Uh… Samyr Destine—"

Francesca spit out what Reg could only assume was a Creole swear word or curse. Reg stopped talking and stared, not sure whether to go on or whether Francesca would explain further.

"I thought when I came here I would be leaving him behind!" Francesca said. "Are you saying he is here? Right here?" she pointed at the warehouse in front of them. "How could this be?"

"I—you know him?" Reg asked awkwardly.

"Yes, yes, of course, I know him. He is a very powerful bokor. He operated out of Haiti for a very long time, as long as one can remember. What is he doing here? I had hoped to escape his influence forever!"

"He's apparently smuggling magical artifacts. At least, that was what he was doing the last time we caught him. Or almost caught him," Jessup advised. "Just how familiar are you with him? You know him personally?"

"That is beside the point." Francesca waved this away with an angry gesture. "We need to get out of here—all of us. There is no way to fight his influence ourselves. We must leave here before we are all ensorcelled by him."

"We can fight him, and that's just what we're going to do," Corvin said calmly. "Between us, we have the tools to do it, isn't that what your friend Harrison said, Reg?"

Reg nodded.

"Harrison?" Francesca repeated. "Who is that?"

"He is… a friend of mine who knows the Witch Doctor."

"And where is he, when there is trouble? Why is he not here to fight?"

"He said that he is not allowed to harm the Witch Doctor."

"Then he is one of them?" Francesca shook her head. "You cannot trust their kind. This is just like them, to play their little games with the mortals and then to disappear when there is a real danger. They are never here when they are needed. Always they are gone." Her lips were tight, her movements jerky. Reg could feel her anger like electricity in the air.

"He said that we have all we need," Reg tried to keep her voice calm like Corvin's. It wasn't even her fight, so why was she getting involved?

But deep down, Reg knew that it *was* her fight more than it was any of theirs. She was the one who knew the Witch Doctor and had faced him before. She was the one the Witch Doctor knew and recognized.

"So what exactly is it that we have?" Damon questioned reasonably.

"Well, we have the police and a warrant so that we can get in," Corvin began, gesturing to Jessup. "Once we are inside, I should be able to access the powers of the magical objects that he is smuggling. That will give us a great deal of power, and gifts that we don't yet know of. We have Reg," he indicated her as if everybody didn't already know who she was. "She has powerful psychic gifts." He met her gaze. "Even stronger than she knows. She has a connection with the Witch Doctor and can pinpoint and communicate with him. She can lead us to where he is and keep him talking and distracted." He gave a little shrug. "Psychically, that is. Then we were advised to bring the two of you as well. Damon has the ability to detect lies and to give visions. I'm not sure how those powers will come into play, but they are apparently important. Unless there is some other gift that you have that you have been holding back and not telling anyone about?"

Damon shrugged and didn't suggest anything. "Lighting objects on fire, maybe?" Corvin suggested.

Damon looked at Reg, brows drawn down. "I'm not the one who can light fires."

Corvin went on. "And then we have Francesca, who Harrison referred to as a charmer."

She nodded.

"Again, I'm not sure what benefit there is to having a charmer with us, but it is apparently important. Harrison said that we were all needed to make this work. But he said that with all of us together, we have the tools needed to fight the Witch Doctor."

"And *win?*" Francesca demanded. "Because beings like him tend to miss the finer points—like that we could get killed in the process. It's all a joke to them, watching the mortals play games. Did he say that we could defeat the Witch Doctor? Or just that we could fight him?"

Corvin looked at Reg. She tried to remember his exact words, but couldn't be sure.

"He said that we could win," she said firmly. They needed as much confidence as they could get. Telling them that she didn't know for sure if they could defeat the Witch Doctor was not the way to go in with a winning attitude.

She saw the doubt flicker across Damon's face at her lie and hoped that no one else had.

"So is everyone ready?" Corvin asked. "Waiting will not prove efficacious in this fight. We need to go in, attack without warning, and have the advantage of surprise."

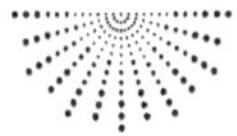

# CHAPTER TWENTY-SEVEN

"You, uh, might have forgotten to mention one thing," Reg said.

"What?" Corvin's tone was irritated. Here he was, ready to bust the doors down without even a plan, without even having briefed his companions appropriately. He must have really been champing at the bit to get his hands on the hoard of magical artifacts that the Witch Doctor was piling up in the warehouse.

"The draugrs."

"Oh." Corvin stopped, and looked at Damon and Francesca, making a face. "Yes. As well as the Witch Doctor, we will be facing his draugar as well."

Francesca rolled her eyes. "That might be an important thing to know. How long has he been raising draugar?"

"We don't know for sure. We've only been aware that was what he was doing for a few days, but it was probably some time before that."

"How many are there?"

Corvin looked over at Reg as if hoping she might have a different number this time.

"Nine," Reg said. "They're probably not all in there. They weren't all in one place last time I checked, but I'm too close right now to discern anything but the cloud around the Witch Doctor. So… hopefully less than nine that we have to deal with immediately."

"But once the fight starts, I'm sure they'll all be on their way," Corvin advised.

Francesca's face was white. Everyone else tried to look unconcerned, but they all knew that they were unlikely to win against that kind of a force, no matter what Harrison said.

"Nine draugar," Francesca said and muttered another curse under her breath. "You know how to pick them, don't you?"

Corvin gave an embarrassed shrug.

"And what form are they in? Human, giant, or kattakyn?"

"We don't know. At least one of them went inside in cat form, but I don't know if he stayed that way. Or what form the others are in. I assume if they are helping the Witch Doctor with physical labor, they must be in human or giant form."

"It will be important to get them into kattakyn form if possible."

Reg looked at Corvin and then back at Francesca. "And how are we supposed to do that? What makes them go into cat form?"

"When they feel the need to hide or take flight, they will shift to kattakyn," Francesca advised. "I will try to entice them as I can. But against so many… I don't know if I will be able to do it. Destine will do his best to keep them in giant form, as that is the most physically powerful. He must be distracted." Francesca pointed to each of Reg, Jessup, and Damon in turn. "That will be your job. Distract Destine in any way you can."

"Okay." That was at least something that Reg could wrap her mind around. "What kinds of things will distract him?"

"That is not my job. That is yours."

Helpful.

"So are we ready?" Corvin asked again.

"Who is going to open the door? Are we going to break it in? Pick the lock? Charm it?" Reg looked from Jessup to Corvin.

"I don't have a battering ram with me, so picking or charming it would be the best. Can you do that?" Jessup addressed this to Corvin.

"Not exactly my area of specialty."

Damon and Francesca didn't offer any suggestions.

"Oh, good grief." Reg pushed past Corvin and got back into her car.

"Regina!" Corvin protested, thinking she had decided to leave.

"Watch and learn," Reg advised.

She buckled her seatbelt, put the car into gear, and, aiming for one of the bay doors at the back of the warehouse, mashed the gas pedal. The car lurched forward, tires squealing for grip on the asphalt, and then headed straight for the door. Reg squinted her eyes almost-shut as she got closer, braced for impact, and drove straight in through the door.

It wasn't as bad as she had thought. Not like driving into a brick wall. The metal of the door burst open like a piece of paper, admitting her car with a long squeal.

Reg sat there for a moment to make sure that she was still in one piece. The airbag hadn't even deployed. She unbuckled her seatbelt and got out. The others ran in through the hole in the door, shouting to her and each other.

"Reg, what do you think you're doing?" Jessup demanded, grabbing her by the arm.

"I'm getting us inside. You forgot your battering ram."

"Well… you could have been hurt! And this definitely isn't something I am going to get commended for in a report!"

"I don't particularly care about your report at this point. I want to deal with this and hope that we survive."

Jessup made a face, but it was apparent she didn't have an argument. She kept her hand on her sidearm and looked around, waiting for the draugrs to burst in on them.

There was no clear leader in the group, everyone looking at everyone else for direction. Reg pointed to the loading dock a few steps up. "I assume we go that way."

There was nowhere else to go. They all advanced. There was

nowhere to hide, nothing to shelter behind. Once they got into the warehouse proper, there would hopefully be pallets of crates to hide behind.

They variously climbed or jumped up to the loading dock platform and entered.

Corvin was drawn like a magnet to the nearest stack of boxes. They were not uniformly-sized packing crates like Reg had pictured, but various boxes, crates, and chests of every description.

Reg followed closed behind Corvin. "Can you feel them now?"

She didn't need to ask. His eyes were glazed. He reached out toward the nearest box and put his hands flat against the side. With an animal-like growl, he shoved it off of the stack, and it went crashing to the concrete floor. The wooden sides broke open and the artifacts spilled out.

Reg averted her eyes at first, half-expecting to see dismembered animal parts as she remembered the endangered species smuggling that was part of the Witch Doctor's business. But she looked back, and it just seemed like garage-sale items. Old urns and bowls and oddly-shaped sculptures. She reached over to pick up an urn to examine it, and Corvin shoved her roughly out of the way.

"Do not touch anything!" he snapped. "Some of them may be cursed, and you do not know how to counter such things!"

Reg flushed with embarrassment. Of course he was right. She didn't have any idea how to sense or fight any curses that might have been cast on the objects. She was, once again, rushing right into the thick of things without any idea of what she was up against.

At least Jessup was still right with her. Jessup was more cautious and liked to check for traps before rushing into danger.

Not that that meant they were safe. They were intentionally entering the Witch Doctor's domain, right at the heart of his enterprise.

Corvin was occupied with the treasures. Greedily touching

each item, his face lit up in rapture. Reg swallowed and moved away from him, repulsed. She looked at the others. "Okay, so he's doing what he's supposed to be doing. Sucking up powers. How about the rest of us?"

"Distraction," Damon reminded her.

"Right."

They walked down one of the aisles. "Can you sense where he is?" Jessup asked Reg. "I assume you have some idea where we're going?"

Reg took a deep breath. She had been fighting against feeling for the Witch Doctor, knowing that as soon as she could contact him, he would see and feel her. And then she wouldn't be able to control anything else that happened. Harrison had already told her that he wasn't going to do anything that would harm the Witch Doctor, so it was up to her and her friends, hoping that their little bit of magic would be enough to fight the tremendous force of the Witch Doctor.

At least Francesca seemed to have some idea of what they were up against. But Reg wasn't sure that made her feel much better.

A shadowy figure loomed up ahead of them.

"Draugr," Reg warned, flicking a hand toward it. Definitely in giant form, he had to be nine or ten feet tall. The others looked at it and then at each other. "Distraction is my job," Reg reminded them. "Not casting spells."

She looked back for Corvin to see if he was joining them, newly empowered and willing to take on the Witch Doctor and his minions. But there was no sign of him.

"Go that way," Francesca instructed, motioning to an adjacent aisle. Reg turned, and Jessup and Damon with her, but Francesca was apparently not going with them. They were down another fighter; only the distraction squad was left.

It was time for Reg to do what she was there for. She closed her eyes and focused on the Witch Doctor. He wasn't far away. She was already in his shadow. She felt his attention turn to her, startled.

"It's the child again," he purred, "I'm so glad you have returned."

"I'm not a child any longer," Reg told him. Though she knew that the longer-lived races certainly considered her one with less than a century to her name. If the Witch Doctor was some kind of immortal, as Harrison and Francesca had implied, then she undoubtedly was a child to him.

"And you are here without your guardian. Making yourself a gift to me."

"No. I'm here to battle you."

His laugh was rich and deep. Reg could see him in her mind, just as he had been the day when her mother was killed. He had been looking for something. Reg didn't know what. He had employed torture as a means to get the information that he had wanted, but he didn't leave it at that. Even when he knew that her mother did not have what he was looking for, he had continued the torture until she had given up the ghost. He had reveled in it.

"You killed my mother."

The laugh continued. "Yes, I did, didn't I? A tasty morsel. Silly, weak humans. Why do you think you can stand up to a being as powerful as I? Your bravery is… inspiring, but misguided."

"Why did you do it? What were you looking for?"

Something niggled at the back of Reg's mind. What had Norma Jean said? Had she told the Witch Doctor something that night? Or had she told Reg, as a little child, something she was supposed to remember? She couldn't quite put her finger on it. She swore to herself.

"Why would I be looking for something?" the Witch Doctor asked.

"You were," Reg insisted. She was sure of that. He had not been there just to hurt her mother. Had he been looking for Reg herself? Reg had been hidden away by Harrison's protection spell, but she didn't think that she was what he had come for. She would have been another tasty morsel for him, but she was so insignificant.

"You think that with my powers I cannot find whatever I want?" the Witch Doctor bragged. "Your limited vision is laughable."

"I know where it is," Reg bluffed.

She felt an immediate shockwave back from the Witch Doctor. He was *still* looking for whatever he had been all of those years ago. Was that what he was filling the warehouse with? He was looking for some powerful object?

But she was wrong. It wasn't a thing. It was a *person*. Norma Jean had tried to tell Reg.

"I know where Weston is."

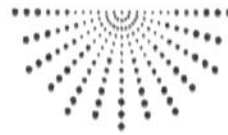

# CHAPTER TWENTY-EIGHT

Immediately, it was as if all of the Witch Doctor's power coalesced around him, like an inverse explosion. Reg watched the darkness gather to form his human body in front of them, a tall black man with long, thick dreadlocks. His eyes burned with fire. Reg could feel her companions draw back, trying to pull her back with them. Jessup was firing her gun. Reg resisted, facing the evil man she had previously cowered before. This was her chance to get revenge for what he had done to her mother and for pursuing her for so many years as a child, from one home to another.

"Weston?" shouted the Witch Doctor. "Where is Weston?"

"What's the matter, Sam?" Reg asked impudently. "I thought you were all-powerful. I thought you knew everything. You could find whatever you were looking for."

He strode toward her, physically intimidating. But he wasn't close enough to touch her.

"You are an ignorant child. You have no idea of our ways! You do not know anything."

Reg imagined the protection spell that Harrison had put around her as a child and in the restaurant. It made his power seem farther away, providing a little comfort. She had the upper hand now. At least for a few minutes, he had to figure out whether she had the knowledge he desired before he could kill her.

He would undoubtedly torture her just as he had Norma Jean. Not that he needed any physical torture when he could reach into her mind and wrench out the information he needed.

Except he wouldn't find it there. She hadn't any idea who Weston was, much less where he was.

But she knew all she needed to; she had distracted him. He was no longer paying any attention to his draugrs or the tiny mortals invading his territory. He wanted to know what Reg knew. She split her attention between the Witch Doctor and her friends. It was easy, now that he was in front of her and she didn't have to worry about accidentally attracting his attention.

Corvin was still somewhere behind them, growing in power. She could feel him strengthening himself. And she could see the draugr individually now, those who weren't already at the warehouse homing in on it, obviously having been called to duty.

The Witch Doctor stalked around her, looking at her, pushing at her mind.

"You do not know anything. You are only mouthing words."

"That's what you say," Reg said with a shrug. She tried to build up the forces of her mind, to put a wall around her brain so that he couldn't dig into it and confirm what he already suspected. "Do you think that after all of these years I wouldn't have investigated it for myself? That I would accept what happened to my mother and not try to find out why? You have a very limited understanding of humans, don't you?"

He prowled back and forth, angry and restless.

"You thought that humans were not worth learning about. They were just vermin and couldn't affect anything you did. But we're not. We can be strong too. We can squeeze through the cracks like bugs and listen and learn and get more powerful."

She was teasing him, seeing how long she could keep him

believing that she had the knowledge that he needed. Until Corvin was strong enough to strike, or at least to make an attempt. Long enough for Francesca to try her charms on the draugrs.

"Humans *are* bugs," the Witch Doctor hissed. "They are nothing more than little worms to be crushed. They have bodies and minds as weak as any animals. Put here on the earth just for our amusement. Put here to do with as we please, because they have no defenses, no way to fight back against us. They *never* have."

"Never?" Reg challenged. She reached for what mythologies she knew. If the fairy tales and the myths that Corvin had spoken of were true at their core, then she should be able to draw some inspiration from them. Humans fighting against immortals? She knew a few stories, but would it be enough?

She could feel Damon next to her again. She wasn't sure if he had moved closer again physically, or if he were nudging her mentally, trying to get her attention. She tried to open herself up to him to see what he wanted.

He was ready to help if there was anything he could do. Reg wasn't sure if she could tell him what she needed from him without addressing him directly. Had she been speaking with the Witch Doctor in her mind or aloud? Had the others been able to hear what they were saying? Or at least what Reg had been saying?

She was careful to speak out loud with her next words. "You are telling me that humans have never challenged immortals? They have fought them through the ages. Hercules, Perseus, Odysseus. They've all fought against monsters and immortals who were more impressive than you. They proved long ago that humans are more than capable of fighting any force that opposes them. Look at how we have spread over the earth now. We're not just a weak little tribe anymore."

She could see the images that Damon started to feed to the Witch Doctor based on her words. Rich pictures of the Greeks she had mentioned and their great battles. She could hear the roar of war and taste the tang of the sea. And the vast tapestry of humanity covering the earth, billions upon billions of human beings, living out their lives, oblivious to the immortals they had squeezed out.

"Stories written by the losers!" the Witch Doctor roared. "Pap! Children's fairy stories!"

"Haven't you ever heard that history is written by the victors?" Reg asked. "It isn't the losers who write the account of what happened; it is the winners. And you don't want to admit that the humans are the ones who beat the immortals. Where are the rest of you? You are living among us, pretending to be one of us so that you cannot be vanquished? You are the one who is hiding. It isn't the helpless little humans that cower and creep into the crevices to hide from your power. You are the one hiding from us."

"I have no reason to hide!"

"No? Then where are the gods and other immortals now? Is it just you? You're the only one who is left? You must be very lonely all by yourself."

He took another step toward her, pulling his hand back in a threat to hit her. "You think I can't kill you with a single blow? Will that be my lesson to the humans today? I can still crush you. I could crush you a thousand years ago, and I can still crush you today!"

Reg took a steadying breath, watching for his attack. She tried to strengthen the wall she had put around herself, but she knew it was pitifully weak compared to what someone like Harrison or even Corvin could construct. She had no idea how it was done. She was like a child building a house out of sticks.

"We are weak?" It was Corvin's voice that rang out behind them. Reg didn't turn to look at him, afraid to take her eyes off of the Witch Doctor and leave herself vulnerable to attack. "Do you think that I am weak now?"

The Witch Doctor recoiled. He attempted to gather his power into his physical form, but he had already done that, and there was nothing more to gather. He turned fractionally away from Reg, his eyes on Corvin.

Reg could feel Corvin approaching from behind her. He was strong, but was he strong enough? Had he left his feeding too early, driven by his sense of duty toward Reg and the others? She tried to weigh the two of them and to sense the balance between them, but it was impossible. Both were strong beyond her ability to comprehend.

"My hoard!" the Witch Doctor hissed. "You have no right to consume my hoard!"

"No right?" Corvin laughed. "Who is making up the rules now? That is what I was born for. That is what I have been seeking to do all my life. My lifespan may be short compared to yours, but I am in my prime. I will continue to drain every last bit of power from these magical trinkets, and I will leave nothing for you! Might makes right. I will be stronger than you. You will be the worm that I crush into the ground."

A tidal wave of visions came from Damon, so real that Reg couldn't sense what was true and what was imagined anymore. Corvin and the Witch Doctor in battle, hurling magical darts at each other, trying to overpower and crush each other. Corvin the victor, triumphing over evil.

The Witch Doctor fought back against the visions, pushing them away. He apparently knew where they came from and advanced on Damon, blasting him with a powerful blow that sent him crashing to the floor to lie there unmoving, unconscious or dead, disabled from feeding any more visions to the Witch Doctor or the rest of them.

"You are liars! Liars and thieves! These things are not yours to consume! You do not have the right to my treasures! And you!" He whirled around to face Reg again. "You are the weakest of all. You don't know where Weston is. Weston is gone the way of the earth decades ago. If he were not, he would have returned to protect his blood. Since he did not, he is either a coward, or he is gone from the earth! He is not here to protect you any longer. He was never there for you when you needed him. He is a coward and a weakling!" The Witch Doctor roared his imprecations and looked around him as if waiting for the building to fall around him or for some other opponent to attack. As if he were daring Weston, whoever he was, to appear and fight him.

But there was no appearance. Not from the mysterious Weston and not from Harrison. There was no one coming to their aid.

Corvin closed in. "Are you going to fight? Or are you going to hide? Fight or retreat, because those are your only two options. Do you dare to challenge me now, in my glory? You have failed. You have no more treasure. Your monsters have been defeated."

The Witch Doctor retreated a couple of steps and then held his ground. "You are mortal. You have not defeated me!"

"Only a mortal could defeat you," Corvin countered. "And here I am. It's time to face your fate."

And then Reg was caught in the middle of a chaos of spells. Unlike the picture that Damon had painted, it was an uncontrolled war of forces that buffeted Reg and forced her to the ground. She looked around for shelter and saw Jessup also on the concrete floor of the warehouse beside her. She grabbed Jessup's arm, and two of them slithered out of the aisle, trying to find some shelter between crates that clearly were not up to the task.

While the Witch Doctor and Corvin didn't appear to touch each other, there were crashes and explosions that felt like they would tumble the warehouse to the ground. Jessup shouted something to Reg, but she couldn't hear what it was. She put her ear right up to Jessup's mouth, straining to hear her over the war going on just inches away from them.

"Damon!" Jessup pointed toward the other warlock, on the floor a few feet away from them. He was gray and still. Reg's stomach turned, fearing it was already too late to protect him.

She nodded at Jessup, and the two of them dashed back out, each grabbed an arm, and with the adrenaline pumping hard through their veins, dragged him back to the sheltered space between boxes. Reg turned her attention back to the fight as Jessup bent over Damon, examining him.

Corvin was stronger than he ever had been, but was that really enough for him to defeat an immortal? How strong was the Witch Doctor? Did immortality mean limitless powers? Or was he still vulnerable to the powers of another?

# CHAPTER TWENTY-NINE

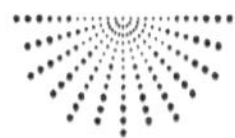

Reg peeked out from her shelter to see how Corvin was faring, though she wasn't sure how she would be able to tell one way or the other. Whether she used her natural eyes or her psychic abilities, she didn't know what she would be able to see.

There were still crashes and shouts, and the air around them vibrated with magical activity. Corvin had his back to her so that she couldn't see his face, but he was glowing with power. Closing her eyes, she could feel him still drawing power from the artifacts in the boxes and crates around him.

He was walking toward the Witch Doctor one forced step at a time, as if he were fighting against a strong wind.

There was a subtle shift in the flow of power to Corvin. The flow from the magical objects slackened like there was a blockage, with Corvin sucking it toward him with increased force, but it was stuck, the suction power building to the point where it almost hurt her ears.

Corvin closed the remaining distance between himself and the Witch Doctor and reached toward him. Reg clenched her teeth and braced herself, remembering the electrical charge she felt when Corvin touched her, and the feeling of opposing magnetism she had felt when she had been in the pixies' shadow-land and had tried to touch someone in the visible world. She expected to see one or both of them jolt with the pain of contact.

But there was no sudden shock when Corvin touched The Witch Doctor. Instead, the stoppered feeling released, and rather than drawing power from the magical artifacts, Reg realized that Corvin had been trying to draw power from the Witch Doctor himself. Once in physical contact, he was successful. The Witch Doctor's head fell back and the magical power flowed from him to Corvin. The Witch Doctor was still on his feet, but it was clear he was utterly in Corvin's thrall. Jessup swore. Reg looked over at her and saw that she too was peeking out at Corvin and the Witch Doctor, her eyes wide and round.

Reg hesitated, unsure whether the fight was now over and it was safe to come out of her hiding place.

There was a starburst of energy from the Witch Doctor, and then he dropped from Corvin's grasp to the floor. The warehouse was eerily quiet for a few seconds. Reg scrambled out.

"You did it!" She was amazed. The human form of the Witch Doctor lay collapsed on the floor, unmoving. She could detect no energy or magical force from him. But then she realized she could still feel it, just not from the Witch Doctor.

"Regina." Corvin reached out his hand to her.

Reg didn't need Jessup's shout to warn her not to let Corvin touch her. She flinched back from him.

"I told you I could do it," Corvin gloated.

"He's not gone—" Reg warned, "—the draugrs!"

His gaze had been focused tightly on her, but at her words, he suddenly looked around, like a dog scenting the air, and realized she was right. He swore and started moving toward the area where the draugrs were gathering. Reg followed close behind him, though she wasn't sure how she was going to fight giant draugrs. She'd been told to distract the Witch Doctor, but now that that job was done—or seemed to be—what was she supposed to do?

She glanced back at Jessup, who appeared to be torn between following them and tending to Damon.

"Stay with him!" Reg shouted back. Jessup had little magic; there wasn't any point in putting her in more danger. She would be in charge of cleaning up and explaining everything to the authorities once they were done.

If they succeeded.

"Why are they massing together?" Reg asked Corvin. "Shouldn't they be spreading out and looking for us?"

"Maybe they have something else in mind."

Reg didn't like the sound of that. She tried not to imagine what they might be gathering together for, but she couldn't help it. She imagined them consolidating their bodies into one huge draugr that could consume them all.

They slowed and crept along the side of the aisle, trying to approach without alerting the draugrs to their presence. Corvin peeked quickly around the corner then ducked back again. He looked at Reg, chuckled, and shook his head.

"What?"

"Have a look."

He and Reg switched places, and Reg took her quick peek. It was a moment before she could process what she had seen. The draugrs were gathering in their kattakyn form, a small group of midnight-black kittens. Reg hadn't been able to feel the Witch Doctor's aura in the cats before, but something had changed when he had sent his energy out, and she could now feel his malevolence even in the kattakyns.

And the thing that was attracting all of them to one place was not the opportunity to combine their powers into one giant, vengeful automaton, but the calls of the fair Francesca. She called to them coaxingly, reaching out her hands, encouraging them, speaking lovingly to them.

Reg bit her knuckle to keep from crying out when Francesca touched them, knowing how full of the Witch Doctor's evil they were and worried about the effect they would have on her.

Francesca petted them, scratched their ears and chins, and let them rub against her. Reg saw Francesca counting them. She called one that was lurking in a corner, watching but not approaching. Her voice was a gentle, melodious purr, so attractive that even Reg felt like following the coaxing voice to its owner. Gradually, the last cat made its cautious way over to Francesca.

Her song changed perceptibly when they had all joined her. Her hands seemed to have purpose rather than just petting and scratching them. It was as if she were gradually wrapping a long, invisible thread around them, binding them to her. The malevolent force of the Witch Doctor started to diminish until Reg could no longer perceive it.

Reg rounded the corner cautiously. Francesca, crouched on the floor, looked up at her.

"It is quite safe," she assured.

"How did you do that? *What* did you do?"

Francesca raised her brows. "I am a charmer. I charmed them."

"And… is this permanent? They won't turn back into the other forms? The Witch Doctor can't re-form?"

She shrugged delicately. "It will last for at least a thousand years. Unless someone is to gather them together and unbind them." Francesca rose, one of the black cats in her arms, purring away like the most contented kitten. "We will need to find them new homes, of course. Preferably on different continents. That will make it less likely for the spell to be undone."

Corvin was coming up behind Reg. She turned, wary of him.

"You've been fed," she warned, "you shouldn't even care about my powers anymore."

He was still glowing, his cheeks fuller than they had been, eyes very bright. "I left room for dessert."

Reg laughed and shook her head. "No way. Stay away from me."

She could smell the roses and feel the same kind of magnetism that she had felt from Francesca when she was calling the kattakyns. A desire to cuddle up in his arms and be in his control.

She tried to raise the wall of protection that she had used against the Witch Doctor. She was getting weak, and she was still only trying to imitate the feeling of Harrison's spell, but the pull toward Corvin slackened slightly.

"There are more artifacts here. You can't have used all of them yet."

"No. But human powers are always more satisfying than those that have been forced into an object."

"Stay away."

"Regina…"

"I mean it. I'll call Harrison."

His expression turned sulky. "And do you think he will be stronger than the Witch Doctor? I banished one, why not more?"

Francesca looked at Corvin and shook her head. "Your power is not without limits. I would not battle a second immortal in one day."

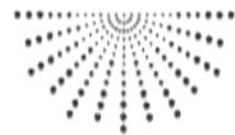

# CHAPTER THIRTY

Reg hurried back to where Jessup was watching over Damon. "Is he okay? If he's dead because I asked him to come and help with this thing…"

Jessup shook her head. "It's not looking good, Reg. Where's Corvin? He might be able to help."

"He was supposed to be right behind me." Reg looked back over her shoulder. "Chatting up cat-girl, no doubt. Corvin!"

Corvin was not quick to saunter into sight. He looked at the other warlock on the floor and made his way over to them casually, looking unconcerned.

"Can you do something?" Jessup asked.

Corvin knelt next to Damon's prone body and held his hands over him. Reg had seen him do this before, both to help her and to help Sarah. He wouldn't be able to complain that he'd been depleted of too much energy this time. Not with the amount that he'd already absorbed and what was still available in the artifacts. Reg watched Damon's face for some sign of improvement. He was pale gray and lay so still that Reg would have doubted he had any life in him. Jessup kept her fingers on Damon's wrist.

Reg thought she saw some color coming back into Damon's face, but maybe it was just what she wanted to see. "You should call for help," she told Jessup. "There's no more Witch Doctor or draugrs, so it should be safe, right? Get some police to secure the place and bring an ambulance in?"

Jessup nodded, not looking at Reg. "I'd rather let Corvin do his thing… and then we need a story to explain this."

"A story that will satisfy the non-practitioners is not going to be easy." Reg rolled her eyes.

"You're telling me."

Damon stirred and opened his eyes. He stared up at them glassily.

"Hey." Reg pushed his hair back from his face, smiling. "How are you feeling?"

Damon groaned. "Not so good. What happened?"

"Well, you were crushed by an immortal," Corvin contributed cheerily. "Most people wouldn't survive that."

"Is he okay?" Jessup demanded.

"Lots of broken bones and internal bleeding. That's not easy to heal in a couple of minutes."

"But will he be okay?"

Corvin nodded, the corners of his mouth lifting. "Thanks to my enhanced powers, yes. Give him a few minutes to get his bearings. Being as good as dead, even for a few minutes, takes something out of a person."

Damon coughed and winced. "I'll be fine," he assured them.

Reg and Jessup continued to sit with Damon and tend to him, much to Corvin's disgust. As far as he was concerned, they should be lavishing their attention on him and giving Damon some space to recover and slink off back to his car.

In a few minutes, Damon was sitting up, leaning on one of the crates. Reg was glad to see more pink in his complexion. He had been gravely hurt, and they did owe Corvin thanks for that. And for his battle with the Witch Doctor. As annoying as it was to owe gratitude to someone so full of himself, he had been the only one who could have gathered enough strength to face the Witch Doctor in battle and even to be able to steal his powers, however much Corvin had managed to take from him.

"What happened?" Damon asked. "Did Corvin kill the Witch Doctor? Did he run away?"

"Corvin battled him until he gave up his mortal form," Jessup explained. "And then…?" She looked at Reg.

"He sent his… power… into the draugrs. I assume the idea was that he could still control them and make them attack us. And then… he'd gather himself into one place again? I don't know."

"And Corvin killed the draugrs?" Damon shook his head, which made him look a little wobbly. "I thought you had to chop off their heads… Even Corvin couldn't chop off nine draugr heads, could he?"

Corvin was still standing close enough to hear them. "I could have," he argued, "if I'd had to."

"I thought that was the only way to defeat them for good."

"Francesca charmed them into cat form and called them to her, and then she performed some spell… I'm not sure exactly what, but she bound them. So now the Witch Doctor can't re-form and use his powers unless someone reunites all of the cats and unbinds them."

"Sounds like a plan," Damon breathed. "I guess your friend was right; you really did need all of us."

* * *

Damon and Corvin had both gallantly offered to escort Reg home, but she refused them both. She wasn't sure that Damon was fully recovered, and she should probably have accompanied him home to make sure that he got there safely. But she didn't offer, not wanting to insult his manhood.

And of course, she had refused Corvin because he was Corvin and she didn't want to have to defend herself against his charms and advances. As powerful as he had made himself, she didn't know how she was going to be able to resist him. She might have to leave town just to stay away from him. The little tricks she was learning to fend him off were helpful, but she feared they would be too weak to keep him away with his newly enhanced powers. Harrison had been able to walk past the wards that guarded her cottage without even a flicker; if Corvin had taken the same powers from the Witch Doctor, then how was Reg going to keep him out of her house?

Reg walked slowly down the path through the yard to her cottage, trying to comprehend all that had happened in the last few days. It seemed like the more she learned about magic in the world, the less she knew about anything. All that she had once believed to be true seemed like just a veneer placed over a chaotic world to make it seem sane and organized.

There was a movement in the garden. Reg froze. She reached out with her mind, trying to identify who or what it was before going any farther. She saw a lithe, black shape, and realized it was one of the kattakyns. Her heart raced and she looked for some escape. Had she miscounted? Were there more draugrs than she had thought? Had the Witch Doctor been able to raise more of them in those final moments when they thought they had him bound forever?

The cat looked at her, head cocked, and Reg felt a familiar warmth. She breathed out in relief.

"Nicole," she said in a voice barely above a whisper. "Come here, Nicole. Do you want to come inside? Do you want to see Starlight?"

Nicole kept looking at her, not running away, but not getting any closer.

"Come on," Reg invited again. She tried to send Nicole thoughts of warmth and food and companionship. "It's safe now. You can come visit with Starlight, and I'll call Francesca."

Reg inched forward, trying to move so slowly that Nicole wouldn't even detect her movement. She would get to the cottage and open the door, and Nicole would be curious enough to enter. Reg could rest easy, knowing that Nicole was finally safe. And hopefully, Nicole would be the last black cat who crossed her path in Black Sands for a long time.

Reg unlocked the door and opened it slowly. "Starlight," she called in the same low, coaxing voice. "Nicole is here. Call her into the house. She'll come when she hears you."

There was an extended purr-meow from inside the cottage, similar to that of a mother cat calling her kitten, followed by a more musical yowl that made Reg's arm hairs stand on end. Nicole's ears perked up, pointing sharply toward the cottage. She eyed Reg, trying to judge her safety. Reg continued to send warming feelings toward Nicole, reminding her of all of the perks of living as an indoor cat. Nicole took a few tentative steps toward the door, then dashed inside, too quick for Reg to grab her.

Reg stepped in and pulled the door shut behind her. She turned on the lights and smiled as the two cats touched noses.

* * *

Reg had been sleeping, exhausted after a long day of fighting draugrs and an immortal, as well as the rest of the energy she had spent on connecting over distance with Corvin to make sure he was alright. She was glad that the destruction of Black Sands had been averted. With the malevolent feelings of dread and doom gone, she knew that she would sleep for a long time.

But she had only been asleep for a couple of hours when she found herself awake again. She lay in bed for a while, listening for any disturbance, reaching out her psychic powers for anything that might be wrong farther afield. But she didn't sense anything wrong. She had just awakened because…

It wasn't Starlight. For once, he wasn't pacing around restlessly and yowling at the window. Now that he had spent some time with Nicole and knew that she was well and safe, he had settled down again. He hadn't appreciated being separated from her again by Francesca, but he hadn't pouted for long, and he was sleeping beside her, a warm, soft pressure against her leg.

She didn't think it was Sarah's comings and goings. She was getting used to Sarah's more active nightlife now that she was well again.

It was something else. She kept reviewing the things that Harrison and the Witch Doctor had said to her. Reminders of the past and the things that had happened to her when she was just a little child. And Norma Jean, curiously quiet since Reg had faced the Witch Doctor. Was it possible for a ghost to be traumatized by the reminder of something that had happened in her past? Or had the stress of the encounter with the Witch Doctor damaged Reg's mind, silencing Norma Jeans' voice again?

Reg closed her eyes as if she were going back to sleep again, but she didn't know who she was trying to fool. Did she think that if she approached it obliquely, she could 'sneak up' on Norma Jean and avoid scaring her into silence?

"Norma Jean, are you still there?"

She didn't say it aloud. Even a whisper would have been too much. And she didn't really want an answer. It was better if Norma Jean *was* silenced. Maybe this was what she had wanted all along, vengeance on the entity that had tortured and killed her. Now that he had been banished, she could rest in peace.

But Reg could still feel Norma Jean stirring. She didn't answer, but she was still there, attached to Reg.

"Who is Weston?" Reg asked her.

There was no answer.

Reg rubbed her forehead, massaging the psychic third eye position on her forehead. It was throbbing and all of the muscles in her face and skull felt tense. She should be sleepy and relaxed and fall back asleep again, but she shifted restlessly, unable to get comfortable.

"Who is Weston? And where is he?"

Norma Jean was silent.

**Did you enjoy this book? Reviews and recommendations are vital to making a book successful.**

**Please leave a review at your favorite book store or review site and share it with your friends.**

Don't miss the following bonus material:
Sign up for mailing list to get a free ebook
Read a sneak preview chapter
Other books by P.D. Workman
Learn more about the author

Sign up for my mailing list at pdworkman.com and get Gluten-Free Murder for free!

# PREVIEW OF THE TELEPATHY OF GARDENS

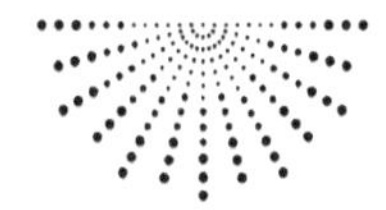

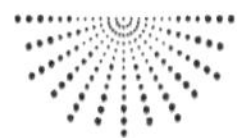

The kittens really were the cutest visitors Reg had ever had in the cottage. Nine pure-black little cats, they were almost impossible to tell apart. Yet they were each starting to show distinct personalities so that Reg could, in fact, tell one from the other. It was hard to believe that only days before, they had been draugrs, undead creatures raised by the Witch Doctor to do his bidding. Now, no one would guess that they had started their existence as zombies.

Francesca laughed as one little fellow chased her shoelace, so intent on it that Reg would have thought it really was a mouse or whatever kind of prey the cat imagined in his little kitty brain. "Come here, little kattakyn," blond-haired Francesca crooned in her Haitian Creole accent, "did you not hear Nicole tell you it was time to go bed? You are getting yourself all wound up instead of ready for sleep."

He continued to romp around her, pouncing on her shoelace and then darting back in retreat. Nearby, the kittens' surrogate mother, Nicole, patiently caught another of the kittens by the neck and wrestled it over to the pile where the others were washing or sleeping. They were too big for her to be bossing around, almost three-quarters her size, but she seemed determined that the little black cats were her own kittens and she would train them to obey her. She licked him and pressed him into place with the others, then approached the kitten that was playing with Francesca, making low meows and purrs as she called to him. He continued to jump at Francesca's shoelace and then retreat as if it were a dangerous snake.

"You are never going to get this one settled down," Francesca warned.

But Nicole was undaunted. She put one long foreleg over the kitten's shoulders, pinning him down, and then dug her teeth into the scruff of his neck to drag him over to the other kittens. While they were acting sleepy and getting ready for their naps, the last kitten was having nothing to do with it. He pounced on the nearest tail, then bit it, rousing one of the others. Nicole again pinned him with a foreleg, and then lay atop him, licking him soundly, forcing him to be still as she gave him a bath. The kitten wriggled and turned his head, but she kept a firm hold on him, all the while licking persistently until his eyes started to shut into slits and they were both purring in unison.

Reg shook her head, her thin red braids swinging around her face. "Well, I never would have thought she could do it. That little guy has ADHD if any kitten ever did. Always distracted by the nearest movement."

"Or shoelace," Francesca laughed.

"Well, you have to admit, it did look pretty lively."

Francesca shook her head, her tinkling laugh filling the room.

Reg felt relaxed and comfortable. She liked the aura that Francesca brought with her. Despite the logistics of bringing ten cats over to the cottage for a visit, Francesca never seemed to be frazzled. Nicole and the kittens themselves also brought a calming, happy presence into the house, like the warmth of a fire. After all of the dread and fear that Reg had suffered as the Witch Doctor raised his draugr army, Reg needed the beneficial feelings they brought.

Starlight was the only one who didn't seem happy with the

arrangements. It was understandable; the tuxedo cat with the mismatched eyes had been pining over Nicole since she had first appeared in the garden. Now that she was back inside and coming over for visits, she should have had plenty of time for him. But Nicole had been smitten with the kittens as soon as she had seen them and seemed oblivious to Starlight's advances.

"Don't you worry," Reg told Starlight, patting the seat of the upholstered couch beside her to invite him over. "The kittens will not be around forever. We need to find them all new homes. Then Nicole will have time for you."

He glared at her and washed his face, blaming her for the arrival of the furry interlopers.

It wasn't Reg's fault that the Witch Doctor had decided to make Black Sands his center of operations, nor that Francesca had charmed the draugrs into their kattakyn form and magically bound the Witch Doctor's life force that was dwelling within them. Reg hadn't wanted anything to do with the dark force from her past. She had been dragged into it by Corvin, much like the kittens being dragged by the scruff of their necks by Nicole.

It wasn't Reg's fault that she'd been recruited to protect Black Sands against zombies.

"We do need to find them new homes," Francesca agreed, watching the pile of black cats snoozing peacefully, Nicole on top of the pile looking very satisfied with herself. "It is vital that they are separated so that no one can unbind them. As long as they are kept apart from one another, Samyr Destine will not be able to re-form, and the world will be safe from him."

"Hard to believe that those little cats are all that separate Black Sands from the Witch Doctor's evil powers." Reg couldn't sense even a hint of the evil and dread that had accompanied the Witch Doctor. His force was completely suppressed by Francesca's spell. She and Corvin Hunter were the ones Black Sands owed their safety to. Without their powers, Reg and the others would easily have been killed, and the Witch Doctor would have gone on acquiring magical artifacts, gaining in strength, and raising more draugrs to do his bidding. Anyone who crossed his path or dared to stand up to him would be killed. It was a simple matter for a draugr to enter into its victim's dreams and to sit on his chest until he suffocated. Reg had only been spared that fate by Starlight's intervention. Reg wasn't sure how a real cat could fight off a dream cat that could kill despite not having real substance—but he had. The kattakyns were no longer dangerous, and it was easy to forget their origin, imagining instead that they were Nicole's natural kittens.

"How exactly are we going to find them homes all around the world?" Reg asked. "Is there some magical network that adopts cats?"

"These are very special cats," Nicole pointed out. "They will make good familiars. Even though the power of the bokor is bound, it is still there, and it will help to magnify the powers of the witch or warlock they are joined to."

"So is that a yes?"

"There is no magical network for cats," Francesca said, "but there are many people who will be happy to take one of these special cats. It is just a matter of finding the right homes. Not every cat is a good match for every practitioner."

Reg thought back to the day she had gone to the animal shelter and picked out Starlight. None of the other cats had responded to her the same way as Starlight. She knew that he was the cat she was supposed to have. The shelter worker's story of how Starlight had recently lost his old master and had not responded to anyone else who had approached him had sealed the deal. Reg needed a cat and he needed her. She hadn't anticipated just how compatible they would be. With the white star in the center of his forehead—his 'third eye,' as Sarah referred to it—his psychic powers were considerable. She was often surprised by how much he could boost her and enhance her psychic abilities when she needed a little extra help.

And he was furry and cute and lovely to cuddle up with when she was alone.

* * *

Starlight stopped washing and looked toward the window, his ears pricked forward.

"Someone out there?" Reg asked. Focusing her attention in the direction Starlight's ears pointed, she could sense Sarah Bishop, her landlord, along with someone else she wasn't familiar with. Sarah didn't seem to be headed toward Reg's door, so she wasn't bringing over a client or someone she wanted to introduce Reg to. Reg leaned over and pushed the curtain back an inch to see the two figures headed toward the garden. She only caught a glimpse of Sarah and the short man who was walking with her. Her seemingly middle-aged landlord was dressed in pink pants and a white shirt, with lots of pearls as accessories.

"Who is there?" Francesca asked.

"Sarah. Somebody else, maybe the new gardener."

"Good," Francesca approved. "That poor garden needs someone to take care of it."

Sarah had thrashed the garden with a broom when trying to shoo Nicole, then an unknown stray cat, out of the yard. The devastation caused by her impulsive act—the result of dementia caused by rapid aging—was significant. When Sarah had regained her health, she had attempted to rehabilitate the battered garden herself, but it was too much for her.

"Do you think I should go out and say hello?" Reg ventured, unsure what the proper etiquette was in a small town. She was only a tenant; Sarah was in charge of the yard and its upkeep, so it really wasn't any of her business.

Francesca shrugged. "You might introduce yourself. He is going to be working in your yard; it could be awkward if you keep walking by without saying anything."

"Okay. Makes sense," Reg agreed.

She got up and made her way to the garden back behind the house. Sarah was standing with the man, pointing out this and that. Reg wondered, looking at her newly-youthened face, whether she had also lost some weight with her transformation.

The gardener was quite short, probably suffering from some form of dwarfism. He was an old man with a wrinkled face and white beard. He had on green coveralls and a red cap. Reg couldn't avoid feeling his pain as he looked over the ruined garden.

Sarah turned, hearing Reg's approach. "Oh, Reg. Come and meet the gardener who is going to get my poor little garden back into shape again." She stretched her hand out in welcome and motioned toward the little man. "This is Mr. Blumenthal."

"Forst," the gardener introduced himself gruffly, holding out a calloused, stained hand.

Reg shook. He had a very strong grip—someone who had spent a lifetime working with his hands.

"I'm Reg Rawlins. I'm sorry this is such a mess." She gestured to the garden. She wasn't taking responsibility for the damage, of course, just acknowledging his pain at finding the plants in such poor condition. He cared very deeply about his work.

Forst gave a single nod. He looked back at Sarah for further instructions.

"Anyway," Sarah shrugged. "This is your area of expertise, so I don't have to tell you what needs to be done. Let me know if you can't find something you need. Come in for a cup of tea whenever you want one and have a break."

Reg was a little surprised that she was inviting a stranger into her house, especially with all of the trouble that a magical intruder could cause. But maybe Sarah had known him for a long time. Or maybe she had special wards or knew something about his magic or lack of it. It wasn't Reg's place to object. But she wouldn't be inviting him into her cottage.

"Nice to meet you," Reg told Forst. "Thank you for helping Sarah to get this fixed up. I know she'll be much happier once it is looking better again."

He gave another nod and said nothing.

Sarah walked Reg back to the cottage door. "Let me know if

you have any concerns," she said. "I don't want you to be disturbed by his work. If he is using a chainsaw during a seance… just let me know, and I'll take care of it."

"I'm sure it will be fine." As far as Reg could tell, there was no reason for Forst to be using any power tools. Sarah had beaten down the flowers and plants with a broom; it wasn't like Forst would need to cut down trees, and certainly not at midnight. He would be cleaning up the bits that were dead and maybe staking the plants that were bent over until they were strong enough to stand on their own again. But then, what did she know about gardening? The full extent of her plant-growing experience was planting beans for early school experiments. She'd never owned a houseplant, let alone tended a garden.

"He seems like a nice man," she told Sarah neutrally.

"They do tend to be very… laconic. Talk with each other, but not to outsiders."

"Outsiders?"

"Well, we aren't exactly his kind, are we?"

Reg came to a stop on her doorstep. "What exactly is his kind? Is he a fairy? A dwarf?"

Sarah laughed. "Fairies do have an affinity to nature and plants," she admitted, "but they are not likely to tend your garden for you. They are much too proud for that. They don't work for humans. And dwarves… you won't see them this near open waters. You're not likely to run into any dwarves outside the mountains, even in these modern times."

"Then what is he?"

"A gnome, dear." Sarah laughed again. "A garden gnome."

Reg had seen fake gnome statues in gardens, but she had no idea that they were really a thing. She shook her head at Sarah. "A garden gnome?"

"Of course. Who else would you get to rehabilitate a garden? A gnome will do it faster and with much better results than any other kind of expert. Those human landscapers that you can hire… well, they would take months to get my garden back to its natural glory. I would never hire a human to do a gnome's work."

"Of course not," Reg agreed dryly. "Who would do that?"

"Exactly," Sarah agreed. "Well, I shall leave you to your guest." A crease between her eyebrows, Sarah glanced at the living room window where Starlight was poking his head out between the curtains waiting for Reg's return. Reg wondered whether she could sense the other cats. Sarah would not have been happy to find so many cats in the cottage. She tolerated Starlight as Reg's familiar but had blanched at even the thought of a second cat around when Reg had started to look for Nicole.

Sarah had an African gray parrot and an affinity for birds, and she did not like cats.

* * *

Reg sat down again with Francesca. She looked at the cats all snoozing in a pile and picked up Starlight to give him some attention while she talked.

"So what do you need me for?" she asked Francesca. "It seems like you've got a pretty good handle on the market for the kattakyns. I don't know anything about giving cats away. I always wanted a cat as a kid, and I tried bringing abandoned kittens or stray cats home more than once, but that never worked out. Foster moms are usually overworked as it is, they don't need another mouth to feed or critter to look after. Even if I promised to take care of all of its needs, I could never convince anyone to let me have one. So I'm not sure how much help I would be to your case."

Francesca smiled, watching Reg pet Starlight, scratch his ears, and rub the white spot on his forehead. "It is not your marketing expertise that I am hoping for," she said with a lilt. "I am looking for someone who can help to match the kattakyns with the right owners. The ones who will suit them the best."

"Oh." Reg thought once more to her tour of the animal shelter, eventually finding Starlight there. She had found the cat that suited her the best or needed her the most, but was that a transferable skill? "I don't know. I've never done anything like that before."

"You are very good with the kittens," Francesca pointed out. "You can see their personalities. You can tell them apart."

"Well, yes, that's true. But they do have very distinct personalities; you've noticed that too, right?"

Francesca shook her head. She adjusted the lay of her sweater, looking uncomfortable. "No, I am afraid not… as much as I try, I only see nine little black cats. We want to be able to match them up with the practitioners who best suit them."

"Okay. Well, I guess I'll do my best."

"You want them to be happy in their new homes. We need them to stay put, not to roam around and find each other."

"Do you think that would happen? It wouldn't, would it? They would get lost, but they wouldn't be able to find each other. They wouldn't know where to go."

"They are bound together. They will eventually find each other. We want to keep that from happening for as long as possible. By placing them around the world, I hope to keep them apart for hundreds of years. The farther they are apart, the less chance there is of Samyr gathering enough power to reform himself."

Reg shuddered. "Okay, I'm in," she agreed.

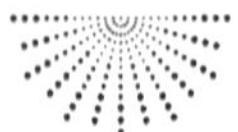

*R*eg helped Francesca carry the cats to her car in a couple of boxes. Since they were half-grown rather than small kittens, they couldn't all be corralled in a shoebox. They scrabbled around in the large boxes, their claws slipping on the slick cardboard. A couple of them started meowing, protesting their situation. They put the boxes on the back seat of the car. Reg smiled at all of the inquisitive black furry faces looking back at her. She pushed a couple down when they tried to climb up out of the boxes and sent them calm, reassuring thoughts. Eventually, they all settled.

Francesca nodded and got into the driver's seat. "Thank you, Reg! I will be in touch when I have had a chance to talk to some of the potential buyers. Then we can sort out which one to send where."

"Okay. Sounds good. Drive slow."

"I do not want to have any accidents with this cargo," Francesca agreed, taking a look over her shoulder at them.

After Francesca's car pulled out, Reg became aware she was being watched. She looked around and saw a white compact car. Not a surprise, since the town was full of white compacts, but she knew by the feeling that started to grow and thicken around her precisely who it was.

Corvin extricated himself from the small car and approached her. His handsome face was sullen. "I've been waiting half the day for you to get rid of that woman and her cats."

"Oh?" Reg gave a careless shrug. That was another bonus of a houseful of cats—it kept Corvin at a distance. "I don't remember you calling or mentioning that you wanted to come over."

He looked like he had tasted something sour. "That would probably be because you've blocked me on your phone."

Reg smiled. "Yeah, that's probably it."

"But I still know where you live. All that means is that I have to come over here in person, which is not exactly a hardship. I would rather see you face to face."

That was a drawback of cutting off phone communications. Reg would have to rethink that. It wasn't like she could get a restraining order to keep him from hanging around her house. He wasn't doing anything to threaten or harm her. Reg also had no desire to stand before a judge and plead her case. She made it a policy to stay as far as possible from police and courtrooms.

Corvin's eyes roamed around. "Why don't we go for a walk?"

He knew, of course, that she wouldn't allow him in her house. Not with his track record. It was dangerous to invite any unknown warlock into the house. All that much worse, one like Corvin whose dangers were known.

"I'm not going for a walk with you. Spit out what it is you want because I'm going back to my house and you're not going to stop me."

"There's no need to be so vehement about it."

"There is every reason."

"I just wanted to talk. You know I don't have very many options of who to talk to right now."

"It's not my fault you are being shunned."

"Well…" He raised his brows. "It is sort of your fault."

"You're the one who attacked me. If you mean it's my fault because I testified against you, then fine. It's my fault you're being shunned."

He didn't look pleased that she had agreed with him. He was looking for a fight. Looking to engage with her. Reg couldn't afford to let him work his wiles on her. She looked at her phone to see what time it was.

"So, what did you want to talk about? Do you actually have a purpose here, or are you just hanging around because you're bored?"

He took a step closer to her, into her comfort zone. Reg took a step back and tried to raise her psychic defenses against him. Sooner or later, he would make his move. She needed to be ready for it. He wouldn't be able to resist trying to magic her.

"I didn't say I was bored," Corvin said, staring into her eyes, his manner confidential and intense.

"Well, good. Then I guess you have plenty to do and don't need to bother me."

"Regina," he crooned her name, correctly pronouncing it, Reh JEE nah, not like the Canadian city. "When are you going to stop this dance? Just admit that the two of us are fated. Stop fighting every word and every move. I don't want to hurt you. I want us to be friends."

"You want a lot more than friendship, and I'm not going to give it to you."

He shifted his feet, looking for a more comfortable position. But he wasn't going to her cottage, they weren't going for a walk, and he was too far away from his car to lean casually against it. He could only stand there, out in the open where everyone could see him, talking with Reg. Because that was all she was going to let him do. As handsome as the dark warlock was, and however enticing he could become when he exercised his charms, she couldn't give in.

Corvin leaned closer. "You realize that things could change very quickly."

She didn't like his proximity. Was he making a threat? Having gained so much more power in his fight with the Witch Doctor, who knew what he could do now. Or was he suggesting something else?

"What things could change?" she asked cautiously.

"The Council is considering commuting my sentence."

Reg felt like she had been punched in the gut. After all of the pain and suffering she had gone through, after having to face the humiliation of testifying against him, they were going to let him get off that quickly? They had said that they would shun him until he proved he could be a positive member of their society. His sentence was indefinite, and Reg had thought that meant it would be long, not short.

"How can they do that?" she asked breathlessly.

"Our encounter with the Witch Doctor proved that I am a valuable asset to the magical community. We saved countless lives and bound a dark force that could have done unimaginable harm."

"You didn't exactly do it for altruistic purposes."

"Who is to say?" he countered with a smug smile. "When I tell the story to the Council members, it certainly will be."

"The only reason you went into that warehouse was so that you could have access to the magical artifacts and consume their powers."

"Not the only reason."

"And to prove that you could defeat a powerful being. An immortal, or whatever he was."

Corvin's smile just grew. Reg shook her head, sickened by his attitude and the thought that the warlock council might reinstate him so quickly. It was beyond belief. How had he been punished for what he had tried to do to her? He had gone against all of the rules imposed on his kind and tried to steal her powers from her by force. If they reinstated him so quickly, it would be a sign that they didn't care what he did. He could go on doing whatever he liked; they didn't care a bit about his victims.

"Reg…" He cocked his head, looking at her like she had hurt him by not being excited about his news. He made a pouty face. "Don't be that way. I don't harbor ill will toward you. We can be friends. Forget the past, and look forward to the future."

"To a future where you can have whatever you want because you're the strongest? Where you can break all of the rules and no one cares about it one bit?"

"Obviously, people care, or they wouldn't have disciplined me to begin with. But I've learned my lesson. I won't let my appetites get away from me again." He blinked and smiled encouragingly. "You and I can get along. Our powers are synergistic. They go together so well, matching each other strength for strength. The two of us together could defeat any foe."

"Oh, that's your new line, is it? Now that you've got the power, you're ready to use it. And it's not to protect all of the innocent citizens of Black Sands anymore. Now it is to defeat all foes and get what you want."

"That isn't what I said. Think of how many people could benefit if you and I combined our powers. Think of all of those people that you would like to be able to help. The two of us together could do almost anything. Think about all of your lost and broken dreams. All of those things that you used to want that you've given up on. You could have them all."

Reg shook her head, trying to rid herself of his influence, like a fly buzzing in her ear. He didn't understand anything about her childhood and her lost and broken dreams. He thought that she had dreamed of money and power. But in reality, she had dreamed of a loving family, stability, enough to eat, and a future. She was doing well in Black Sands, but it was only a matter of time until that dream ended too. They would come for her and she would have to run again if she wanted to avoid incarceration. She would be on the skids once more, looking for a home and a stable income somewhere else where people had never heard her name.

"Reg." He reached out to touch her cheek. "You look so sad. You can have anything. Think about it. Whatever you want."

She could feel his warmth even before his fingers touched her skin. She swallowed and closed her eyes, wishing that she could swim into the warm, safe feeling that he promised. But she knew how she would feel if she surrendered to him. When he was done with her and had stripped away all of her gifts, she would be left an empty husk, with a hollow, echoing space in her head that used to be filled with voices. She would be more alone than she had ever been before. She pulled back from his touch, forcing herself to withdraw instead of leaning into him.

"Corvin…" She rarely addressed him by name, rarely told him anything about her past or how she was feeling. "You have no idea what it's like for me."

She opened her eyes and looked at him. Corvin frowned, wrinkle lines forming between his eyes. He pulled back his hand. "Then tell me. I know what it's like to hold those powers. I don't know how you could be unhappy with the richness of the powers in your possession." It was his turn to look at her longingly. He had untold powers after consuming many of the magical artifacts at the warehouse and the powers of the Witch Doctor himself. Anyone else would have been satisfied with that. But not Corvin. He had to have it all. He had to have Reg's powers too.

"How could you still be hungry?"

He shrugged and chuckled. "You know how you can spend a couple of hours eating at a buffet, until you're absolutely stuffed, and still want the dessert afterward?"

"And I'm your dessert?"

"Well, not you, but your powers."

"It's the same thing. I don't want to be consumed. You don't know what it feels like."

"Oh, but I do," Corvin reminded her. He had told them all at his hearing how his father, also a power-drinker like him, had consumed his powers multiple times. Because Corvin could gain power from other people and magical objects, then unlike most of the practitioners in existence, he could have his powers stripped away more than once. Reg looked away from him, embarrassed to remember his vulnerability.

"If you know what it's like, then how can you do it to someone else?" she demanded. "How can you do that, knowing how empty they will feel after you take their powers?"

"Because I need to do it to survive. Do you like the fact that animals are killed for your consumption? That to survive, you kill other living creatures?"

"Well… I don't like to think about it, no. But it isn't like I'm killing them myself. And if it weren't for the agricultural industry, I wouldn't eat them at all. It's just because… they are there. If I stopped eating animals, it wouldn't change anything in the industry."

"So if you won't stop killing other creatures to fill your appetites, then why would you criticize me for doing what comes naturally for me? I need to consume others' powers for my survival."

"I could decide to be vegetarian; then I wouldn't be eating animals. You could choose to just consume the powers from objects, not from people."

"Think of the pain you would be inflicting on the plants you ate. Is that any better than killing animals? You consume them alive!"

"Plants don't have feelings!" Reg rolled her eyes.

"Tell that to a nature guardian. Those who tend to the plants know better."

Reg shifted uncomfortably. She looked at him, squirming. "You don't need my powers right now. You don't need anyone's powers right now. You're still full from the buffet. With the amount that you filled up before the Witch Doctor gave up, you shouldn't need to feed again for about a century."

"You don't know anything about how long it will last," Corvin pointed out grumpily.

"I know that you're full right now."

"And did I say I was going to consume your powers? I suggested that the two of us could work together. That's all."

"And that you would still like dessert."

"A man always wants dessert."

"I'm going inside. I really don't want to talk about this anymore. I'm not about to become Bonnie to your Clyde, so you can forget about that. You're on your own."

He mouthed the words, Bonnie and Clyde, like he had no idea what she was talking about. The magical world could be so isolated from the real world. They just lived in their own little pockets, ignoring the rest of the world. Some of them didn't have any electronics. No phones. No TVs. Reg had no idea how they could survive without modern conveniences. It was a modern world.

"The answer is no, Corvin. I'm not teaming up with you. I wasn't happy about being forced to team up with you against the Witch Doctor. I'm done."

Corvin blew out his breath, frustrated. "You owe me. You just remember that. We are bonded together until you repay me your part of the covenant."

Reg swallowed. "You took my powers. The contract was fulfilled."

"I returned them to you. That means you still owe me. You agreed. You made a covenant. And until you fulfill it, we will be fated to cross paths."

"Ick. I'm going home. You can sit in your car and wait for me to come out again. Or you could go home and do whatever warlocky things are on your magical to-do list."

Reg pulled back, forcing herself to leave his circle of influence. The cooler air caressed her skin and she was able to take a full breath again. She had failed to notice just how much he had been stifling her.

She went back to her cottage, looking back once or twice to make sure that Corvin wasn't following her. He stayed out in front of the main house.

* * *

*The Telepathy of Gardens, Book #5 of the Reg Rawlins, Psychic Investigator series* by P.D. Workman can be purchased at pdworkman.com

# ABOUT THE AUTHOR

Award-winning and USA Today bestselling author P.D. (Pamela) Workman writes riveting mystery/suspense and young adult books dealing with mental illness, addiction, abuse, and other real-life issues. For as long as she can remember, the blank page has held an incredible allure and from a very young age she was trying to write her own books.

Workman wrote her first complete novel at the age of twelve and continued to write as a hobby for many years. She started publishing in 2013. She has won several literary awards from Library Services for Youth in Custody for her young adult fiction. She currently has over 60 published titles and can be found at pdworkman.com.

Born and raised in Alberta, Workman has been married for over 25 years and has one son.

* * *

Please visit P.D. Workman at pdworkman.com to see what else she is working on, to join her mailing list, and to link to her social networks.

* * *

If you enjoyed this book, please take the time to recommend it to other purchasers with a review or star rating and share it with your friends!

facebook.com/pdworkmanauthor

twitter.com/pdworkmanauthor

instagram.com/pdworkmanauthor

amazon.com/author/pdworkman

bookbub.com/authors/p-d-workman

goodreads.com/pdworkman

linkedin.com/in/pdworkman

pinterest.com/pdworkmanauthor

youtube.com/pdworkman